# THE GLITTERING STAR

## SWAY OF THE STARS BOOK 2

## FRANCES DALL'ALBA

Poinsettia
Publishing

# Also By Frances Dall'Alba

This is a work of fiction. Names, characters and incidents are the product of the author's imagination. Any similarities to a name, character, or history of any actual person, living or dead, is entirely coincidental.

THE GLITTERING STAR

ISBN: 978-0-6451162-7-4

*For the many volunteers of TREAT.*
*The right tree in the right place for the right reason.*

# PROLOGUE

*2 8 Years Earlier*

Lily grunted in the darkness, tears gushing down her cheeks. Sweat dribbled down her back as the small digging shovel slipped from her fingers. She stopped, resting her aching arms and took a deep breath to regain her strength. A slight breeze rustled through the branches, giving her heated cheeks a brief reprieve when it brushed against her moist skin.

She swiped a grubby sleeve across her face before lifting the battery-operated torch from the leaf litter. She swung it over her efforts, inspecting the progress. The torch wobbled in her trembling hand, casting an eerie glow on the forest while her heart thumped with every scurrying noise that sounded nearby.

She carefully positioned the torch against the base of the giant kauri pine tree, the quiet of the dark of night only broken by her heaving breaths. The realisation that her life had changed in an instant struck again, and a sudden bulk of apprehension swept her back, and she collapsed against the rough bark of the ancient tree. The tree's rough surface poked into her back through her flimsy cotton shirt, but that was the least of her worries. Racking sobs sought escape which she tried to muffle with her still-shaking hand. If the others chanced a late-night cigarette out by the lake, she would need to stay quiet or risk being discovered.

She moved her hand against her flat stomach, where the tiny seed of a new life was forming. In order to make her choice, she'd need to bury all the memories of the past six months first.

It was what she deserved. No good ever came to those who broke the rules. And she had. Dead was one thing, but there was more. Her secret would need to remain as such forever.

Biting her bottom lip, she made a herculean effort to stem the flow of tears and harden up. She would bury this memory amongst the roots of this monolith, leaving it behind and picking up her life from where she'd left off. The pain would never go away. She didn't expect it to.

So, she kept digging. She was intent on going as deep as she could, working around the timeless roots of the giant tree. When she deemed the hole deep enough, she picked up the small box. Nestled comfortably on her palm, she tightened her hold on the memories it represented one last time.

She was seconds away from pushing it into the depth of the hole and covering it with dirt, leaf litter and branches. Moments away from hiding everything that the past six months represented. But she wanted one last look. One last glimpse of the glittering white sapphire. One final moment to experience the rush of what he'd meant to her the day he'd gifted her this precious promise of his love. She'd almost given it all away.

She fumbled with the small catch before prising open the sturdy plastic box. Grabbing the torch again, she held it over the star-shaped gemstone. Shimmering light glittered in the dark forest, piercing her eyes, opening the floodgates once more. Tears dripped onto its clean, geometric lines, accentuating the hard work he'd done to shape and reset the stone he'd found fossicking with his family.

She slammed the lid shut, her fingers closing around the tiny box, her tears laid to rest on the stone for eternity. Shoving the box into the deep hole, she hastened to shift the dirt back in place before feathering the top with leaf debris. Sitting back, she allowed one final wretched sob to escape before rising on shaky legs and walking away.

Leaving everything behind.

# Chapter 1

*Present Day*

Roberta Mintello rounded a bend on the narrow road and slammed on the brakes. Her screeching tyres had her heart beat ramping up as she gripped the steering wheel. "What the heck?" *An accident?* She raked a shaking hand through her hair before rubbing her tired, bloodshot eyes. Surveying the car only metres away, her heart continued to thump uncomfortably inside her chest. That was too close, dangerously close. She took a moment to calm her breathing by taking small, shallow breaths, her leg still shaking as she put the car in park. She'd given herself five days to make the trek from Melbourne to Malanda, and she should've stopped three hours ago for a rest.

The sounds of Dean Lewis floated inside the car as she engaged the handbrake and eased her foot off the brake. Dean's music talked to her over the past five days. The 'I'm feeling sorry for myself, why can't I get my life back on track?' pervaded her life of late. The short-lived stint with Antonio from the Frevannini dynasty was the last time she'd felt alive. But that had died a quiet death. Worlds apart and all that.

Which had nothing to do with why she was here. Once she'd made the decision to fulfil her mother's ridiculous wish, she arranged for time off work. With six months of overdue leave approved, the mantra running around her head for the past two weeks was: pack a bag, sort the playlists, get in the car, drive, get the music blaring, watch for idiot drivers and stop when tired. Simple. If only she could push back the crap of what her mother had told her, including the mission her mother expected her to accomplish. Yeah, right! Her mind and body had gone numb since receiving the news. Nothing like royally screwing up her life.

Roberta squinted into the distance. It didn't look like she was going anywhere in a hurry. With about a dozen cars already stopped ahead of her, she turned the ignition off along with the music. The quiet inside her reliable Mazda 3 scared her for a moment, sending a shiver down her spine. If she wasn't careful, it would allow a tiny bit of space to expand inside her head. If she allowed herself to think, even a little, she might go places she wasn't prepared to, and then all hell would break loose. *Don't think, girl.*

She opened the door, and a rush of cool air eddied around her cheeks. It was time to direct her thoughts to other things. Her fuel consumption had been good on the drive up, and she could thank her dad for teaching her all about that. But—oh heck, that wouldn't work anymore. Who would teach her new things now? At twenty-seven, she still needed her dad for so much. How was a child expected to learn all the practical stuff a person needed to navigate a full and successful life?

She had always been so proud of his Italian heritage, except he wasn't her biological dad. Not anymore. Irrelevant now that he was dead. Too bad some drug-induced lunatic decided to T-bone her dad's car. So senseless and unfair, it had the power to swamp her under its anger. She had to let it go. Time to steer away from those thoughts.

Thanks to her mum, there was another monster to confront. She had no idea how she was going to go about achieving that assignment. In typical Roberta style, she instructed herself to get up to Malanda and come up with a plan. She had one item on the list and hoped it worked in her favour. Oh, and she had to keep all this from her younger brother for now. Well, half-brother, apparently.

*Thanks, Mum.*

She got out of the car, stretched the kinks out of her legs and took a good look around. As she stifled a yawn, she glanced at her watch—it was getting on to three pm. Sally was expecting her soonish, and it would be so good to see her again. Damn! She was so close to the end of her trek, and this would be the first major hold-up the entire drive north. *Quit your moaning. It could be a serious accident up ahead.*

It'd been nearly two years since she'd visited these parts. Meeting Liz on the train in Italy. Escorting Liz home after her attack and hospital stay in southern Italy. Meeting Liz's cousin, Sally. Those jewels. What a story that was. What a love story, too for Liz and Connor. She grimaced. Yep, some people have all the luck going around.

Only moments earlier, her GPS told her she was somewhere along the Palmerston Highway on the way to Millaa Millaa. Then Malanda, the small town where Sally lived. She couldn't hear any approaching sirens or see anything sinister. Peering up ahead, it didn't look like an accident. *What the heck is going on?*

She'd stroll up in a minute if there was no further action and see what the hold-up was. For now, she wanted to declutter her head of the encroaching fatigue that only five days of driving could create. Inhaling a good lungful of fresh, clean air, she rotated a slow three-sixty-degree turn. They weren't wrong when they described this region as a green, rolling hill kind of place. They were all she could see in every direction if she looked past the thin haze of mist or drizzle or whatever was hanging overhead and connected to the dense clouds.

No blue sky here today.

Her stomach rumbled; she was due for a food break. Opening the backseat door, she reached in for the small cooler where she kept her snacks chilled. She took out a homemade granola bar and munched on it slowly, trying to think of nothing except for the sound of her chewing.

"Bloody greenies. Don't they have anything else better to do?"

Roberta swivelled towards the car stopped in front of her. The male driver casually leant against his door and was speaking to a female passenger over the top of the car.

*Greenies?* Why on a major highway? Didn't they normally tie themselves to a tree or glue bits of themselves to a footpath?

"How the heck are we supposed to make the doctor's appointment in time?" The driver's anger was apparent in his curt and clipped tone.

"And pick up Annabelle from school." The female passenger fumbled with her phone, a worried frown between her brows. "I better let the school know we're going to be late."

Roberta quickly picked up on the dilemma. She shut the rear door, grabbing her water bottle resting in the pouch of the driver's door. After a couple of mouthfuls, she put it back, locked the car and pocketed the keys.

A glance behind her showed a growing line of vehicles. The idiots blocking the road needed a wake-up call, and if Roberta was riled up enough, she wasn't one to hold back.

She gave an understanding wave to the couple in front of her as she walked past. "I'll sort out these clowns for you."

The male driver grunted. "I just spotted the first police car arrive, but they can't do a thing. These bastards are too bloody precious, and the police are not allowed to touch them. Too bad there's no way around the block they've put across the road."

"How do you know this?" Roberta was curious, raising her eyebrows. She'd only just rocked up, and this couple couldn't have been in the queue for too long.

"I've been talking to my brother. His mate is one of the local councillors. The police notified the council of what was going on, and word quickly got around. It'll make the national news, of course, giving these imbeciles more fodder to work with."

Roberta nodded, skirting the rough edges of the narrow two-lane major highway. Well, how a major highway looked in these parts. A few metres ahead, the number of potholes had her frowning. *If I was the local councillor, I'd be raising this issue next.*

As she walked past the other cars on her way to the dilemma up ahead, others waited outside their cars. Angry outbursts and disgruntled discussions filled the air. The general discontent was palpable. These people had places to go, lives to live and children waiting for them.

As a chill ran through the air, she tightened her jacket across her chest. She was in tropical Far North Queensland, but someone forgot to mention it up here on the mountaintop. To be stuck on this road on such a blustery day was only going to add to the angst of all those caught up in this debacle. Her included.

With each step she took towards the confrontation, her state of mind was brewing up something chronic, and when she spotted their roadblock, her jaw dropped. In amongst the confusion of vehicles lined up and the police car parked haphazardly, there was a massive, dirty yellow bulldozer parked horizontally across the road. Its bulk reached past the rough edges on both sides of the broken tarmac. It was impossible for any vehicle to drive around. The protesters chose the perfect site for this ambush, with the banks dipping steeply on either side. It looked dangerous and slippery the closer Roberta came to the scene of the crime. No driver would be crazy enough to attempt to go around the roadblock.

Two police officers stood at a respectable distance from about half a dozen activists. Roberta squinted into the haze, trying to read the placards they held.

*No more windmills.*

*Do your research first.*

*What about native life?*

*What will happen in 25 years when they're old and broken?*

Roberta had seen wind farms—their tall, white windmill-looking structures standing out like a beacon in the countryside—along her drive but hadn't thought too much about them. As no one halted her progress, she kept marching, making for one male protester who looked to be about her age. At least his hair was not dreadlocked and tatty and his clothes looked like they might've been washed at least once in the last month. Unlike the other campaigners with their long flowing pants and tie-dyed shirts that had seen better days.

She dived straight in. "What's your name?"

The man swivelled in her direction, a look of surprise coming over his face. As she wasn't wearing a police uniform, maybe this caused his reaction.

He recovered swiftly. "None of your business; now get out of the way."

She guessed demonstrators were prepared for anything, but his response peeved her something pretty.

"Excuse me," she spat, hands on her hips, boring a hole with her glare. Lacking a decent night's sleep wasn't helping. "What is wrong with you people? Isn't this what you lot are driving at? Clean environmental changes so we can close every goddamned coal mine?"

The sandy-blond-haired man towered a good foot above her. He menacingly took a step closer, sending daggers her way. He clipped every single word he spoke. "As you don't understand much, I suggest you move away."

"I'm trying to, you dolt, but a bunch of losers are blocking a major highway, just in case you haven't noticed."

The man darted a look over her shoulder, and Roberta flicked a glance behind her. Dozens of trapped drivers were merging on the median strip and striding towards the group of protesters. On closer inspection, they were doing the same from the other direction, too. *Shit, this is not going to end well.*

"You need to get out of the way, or you're going to get hurt." The protester was so close she could smell a hint of coffee on his breath.

"I don't think so. You and your so-called mates are going to get hurt. I'm here to remind you there are people stuck here with places to go. There's one couple whose child is waiting to be picked up from school and a doctor's appointment they're going to be late for."

"Get out of the way before you get hurt," the man growled.

The lack of police numbers was looking like a distinct disadvantage, and this man was probably realising that the activists were outnumbered by the angry mob approaching on both sides.

With a sudden motion, the man grabbed her by the arm, trying to shove her to the side. She held firm by digging her heels in, refusing to be pushed about. A camera flashed in her face at the exact moment she was propelled enough to trip and fall on her backside. He cast her one quick look, swore once and then turned away.

"Everyone, hold up your messages," the man shouted to the others, and with a synchronised effort, they raised all the placards in the air.

In all the angst, Roberta didn't notice the arrival of the television crew. She was up on her feet in a flash, angrily snatching one placard and hurling it down to the ground. This was what they were waiting for, their five minutes of fame to get their message across. She was going to make it as hard as possible. Again, someone shoved her to the side, but this time, she couldn't tell by who. Oh boy, her tired brain was certainly not thinking straight, and she was up again trying to grab another placard.

The wail of sirens sounded close by and what looked like the arrival of more law enforcers. She breathed a sigh of relief. The police would certainly need this extra help as the restless and angry crowd surged closer.

What seemed like an ocean of law enforcers, heavily clad in protection gear, they approached the demonstrators, rounding them up with handcuffs. An officer yanked her from the group, pushed and shoved her before finally restraining one hand in the handcuff and twisting her arm behind her back.

"Take it easy, okay," the police officer advised. "We're taking you lot into the local watch house."

"What the?" she shouted, trying to twist out of the officer's hold. "I'm not one of them. Let me go!" She tried to shake them off, the people around her a blur of visions and voices. Over and over she shouted to be freed.

As she shook her head to make sense of the situation, another officer grabbed her arm and painfully tugged. Amidst the chaos of being dragged towards the police wagon, she stole a quick glance at her restrained hand, only to find that *he* was handcuffed to it.

"Don't make a bloody scene, you idiot. I told you to keep away."

Roberta's blood boiled. There was too much happening lately for her to be rational about anything. This imbecile making out as though this was all her fault was the last straw in a short life that had taken an awful turn of late. She had an urge to hurt someone. Someone in close proximity.

She targeted his feet wearing well-worn Converse sneakers. As they were pushed and pulled towards the police vans, she took the one moment where they were halted for about two seconds to stamp his foot with her trail joggers, being sure to grind the rough edges for good measure.

"Ouch!" He groaned, his face transforming into an ugly scowl. "What was that for?"

A momentary glimmer of success shimmied across her chest. "I don't know. Why don't you try and work it out."

"Stop! Hey, stop. Don't take her!"

Roberta turned to the agitated voice, realising it belonged to the male driver of the car who'd stopped in front of her.

"She's not with this crowd. Let her go." The driver came to a stop in front of them.

"Look, mate," the police explained politely, "she was part of the confusion, and they can sort it out at the station."

Roberta fished her keys out of her pocket, throwing them in the man's direction. "Thank you so much. Could you drive my car to the station?"

He caught her keys but fumbled. They dropped to the ground, and he crouched to pick them up. When he looked up, she shrugged before being bundled into a wagon and shoved up hard against *him*.

As the others were piled in too, there was little chance of moving away. The handcuffs wouldn't allow it anyway.

Not one to do meek, she locked eyes with him, her meanest look scrunched up on her face. Instead of a similar look returning as expected, she spotted what looked like a hint of amusement wavering at the edges of his mouth.

He couldn't be that stupid to laugh outright in her face, could he?

She turned away with a huff. On second thoughts, she didn't need to look at him again.

Ever!

# Chapter 2

Seven people sat squashed in the back of the police wagon. Roberta shifted uncomfortably, her knees almost in her face. She didn't dare move her arm attached to *him* by handcuffs. At this point, if she put all her concentration into the task, her skin wouldn't touch his at all.

"We got the airplay we were after, Nate. That's one positive for the day." One of the conspirators spoke up after they'd been driving in silence for about twenty minutes.

Roberta whipped her face up, her hand jostling against Nate's for a second. *So, he has a name.*

"Look, Brent, it's already made the local social media pages. Great going, guys," another conspirator added as he swiped his phone screen and showed it to the man sitting beside him, the one bragging about the airplay.

"Let's hold off all discussion until we're back and away from strangers." Nate gave Roberta a side eye before focusing back on his buddies.

"How did you manage this?" Another man sitting in the front shadows pointed to the handcuffs joining Roberta and Nate together.

"What is it with you lot?" Roberta burst out. She understood she was a traitor in their midst, but did they have any idea of what havoc they'd caused?

"What exactly do you mean?" Nate turned slightly, the handcuffs jiggling between them. There was no mistaking his ugly frown this time. No niggling sign of mirth or anything human.

"Putting on a stunt like that is so stupid." She hated they were so well spoken, which meant they were probably well educated—stupidly educated—with no idea of the real world.

"Why would that be the case?" Nate raised his joined hand, raking it through his hair and taking her hand with it.

With a swift motion, she yanked hers back by her side and offered up an evil glare. He could use his other hand.

"Firstly, I came around the bend doing the allowed speed and almost ran into the car stopped in front of me. Trust me, it would've gone down a treat if I'd hit them. Just so you know, that same car carried a mum and dad. Their child was waiting to be collected from school so they could make a doctor's appointment in time."

Nate harrumphed.

"You absolute losers have nothing better to do than mill around creating havoc. Even little old me from Melbourne summed up the situation in a flash."

"That figures. Someone from the city wouldn't know the first thing about preserving our environment for future generations."

"But isn't this what you idiots want? What you keep campaigning for? Green solutions, no coal, no gas. Does someone have their wires crossed?"

"Except they haven't done their homework properly, that's what," Nate spat.

"They're springing up everywhere, and *now* you say they haven't done their homework? Where have you been for the past twenty years?"

"Calm down, you pair," Brent advised.

"No, Brent, I can't. Big mouth here"—he rattled the handcuffs to be certain everyone squashed in the overheating van knew who he was talking about—"obviously doesn't know much, so she needs to be educated. Like now."

"Cool it, Nate. We got our media coverage. We can only hope they'll come to the next meeting prepared to listen." Brent advised, rattling his own manacled hand.

"Those bastards will never listen because they're fools like this one." Nate pointed a finger in her face. She desperately wanted to slap it away.

Instead, Roberta shook the handcuffs. "Watch who you're calling what."

"Exactly. This one"—he wasn't talking to her but over her towards Brent, like she didn't exist—"what does she understand about how wind farms can only be built in remote locations, which then destroys the visual aesthetics of that landscape? What about the impact they have on our unique local wildlife? Yep, these big corporations don't give a toss about any of that. What happens in twenty-five years when they've lived their useful life and need to be disposed of? Where are they going to dump them all? Christ almighty, there are already so many of them set up around the world it's going to be a nightmare when the time comes."

"I know, I know, mate. Try and cool it until they sort us out at the station and let us go," Brent said.

"Why would they let you go? Who do you think you are?" The audacity of these people to think they could carry out today's event without facing any consequences. "Do you have any idea what resources you've wasted in just the past two hours? I bet you didn't leave them the keys to the bulldozer either so they could move it along. Of course not! And where did you get it from? Um ..." Roberta tapped her mouth with her index finger as though thinking deeply. "Let me guess. Oh, right, you stole it. Yeah, what a good idea. Why didn't I think of doing that?"

Someone laughed in the back corner of the van. Roberta swivelled towards the sound of the female voice. "Don't you people have a job? What do you do all day, or is it the poor taxpayer footing the bill for your laziness, too?"

"*When* they free you, don't forget to turn back and drive all the way to your ugly concrete jungle and live happily ever after. We don't need your type up here. We sure as heck don't need you telling us what's best for our part of the world. You guys have already destroyed your part of the world, so leave us to take care of ours." Nate tightened the slack in the handcuff, tugging it towards his chest.

She turned and glared at him, baring her teeth. She knew what he was up to and wasn't backing down one iota. Not wanting to risk having her hand sit on his lap, she tugged back even though the metal dug into her skin. No different to an arm wrestle, she wasn't giving him one single inch of chain.

The same female sniggered again, causing Roberta to straighten her back and clench her handcuffed fist. Hissing, she said, "Over my dead body will you tell me what to do."

There was one small window hatch in the back of the wagon which cast enough light so Roberta could see Nate's face clearly. His was deadly serious; no doubt hers was too. The connection between his glare and hers strengthened, neither wanting to be the first to back off.

Until his blue-lake eyes blinked and softened for one second, and she almost plopped into their depths. Her jaw dropped at the same time Nate looked away to cover whatever the hell just happened. She swallowed painfully to cover her confusion, not sure where to look. Their hands went limp simultaneously. When his finger accidentally grazed hers, a bolt of awareness jolted up her arm. She stiffened, not prepared to move another inch until they arrived at their destination.

*God, how many more minutes until I'm unlocked from this nightmare?*

⁎

Someone was listening to her because, within a matter of minutes, the wagon slowed. Which hopefully meant they were close to somewhere. The cloying air of so many cramped bodies was stifling and she breathed in through her mouth only.

After another few minutes, the van came to a halt and the engine cut out. Light flooded the rear of the van when the back doors opened, and she blinked a couple of times for her vision to adjust.

"Okay, everyone," the police officer said, "make your way inside the station. We'll get your statements first. Once you've been interviewed, you'll be released from the handcuffs."

They all shuffled out of the van and followed the officer, surrounded by another half a dozen flanking their exit. Roberta decided there was no point in trying to make a run for it like they did in the movies. Staying put was the lesser of the two evils. Running away attached to Nate forever would land her in a psych ward within five minutes.

Now to explain her way out of this mess. Roberta grimaced. Heck, she'd been in worse places in her short life, but this topped the list.

At least her phone was still in the pocket of her jacket. Sally would be at her wit's end if she didn't contact her soon, but inside the van hadn't been the time or place to pull it out. They'd been in touch the entire drive up and when she didn't turn up on her doorstep soon, Sally would probably think the worst.

Shunted into a small, airless room with one window, they were made to sit on the plastic chairs placed around the stark walls. Roberta looked out of the heavily barred window and fidgeted. All she could see was a tree and one of its branches gently tapping the window with the slight breeze. Nate was tugging at her arm so he could take a seat, but Roberta ignored him. He could wait until she was ready.

With her free hand, she unzipped her jacket pocket, taking out her phone. Nate tugged harder this time, and she continued to resist. Quickly tapping on her most frequent phone number, she waited for Sally to answer.

"Can you make an effort to move closer to the chairs?" Nate hissed his demand through clenched teeth.

"Can you wait until I'm ready?" Roberta barked back.

She must've accidentally tapped the speaker button because everyone in the room heard Sally say, "Roberta, is that you? Where are you?"

"She's being a pain in the arse and deserves everything happening to her," Nate answered Sally.

"Shut up, you nitwit, and mind your own business," Roberta retaliated, yanking hard enough for Nate to wince.

"Roberta!" Sally sounded hysterical. "Where are you?"

Before Roberta got another word in, Brent shouted from behind, "She's at the Atherton watch house, handcuffed to our leader. I don't think she likes it one bit."

Brent and the others chuckled, and Roberta's lips straightened as she glared at him.

"Sally, I'm fine. They made a mistake. I'll sort this out soon."

"She should've minded her own business and walked away when I told her to," Nate said.

"*You* shouldn't have done what you did, you bloody moron. I can't believe I had the misfortune of stumbling across your stupid prank." Roberta's voice ratcheted up an octave, and when Sally didn't reply, Roberta assumed she'd hung up.

"You had no right to interfere, especially when the television crew turned up. We need every bit of media coverage we can so our message gets out there. You're an interfering, silly moron who should've stayed in your concrete jungle where you came from."

Oh boy, Roberta's face seared at the accusation, her nostrils flaring at the injustice of it. And calling her a moron ... "*You* need to realise the world doesn't revolve around you. There are a lot of different people, cultures and beliefs that need to be juggled to make the world a happy place. Putting up with the likes of you who believe only your views are correct is what's wrong with the world."

They were full on shouting at each other, faces close together, the accusations flying the short distance the rattling handcuffs allowed.

"Quiet!" A gruff shout reverberated around the small room.

Roberta and Nate did just that, their chests heaving as they slumped back into their chairs.

"Aren't you pair on the same team?" The police officer—with the name tag Officer Molloy—filled the doorway.

"No!" they shouted in unison.

This was the opening Roberta needed to get out of there. "I was caught up with these idiots by mistake. My car is probably still sitting on the highway if you want to go and check. Please unlock me from this man as I have absolutely nothing to do with him or this ridiculous protest."

"But I was the one who handcuffed you. You were amongst this group."

"I was trying to ruin their five minutes of fame. Why the heck did you allow them to get that far? You should've mowed them down a lot earlier so everyone was able to continue with their busy lives and not be held up because of this lot."

Nate growled, his seething look brushing her with nasty, angry flames. "One day, when you're old and miserable and hardly able to breathe because narrowminded people like yourself have completely destroyed the world, you might actually think back on this day and regret every single word you're saying."

"Next!"

Another police officer opened the door of the interview room, gesturing for the next two protesters to come in and give their statements.

"I think it might be safer if I leave you pair handcuffed for now," Officer Molloy added with a straight face.

"Noooooo," Roberta wailed, thrashing and flinging her arms about, causing enough distress that Nate physically had to take her in his arms to calm her down.

"Roberta!" Sally's voice somehow pierced higher than her wailing. "What is going on?"

Roberta stopped her thrashing and pulled out of Nate's stronghold, her jaw dropping. How had Sally got here so fast?

"Before you ask, I was already in Atherton and on my way home to Malanda when you phoned."

"Wait! Wait a minute!" a voice shouted into the mayhem. The male driver of the car parked in front of hers on the Palmerston Highway raced into the room. He shoved Sally aside, dangling Roberta's set of car keys. Lucky it was a small country station and anyone could just walk in.

In an instant, all the noise dropped, and no one moved. The male driver was heaving like he'd physically pushed her car all the way from the top of the Palmerston Highway to Atherton. "This woman is innocent of any crime. She was parked behind my car at the blockade and walked up to see what the issue was. Her being brought here is wrong. I suggest you release her." His words came out in a rush, and he had to stop talking for a moment to take a couple of steadying breaths. "She's done nothing wrong and only had time to fling her car keys to me before she was taken away. Otherwise, her car would be stuck on the highway causing more havoc."

The male driver took a hesitant step closer, holding out her keys. Roberta yanked her hand enough so Nate was dragged with her as she stepped forward to collect them. "Thank you. I really appreciate this."

"No worries, it was a pleasure to meet you. You're one fierce young lady. I'd be proud to have you on my team. Now I better get going; my wife and child are waiting outside for me." Turning his gaze to Nate, he added, "There's been enough inconvenience caused today."

As he turned to leave, Roberta thought of something. "Hey, how did they shift the bulldozer?"

"A couple of blokes in their utilities used tow ropes to straighten it. Enough for one lane to open and allow the traffic to keep moving."

"Ah, wait a minute," Officer Molloy asked, holding up a hand. "What's your name?"

"It's Mark Cummins."

"Thanks, Mark, for your assistance today. Could you please leave your contact details at the counter on your way out in case I need to get a statement from you at some stage?"

"Sure, Officer. No problem." Mark turned back to her again. "Your car is parked out the front on the street."

"Thanks, Mark."

With that, he turned and left the room.

"Officer, can you please tell me what's going on?" Sally directed her question to Officer Molloy who was standing in the middle of the room.

Sally came over and wrapped her arm around Roberta's shoulder, squeezing her tight. "Nothing like Roberta to announce her arrival in the north with trumpets blaring."

Roberta chuckled. "Can you ask him nicely to unchain me from this monster?" She thrust her thumb towards Nate. "Then we can go get a coffee, and I'll tell you everything about my nightmare."

Sally raised an eyebrow in Officer Molloy's direction.

"We'll need a statement from her first. Sorry, but she's too involved for us to ignore. They can go in next."

"Do we have to go in together?" It wasn't beneath Roberta to plead.

"Can you be trusted to stay calm if I release you?" Officer Molloy raised his eyebrows expectantly.

"I'll only stay calm if you can reassure me these halfwits will pay for the disruption they've caused us all."

"That's up to the court system to decide their punishment. Our job is to collect all the information and complete our investigations as fully as possible. So, if you want to do your part, be sure to tell them everything you can in your statement."

"Yes, sir, gladly."

Officer Molloy turned to Nate, his stern expression causing the room to fill with palpable tension. "I've known your family forever, Nate. Unfortunately, you won't come out of this unscathed. I hope you know what you're doing. Your grandfather was always a good community man and your intentions have always been good."

Nate nodded solemnly. "Thanks, Officer."

"Hold out your arms, you pair," Office Molloy instructed. "I hope to God you never run into each other again. I don't want to be responsible for cleaning up that mess."

Sally chuckled beside her and whispered loud enough for Nate to hear. "He's cute."

Roberta looked up at the same time Nate did, their gazes clashing.

A shiver ran up her arm when she was unable to read what she saw in his face. "I'd rather die than admit that, thanks, Sal." She made sure she said it loud enough for all to hear. The clank of the chain signalled their release and, looking away, Roberta was able to break the connection with Nate and breathe again.

"Okay, let's keep things moving here." Another summons came from the police officer still standing in the interview room.

"Off you go, young lady," Officer Molloy said. "The sooner you're done, the sooner you can go. Good luck."

"Thanks, Officer, but I think it's him you should be wishing all the good luck to. I did nothing wrong, remember?"

"You think?" was Nate's parting shot as he sent her one last withering look.

# Chapter 3

Giggling, Roberta took another sip of her coffee. "Okay, today takes the prize. Funny, now that I can calmly look back, but Sal, I was furious when they handcuffed me."

"I bet you were. Who wants to be branded a criminal?" Sally chuckled.

They'd left the Atherton police station with Sally driving ahead. She chose a delightful café at a strawberry farm for Roberta to calm down with a coffee. The vista from their table looked out over neatly manicured flower gardens, with the strawberry fields further and beyond.

It was the start of spring, and all the shrubs and greenery looked lush, healthy and eager to leave winter behind. A bit like herself. Beginning to feel better, Roberta inhaled the mixed aroma of coffee, delicious food and the intoxicating smell of rich volcanic earth reaching her inside the open-air café. You'd never find a charming café like this in Melbourne.

The weather was a whole lot better than the blustery conditions at the top of the Palmerston Highway. The warmth from the late afternoon sun tingled along her bare arms as she eyed the startling blue sky from where she sat. Redness from the handcuffs had faded and her wrists no longer stung. Roberta brought her mug up to her mouth again. Before taking a sip, she asked, "Do you know who he is?"

"No idea. I've been racking my brain trying to place him. If his grandfather is such a community man, then it shouldn't be too hard to work it out. I don't recognise him from our school days, so chances are he must've gone to one of the other schools."

Roberta harrumphed. *Arrogant bastard.* Despite the man's good looks, which on any other occasion would've triggered her womanly wiles, she had no wish to ever run into him again!

"So, tell me a little more about your plans. For the Roberta I know, you've been a little vague."

A mischievous smile crossed Roberta's face as she chuckled. Sally was spot-on. Unlike her usual chatty self, she was keeping her news close to her chest for a change. Sally already knew about the death of her dad, Sam nearly six months ago, but she wasn't ready to share the hurt and pain of what she'd recently discovered. But Sally was a good friend. Together with Sally's cousin Liz, they'd shared some remarkable days between them.

Liz and Connor's wedding in Canada was memorable and priceless. Their time in Falerna for the unveiling ceremony after the discovery of the lost jewels added to their shared memories. Sometimes Roberta pinched herself. If Liz hadn't stumbled onto the train that day in Lamezia Terme, with only seconds to spare, who knew how her life over the past few years might have panned out.

Her short but wild experience with Antonio would never have happened. She wrapped those memories warmly within. She never expected it to last, but it was worth every single day she'd spent with him. Oh, what a life it would entail. Wealth and too much money, that's what. Sounded good on most days, but yeah, nah. She couldn't live like that. The short stint had been refreshing, and they'd parted as friends.

"I needed some time off to process some news I didn't like, so I hightailed it out of the big smoke for some downtime up here. Once I get my head sorted, I'll try and explain."

"Oh, that sounds heavy. Will you be okay? The offer to stay with me is still open."

"Yeah, look, I won't do that to you. I'm a real pain in the arse, and you'd have no choice but to kick me out after the first week."

"Aw, Roberta, I don't think so. Whenever you're around, my life suddenly looks brighter and more exciting."

"Not anymore, girl. I'm all grown up now. Responsible, hardworking, and I never sleep in till lunch anymore."

Sally snorted, choking a little on her coffee. "I'd have to see that to believe it."

They giggled and chuckled like school girls. Being together would be good for Roberta, if she could sort through the crap crowding her head. The irony her mother had once visited a school friend from up this way, only to land in more trouble than what she'd planned, hadn't gone unnoticed. Yet, *she* had to be the responsible one!

Roberta inwardly groaned, annoyance settling in the pit of her stomach. Oh, fun times ahead.

"I thought I'd get a part-time job while I was up here."

"Really?" Sally raised a surprised eyebrow. "Is work stressing you out?"

"Nah, it's perfectly fine, and I do enjoy it, but I have a hankering for the good old days of when I was a student. It might help pass the time while I'm sorting out my mother's shit."

"Oooh, now I'm curious." Sally raised her hand understandably. "I won't press for more details. This is Roberta, after all. Queen of no filters. When you're ready, I know I'll hear *everything*. Probably too much."

This statement was so true it was enough to set them off again. They laughed so much when they were together, and it looked like nothing had changed between them. "I might have a surprise for you too." Sally tapped her finger against her mouth. "But mum's the word."

"Oh, poop, Sal, you know I hate surprises."

"I do," Sally said with a mischievous glint, "but I'm still working out the details. You'll be alright, though, won't you? All grown up and stuff. Didn't you say patience was one of your new virtues?"

"No, I didn't. I said I was older, wiser and more responsible. *Nothing* about being patient, thank you very much. That's never gonna happen in my lifetime."

They continued to chuckle, taking leisurely sips of their coffee. She was spending two nights with Sally but hoped her plans would come to fruition. Everything depended on her interview the next day. This sobering thought had her seriously frowning.

"What's up?" Sally asked. Roberta winced, damning Sally for picking up on the vibes.

"Nothing much," she lied, which she hated doing, especially to her fondest friends. "I've organised an interview tomorrow at the Lake Barrine Teahouse, and I know nothing about the place."

"Teahouse? No nursing requirements there."

"Yeah, I know, but I'm revisiting my old hospitality skills. I hope I'm not out of touch with what's required these days. But they're short-staffed and struggling to find replacements, so I'm hoping they'll take me on warts and all. They even have a small cottage tucked into the rainforest and a room I can use. Which is why I won't have to impose on you for too long."

"But you haven't got the job yet. You might still need to stay with me."

"She practically gave me the job during the phone interview. I have high hopes." Roberta flashed Sally a confident smile.

Sally's frown didn't budge. "Why the teahouse? We never got the chance to take you there when you were last here, did we?"

"The ad popped up on a job search page." Not exactly the truth, but close. "I searched for images of the place; it looks very special. Is it really that pretty?"

"It is one of our most popular tourist attractions. A lot of interesting history surrounds the lake and the family who's owned the teahouse for close to one hundred years. I don't get out there often, but occasionally, I'll do the five-kilometre walk around the lake, then splurge on scones and jam. Always a busy place, so you'll have your work cut out for you."

"The good news is the hours are only nine to three. This will leave the nights for partying. What do you say, Sal?"

Sally groaned, placing her cup down. "Oh, Roberta, I'm too old for that." She sat back and stretched her arms behind her before drawing them back in. "Liz used to say that all the time when she was saddled with the responsibility of taking care of her grandparents. God, I used to feel sorry for her, and now it's me saying it."

"And look at her now," Roberta added. "Jetsetting around the globe and probably having sex every single night."

Sally let out a soft chuckle but sobered up quickly. "She deserves it. I just wish luck would come my way one day. Can get lonely sometimes."

"Look, Sal, we'll find our happy ever afters soon, I promise."

"I hope so, girl. There doesn't seem to be any man out there who comes close to what I want. Maybe I'm being too picky?"

An image of Nate flashed up, and Roberta grimaced. "Yeah, I hear you."

# Chapter 4

Nate scowled at the image on the front page of *The Express*. It was good media coverage, except for the photo they'd chosen. Why? Nate wished for one wistful moment that he had control of which one they'd picked.

Of course, it had to be the one with Roberta, the loud-mouthed, interfering southerner. The camera flashed at the very moment he'd shoved her out of the way so the media could get decent shots of their placards and banners. The moment she'd torn the placard from him and fallen on her backside. His face, contorted with anger, bore down on her, and it didn't look good. *Great job, mate!*

It peeved him no end that he hadn't been more controlled. Their motto was for calm protesting, so the message was clear and not muddied.

He sighed, folded the newspaper and slid it to the other side of the small kitchen table. He leant on his elbows and raked his hands through his hair. Despite occasional bouts of despondency when it seemed their efforts were wasted, at least the write-up had favoured their argument.

He rose, remembering his only sister Natasha was interviewing a possible new staff member which included a room in the cottage as enticement. He was the only person living fulltime at the lake. After all the crowds left and the teahouse closed for the day, he wouldn't mind the extra company.

He pushed his chair in, deciding to do a quick tidy up before his break ended. He hoped this new person was a stayer. He didn't care if they were male or female, just someone prepared to work. Natasha, in charge of the teahouse and scone making, had struggled of late to secure good, reliable staff. Nate didn't understand why. The work wasn't difficult, except it did get busy. Working nine to three wasn't too much to ask, was it?

Since he had a habit of keeping things tidy, there wasn't too much to do. He'd been expecting someone to move into the cottage at a moment's notice, so he kept the bare minimum there. Travelling with a backpack taught him how to live frugally. Before leaving three years ago, he'd disposed of most of his property. What he couldn't part with, his parents willingly stored for him until he settled in his own place one day.

About to return to work, he did a final inspection of the open-plan kitchen and living area, pleased it was ready for a new roommate.

It was almost time to launch the boat for another load of tourists. Three coaches full of visitors had arrived for the morning rush. Not unusual for their teahouse. Situated on the banks of the iconic Lake Barrine, there were many days on his travels abroad when he'd missed it intensely. Six months ago, he came home, not regretting his decision at all. With his sister at the helm of the teahouse, it was his duty to share the workload and continue with his great-grandfather's vision. He wouldn't be the one to break the one-hundred-year-old family cycle.

He closed the door of the cottage behind him, taking another moment to appreciate his home. Midmorning sunlight danced along the surface of the sapphire-blue lake. The fringe of tropical rainforest added shadows to its edges, but the real beauty lay in being able to breathe in glorious, clean air. Not always possible in other parts of the world. Being away from where he was raised taught him so much. His home was a priceless treasure to protect until his dying breath. He was proud to continue his family's vision. That included protecting the lake and surrounding tropical rainforest while allowing others to enjoy its beauty in a sensible and smart way.

Secretly, he'd missed home badly. He had pined for the calm waters of Lake Barrine. Had taken his first steps here. Taken control of the wheel of the flat-bottomed tourist boat on his grandfather's and father's lap before he could walk. Kissed his first girlfriend while they swam and paddled in the water. He loved everything about his unique home, and he wanted the rest of the world to enjoy such pristine environments the world over for eternity.

His heart thumped extra hard every time he realised how much work this entailed. There were so many short-sighted people who only looked at the financial gain. The one that would line their pockets. Never about the lasting environmental damage for decades to come.

Walking down the concrete steps leading to the jetty, he fisted his hand. Thumping it against his khaki shorts, he vowed he would fight tooth and nail for this.

Which reminded him of the debacle with the woman, Roberta. The sudden popping up of wind farms across the world took his breath away. They hadn't done the proper research yet. The entire idea of wind energy sounded like the green and safe thing to do, but there were so many negatives too. Nate scrubbed a hand over his face. It made his blood boil. Who would clean up the mess twenty-five years later when they reached their useful life?

With his mind bursting, he veered away from the jetty and made for the back door of the teahouse. The food cooler would be waiting for him to carry to the boat. He'd momentarily forgotten about it. Guests on the forty-minute cruise enjoyed a cup of tea or coffee, including a selection of scones with jam and cream.

"Hi, Hannah. All ready?" Nate asked the closest server.

"Sure is, Nate. Lots of visitors milling around. Hope we put enough in."

"Where's Natasha?" Nate flicked a quick glimpse inside the kitchen.

"She's trying to fit in that interview with the new girl before the lunchtime rush."

"Oh, okay. I thought it was for later this afternoon."

"Nope, it's happening now." Hannah smiled her dimples at him before turning back to the busy kitchen. "Sorry, gotta go. Can't talk right now. Have fun out there today."

"I will." Hannah was a terrific worker and one young woman going places. They'd lose her one day. This job was a stepping stone for her as she studied part-time and played her guitar on weekends. With a gifted voice, sometimes she wowed the crowds on their boat cruises on the days they could afford to do without her in the kitchen. Didn't happen often, but it should.

He picked up the esky, then headed towards the steps leading to where the boat was moored. Flat-bottomed and made of fibreglass, it wasn't the first boat their family had launched on the lake. There were a progression of designs and sizes over the decades, with this current boat able to carry over one hundred guests. He crossed the gangplank, jostling the esky in its place. The popularity of their cruise around the lake never diminished, and he could thank the amazing natural wonder of this volcanic-formed lake. Mother nature at its best with an abundance of wildlife and bird species, surrounded by only the best tropical rainforest. How had they got so lucky?

He made his way back off the boat, smiling as visitors milled around the jetty. Hopefully, everyone read the sign advising that cruise tickets were to be purchased at the teahouse. With fifteen minutes left until the boat departed, all the usual preparations were done. Two cruises a day, one midmorning, one midafternoon, and a manic lunchtime rush, three o'clock raced towards them every single day at great speed. But his day didn't end there. With a continual list of maintenance jobs to be done, he didn't envisage ever having any downtime. He didn't mind. Three years of wandering had staled by the end. He liked being busy, and he loved that visitors enjoyed their teahouse and boat cruise.

He loved his home.

With ten minutes left, the passengers began boarding with a welcome smile and a check of their tickets. Sophie from the teahouse would be along any minute to take control of serving the Devonshire teas. His phone vibrated in his shorts pocket as Sophie arrived. Taking his phone out, he signalled with his hand for Sophie to take over the boarding of passengers.

"What's up, Tash?" Busy with their own chores, they often communicated by phone, even if the distance between them was barely fifty metres. It was easier than traipsing all over the property.

"I've finished interviewing, and I'm sending her down to get a taste of the boat cruise. She's moving in and starting tomorrow. Give her a few minutes to get down there and do your usual welcome thing."

"Okay, no worries. Hopefully, she's a stayer."

"She sounds keen. Anyway, gotta go. There are people everywhere here."

Natasha ended the call before he had a chance to reply, which didn't worry him. For now, they had guests in the teahouse and visitors boarding the cruise boat. Plenty of time to talk later.

"Thanks, Sophie." He took her place again, waving her onto the boat to start the morning tea preparations. Chatting with visitors came naturally to him, and before long, he was asking questions about where they were from and putting them at ease. As calm and smooth as the boat cruise was, some guests still got queasy. He wanted to reassure them he was there to take care of them.

When all the passengers were boarded, he was just about to put the chain across the boarding deck when he spotted a figure coming down the steps from the office door at the back of the teahouse.

She wore a wide-brimmed straw hat with dark, bouncing curls falling over her shoulders. *That's right, the new staff person.* He'd momentarily forgotten about the call from Tash, but no harm done. He hadn't left yet.

The woman wore sensible joggers with neat thigh-length black shorts and a long-sleeved sun shirt the same colour as the water. She must've changed into something casual for the cruise. Nobody did a job interview dressed this casual.

Concentrating on the steps, she only looked up with a welcome smile when she arrived at Nate's feet.

Nate's hand froze around the chain he was holding. "You!" he spat.

It'd taken her an extra two seconds to make the connection. Her smile, which dazzled him for a second, was gone and she drew her lips together in a straight line.

"You're not coming on board," he hissed through his tightly clenched teeth. He was surprised he could speak at all.

Roberta squared her shoulders, looking him straight in the eye. It appeared she wasn't stepping back. "Your sister employed me, thank you very much, and I am doing as I've been instructed to do. So, move aside and let me on."

She was smart enough to keep her voice down; he was impressed, but oh boy, they were supposed to be sharing the small cottage? Over his dead body. He had no choice but to deal with this later with Tash. There was no way this woman was working a single day at their teahouse. She would get her free boat cruise today, and that would be the end of it. He'd make sure of it. Or die trying.

Without breaking the searing, all-consuming way she staked him out with her glare, he moved stiffly to the side to allow her to walk along the gangplank and onto the boat. The breath jammed in his throat, escaped via a hiss when their gazes cracked. Then he secured the chain and followed, his heart booming and his hands shaking from the experience.

A trip to hell sounded like a better option.

# Chapter 5

For the first time ever, Nate struggled to find his mojo. Roberta's presence rattled him completely. The boat knocked into its mooring before he realised he hadn't put it in reverse. *Bloody hell!*

"Everything okay, Nate?" Sophie mouthed, her back to the boatload of guests.

Nate gave himself a mental shake and gripped the wheel tighter. He sent her an apologetic smile, slipped his sunglasses back down and pasted on a sunny smile.

Reversing the boat away from the mooring, he flicked on the speaker system before half twisting in his seat to face the passengers. "Good morning, everyone. I'm Nate. Welcome to Lake Barrine and our iconic boat cruise."

Pausing for a moment, he straightened the boat's position and shifted it out of reverse ready to start the cruise. "A little about myself and our family. We've been involved with Lake Barrine for nearly one hundred years, operating some form of boat cruise for many decades. So, make yourself comfortable as we set off on one of nature's most impressive examples of a maar."

Steering the boat towards the far-left side of the lake, he sidled up close to the rainforest for any sighting of forest wildlife. "And what is a maar, you ask?" Nate continued with his commentary, slowly getting back into the swing of his spiel. It usually took a few minutes before some of the more confident and chatty passengers interacted with him. When no one raised their hand, Nate smiled. "Okay, a maar is a volcanic crater formed by a massive explosion from the superheating of groundwater. Now, I'm sure most of you already knew this, but you're all acting up and pretending to be shy."

The mostly retirement-aged group of tourists who were settled in for the pleasant ride rewarded him with some laughter and chuckles.

"Did you know that there are two other examples of maars close by to Lake Barrine? We're so lucky here on the Tablelands to have such magnificent natural wonders."

Once Nate had the boat cruising at a nice steady speed, he made for the shallows where reeds poked their thin stalks above the water level in little clumps and water lilies spread their plate-like leaves in amongst the mayhem of the reeds.

"Everyone, this is Sophie, and she's very important." Nate pointed to Sophie, who gave a small wave and a chuckle. "She will be serving Devonshire teas in a moment, so please feel free to come up and help yourself. You can move around the cabin freely, go upstairs to the deck for a better view, but we ask that tea facilities remain downstairs."

Nate continued his spiel regarding safety and what to do in the unlikely event someone fell overboard and needed assistance. He didn't once glance towards Roberta. Why did he consider her such a threat? If he couldn't see her, she wasn't there. Hopefully, she was ignoring him because he had every intention of doing the same.

Passengers milled around the downstairs lounge, their chatter upbeat as they headed for the tea facilities. Nate took this as his cue to concentrate on his driving until he needed to provide his next lot of commentary.

The general hubbub of noise washed over him. Seeing Roberta again only reminded him of the ugly image plastered all over the front page of the local newspaper. His gut clenched into a tight knot. It did every time he was reminded of it. He blamed her for everything that went wrong yesterday, including the hefty fine their band of supporters were slapped with.

In the past, they'd always talked their way out of a fine, able to agree on a sensible outcome. Even the farmer who'd loaned them the bulldozer received a nasty fine. This all added up to an intense dislike of this woman, and he wanted her as far away from Lake Barrine as possible.

Sharing the same small cottage? Not in this lifetime! He would move out if he had to.

He gave Sophie a few more minutes to serve the Devonshire teas before slowing the boat alongside a massive fallen tree partly exposed above the waterline. Cutting the engine, the boat glided a little further before resting on the water's surface. The wildlife lovers aboard that day would get an opportunity to snap many pics.

Talking into the microphone, he directed everyone's attention to a massive scrub python curled up in the fork of the fallen tree's branch. "Okay, folks, time to get your cameras out, this is a great spot for pics." Without fail, his mate, as he liked to think of him, made himself comfortable on this tree most days, dozing in the sun.

He gave them a few minutes before pointing out that if they looked into the water, they would see plenty of saw-shelled turtles. There weren't any eastern water dragons sunning themselves on the exposed trunk, but that was usually a hit-and-miss sighting.

"Any bird lovers here today?" Nate asked.

A few hands went up. "Well, you're in luck today." Nate pointed to a tree on the edge of the water. "If you look up onto those branches, I can see half a dozen Australian king parrots."

There was an immediate bustle as the bird lovers moved to the outside rail, craning their necks up for a better look and aiming camera lenses. The contrast of green and their red-orange chests was always a glorious sight and such natural awe always managed to calm him. For a split second, he forgot about Roberta's presence. Despite taking a quick glance around, he still couldn't see her. She must've gone to the upstairs deck. Out of sight was a good thing.

After another five minutes, Nate started the engine and continued steering towards another spot where a family of eels usually swam just below the water's surface. If they were lucky, a musky rat-kangaroo might poke its head out along the forest's edge. They'd see some scrub turkeys for sure. They always did. For now, he continued his commentary, pointing out some of the duck varieties bobbing on the water's surface. Today, there were black ducks, plumed whistling ducks and a handful of dusky moorhens.

As the boat gently glided along, he told everyone to look back towards the teahouse and pointed out the two one-thousand-year-old kauri pines, clearly visible, protruding from the forest canopy. "If you haven't already done so, be sure to take a stroll to the viewing platform less than a hundred metres from the teahouse."

There was a general mumbling from the passengers. This usually meant that some passengers had arrived early and already viewed the trees. "For the more active, there is a pleasant five-kilometre walking track around the lake. Lots of birds and wildlife to feast your eyes on."

The shock of seeing Roberta again continued to reverberate around his body, but he pushed it aside for now. All he needed to do was remind himself of how lucky he was. There had been many days on his overseas travels where nature wasn't at its best. Crowded cities, pollution, destruction. It took leaving his childhood home to finally appreciate the gift they had. No way would he let a chit of a woman stand in his way. A quick chat with Natasha, the moment he docked the boat, would sort the issue out.

⚜

Roberta straightened her back at the mention of the kauri pines and looked back towards the teahouse. Once pointed out, it was obvious where they were. She noted how close they were to the teahouse and the small cottage tucked in behind where she would be living.

Nate's commentary from the upstairs viewing deck was easy to follow. If she forgot who was talking, it was easier to enjoy the cruise. Now, to come to terms with the shock of seeing him again. *Damn!* Her gut was telling her this was bad news for her plans.

She mulled over options, needing to find any means of locating the damn box her mother had buried twenty-eight years ago. Her issue was that Lake Barrine was a national park, so visitors came at any time of the day or night. Finding a window of opportunity where she could dig around the tree would need to be done in the dead of night. In total darkness. A proposition that scared her to the core.

Now, to curb the churning in her stomach. It wasn't from the gentle gliding of the boat as Nate put it back in gear and steered away from the bank towards another spot.

It was from an incident that happened years ago. Stupid, really, what a group of teenage girls got up to when looking for fun. On a school camp in the wooded snow-gum forests of Mount Buffalo, the group of five sixteen-year-olds snuck out in the dead of night.

They were giggling so much that no one heard or saw the group of wild brumbies. Roberta couldn't even remember what their plan was. Was it to prove they could sneak out? She frowned, lost in thought as the breeze whipped across her cheeks, flapping the brim of her hat. Most days, she pushed the incident to the back of her mind, but when confronted with needing to go outside in the dark alone, it reared its ugly memories, causing all her old fears to rise again. She would never unsee the mangled body of one of her best friends. The one that never made it back to camp that night.

Nausea threatened now as she gulped it down. She gave herself a mental shake and stood on shaky legs as the boat picked up speed. She would need to quell this fear, or she may as well drive back to Melbourne and apologise to her mother for not being able to carry through with the plan.

Her knuckles shone brightly as she grabbed hold of the stainless rail surrounding the top deck. There was no choice. It had to be during the night. If it wasn't tourists viewing the kauri pines, it would be joggers completing a circuit of the lake—in the early mornings or late dusk.

Inwardly groaning, she slapped her palm against the rail, deciding to go back downstairs and confront the monster of seeing Nate. She might even give Sophie a hand to clear up the morning tea mess. Nate wasn't her employer, Natasha was, and she had to remember this. No cowering allowed. She was strong, and she would do this. This job was a means to an end. Hopefully, her mother's madness would end once she retrieved whatever it was hiding in the box.

Roberta used the chrome rail on either side of the narrow half-a-dozen steps for support, swaying slightly with the movement of the boat. Cameras and phones were out in full force again as passengers at all vantage points, both upstairs and downstairs, snapped the view of the lake in all its morning glory. The glint of the sun turned the water into a turquoise wonderland, and a feeling of nostalgia claimed her attention for a moment. She straightened her back, pushing the ugly memories away. The idyllic time she'd spent with Antonio and the gorgeous seas surrounding Italy only served to remind her of the rut she was currently in and unlikely to leave until she sorted this mess out.

A splash broke the water's surface, quickly followed by a piercing scream, then a panicked voice. "Man overboard!"

The boat's motor instantly cut.

# Chapter 6

Roberta ripped her sun shirt off, followed by her shorts. She wore a bikini underneath for a swim later, and without hesitation, she leapt over the side of the boat. The coolness of the water rushed over her skin as she glided beneath the water and swam towards the man.

The man wasn't flaying his arms. Roberta's training suggested a medical condition might have caused him to topple over the side. As she took hold of his chin to keep his head above the water, he still wasn't responsive.

Close by, another splash sounded, causing Roberta to whip her face around. Nate was in the water with a ring-shaped lifebuoy. Sophie held the other end of the rope. With Nate's help, she placed the buoy over the middle-aged man's head and down his torso, pulling his arms over the top. She signalled with a tilt of her head for Sophie to pull them in.

Many helpers were stationed at the rear of the boat, ready to haul the man onboard. A passenger had taken over the rope duties, and Roberta lost sight of Sophie.

"Quick, lay him down. I'm going to do CPR," Roberta said. Everyone scattered once the man was lying on the deck. Sophie returned with what looked like a first-aid kit and an automatic external defibrillator. *Good job!* Sophie seemed to know how to use it as she opened the case and spread the contents out.

A female passenger towel-dried the man while Roberta unbuttoned the front of the man's shirt and began CPR. Water dripped from Roberta's hair onto his chest, but she pushed her long strands out of the way, continuing her compressions.

Nearby, a woman wept while others tried to comfort her. Despite presuming she was the man's wife, Roberta blocked out the distraction and concentrated on the number of compressions and breathing into his mouth.

In the next instant, Nate was beside her. "I'm going to turn the boat around. Natasha will contact triple zero and get an ambulance on its way. Will you be okay here with Sophie's help?"

Roberta risked a quick glimpse up at Nate. "I'm a nurse. I've done this before."

Nate squeezed her shoulder. His touch surprised her, jolting her with extra confidence. A man's life was in the balance here, and she needed the boost.

Sophie continued to dry the man's torso before placing the defibrillator pads on his chest. Roberta didn't stop with her CPR, knowing every second counted.

"Ready when you are," Sophie said with an encouraging smile.

"Ok, we don't have a response yet. Let me do one more set of compressions." Once Roberta had done so, she shouted, "Clear!" to ensure no one was touching the man before they pressed the 'shock' button on the defibrillator.

On her knees, Roberta swayed with the motion of the boat, using her hand to steady herself. Nate was pushing the boat as fast as it should go and, in her periphery, Roberta caught a glimpse of the dock. They were close now.

As soon as the defibrillator delivered the shock, Roberta continued for another two minutes of CPR as instructed by the voice prompts from the machine.

Roberta lost track of time as she and Sophie continued to follow the prompts and perform CPR. The moment the sounds of sirens pierced the air, she realised the boat was no longer moving. *Don't stop compressions!*

she instructed herself. There was still a chance to save this man as he was getting medical attention within minutes of the incident.

All the while, she had a sixth sense of what Nate was doing. With the boat tied to its moorings, he was guiding the passengers off with calm efficiency and an apology. One passenger commented that Nate had invited them back that afternoon for a second chance to complete the cruise. No one raised their voice or sounded angry. No one was that stupid.

Then the paramedics were there, taking control of the situation. They fitted an oxygen mask over the man's face just as Roberta felt the jolt of a heartbeat under her palm.

"He's breathing!" she shouted.

"Great work," one paramedic replied. "Now to stabilise him for moving."

The logistics for getting this man up to the ambulance was no mean feat, but in no time at all, with the help of the two paramedics and Nate, the man was on the gurney.

Roberta collapsed onto her backside, utterly exhausted. She rocked to and fro with her arms wrapped around her legs. She'd come a long way from that one night when no one had been skilled enough to treat their friend after a pack of wild brumbies stampeded past them. Maybe her need to be a nurse stemmed from that night. She would always carry the guilt she'd been useless and incapable of doing anything to help their injured friend. She shivered, suddenly cold, when a slight breeze eddied around her bare bikini-clad body.

From her vantage point at the rear of the boat, she watched the progress of the three men as they wheeled, lifted and carried the gurney up the concrete steps to the car park.

"You did great. Since we're going to be working together, what's your name?" Sophie was on her knees packing up the defibrillator. "I saw you coming out of Natasha's office, and she told me you're starting tomorrow." She smirked. "I'm sorry, no secrets here."

Roberta smiled at the young woman. "I'm Roberta, and I wasn't told this job expected some sort of initiation."

Sophie chuckled. "You saved a man's life, you know. I heard you say you're a nurse. That's a special skill to have."

"I hope he comes through okay. It's always a hard pill to swallow when you lose someone."

"I've never been in such a situation. Not sure how I'd react," Sophie said, rising with both kits packed up. "By the way, you were awesome. Just saying, and this calls for a coffee and scone break. Natasha won't say no, but let me do a quick pack up of the Devonshire tea stuff and get it back up to the teahouse and into the coolroom."

While Sophie stowed the kits away, Roberta went looking for her clothes and found them neatly folded on a chair near the bottom of the stairs, along with her tote bag beside it. She slipped on her shirt and shorts, grateful for the considerate passenger who must've seen her throw them off before she dived into the lake.

Back by Sophie's side, Roberta helped her stack all the morning tea things back in the food cooler. Once the top of the food cooler was back on, Roberta lifted the handle on one side. "Do you think we can carry this up together?"

Sophie, with her youthful exuberance and twinkling hazel eyes, took the other side. "I'm sure we can. Lead the way."

⁕

The teahouse was buzzing with excited tourists, and Roberta didn't doubt Sophie would need to pitch in. They placed the food cooler inside the kitchen, and another kitchenhand started unpacking it. "Hey, Sophie, I might go for a quick stroll and look at the kauri pine trees."

"But—"

"You guys look busy here for the next little bit. I'll be back soon for that coffee and scones. I promise."

Sophie's short honey-brown curls bobbed around her face when she smiled. "Okay, fair point. Off you go. They're amazing trees to look at."

*What about digging around them?* Roberta inwardly groaned, chewing on her thumb nail as she worried over this. The more she dwelled over her predicament and her promise to her mother, the more stupid the idea sounded.

Natasha dashed into the kitchen, causing her to come to a sudden halt. "Roberta, wait!" She rushed up, enfolding her in a squeezy hug. "Thank you so much. Oh, my God, it could've been so much worse." She stepped back and waggled her finger. "Welcome to the team, girlfriend."

Roberta laughed. "I'm just going to take a look at the giant trees; I'll be back soon."

"You make sure you do. Coffee and scones are on us today."

"I've already told her this," Sophie piped up from the other side of the kitchen island bench.

"Good girl, Soph, now go and enjoy, Roberta. We'll keep you busy enough tomorrow."

Roberta left the hustle and bustle of the kitchen and walked out towards the crowded midmorning-filled teahouse, taking a moment to wander around and look at all the memorabilia displayed on shelves and walls. Photos of days gone by and an impressive old piano with a sign saying 'Please feel free to play'.

Roberta could play the piano quite well and enjoyed it when she had free time. It was one way she unwound after a tiring and hectic day. Running her fingers along the polished surface, she admired the unique timber grain of the upright. Her shoulders wilted as she looked away, taking in the view of the serene and picturesque lake through the dining room windows. Once this stalwart and proud family realised she was an imposter in their midst, the last thing they'd want her touching was this grand old beauty.

And forget about making a connection. She muttered incoherent words, loud enough for some of the diners to look her way. Straightening up, she plastered on an apologetic smile and walked down the polished staircase towards the water's edge, her hand sliding along the rail. She considered this one attribute of her personality a downfall. Put her in a new situation with different people, and they'd be besties in no time at all, creating lifelong friends. She couldn't afford for that to happen here. Unearth the damn box, cover up the evidence and get the hell away. Finding it would sure as heck open another Pandora's box, but a reminder of how distraught her mother was when she revealed her secret wouldn't go away.

Stepping out into the sunshine, she gave herself a moment to soak in the warm rays. As she swung her tote bag over her shoulder, she spotted a sign pointing to the path to view the twin trees and walked towards it, cursing her mother every step of the way.

# Chapter 7

The kauri pines were barely a hundred metres from the lake on a
well-maintained path. At the viewing platform, Roberta hugged her
arms around her chest. The lack of sunlight penetrating through the thick
forest sent a chill over her skin that had nothing to do with the actual
temperature around her. Craning her neck, she looked up and up, inhaling
the rainforest smell, strong with moisture and damp leaf litter. Filling her
core with its pungent aroma, she closed her eyes for a moment, willing
success to come her way. How, was any man's guess.

Opening them again, she set her sights on the top branches clearly
visible from the cruise boat that morning. With a rough swallow, she
couldn't help but feel small and insignificant. This job required a strong
woman. She'd been told before she was strong. Didn't fully understand
what that all meant. She got things done; could that be it?

Snapping her attention back to the base of the giant trees, she
considered her other issue. Yep, time to stop agonising. Time to get things
done. Her mother hadn't said anything about how impossible it would
be to reach either of the bases. It wasn't a case of just walking up to the
base of either tree. A mere three decades was nothing in the life of these
1000-year-old beauties, but the viewing improvements put in place by the
national parks since put an entirely new spin on everything.

Roberta eyed the purpose-built viewing platform painted mission
brown to blend in perfectly. A visitor viewed the trees without trampling or
disturbing the forest. Meaning to get anywhere close to the base, Roberta

would need to physically climb over the rails and slide down the supporting posts for a couple of metres without killing herself. Or her mother when she returned to Melbourne. These murderous thoughts momentarily disturbed her.

"Hey."

Roberta spun around.

Nate frowned. Roberta tried to change the scowl she was sure she sported by lifting the corners of her mouth to some degree. After all, wanting to murder her mother and a reminder she and Nate were enemies tied in perfectly with how she probably looked. Discovering they would be working together only added to her dilemma. Nothing to smile about, but she tried.

"Everything okay?"

Roberta chuckled wryly. *If only you knew.* "These trees are something."

Nate watched her warily.

*Sheez!*

"Are you okay? Er ... after what happened?"

*Did something happen?* She was already past that and onto bigger and greater things, so to speak. Squaring her shoulders, she needed to say something to placate Nate. "Yeah, all good. It's not the first time I've been in that kind of situation. I handle it okay these days."

Her heart did its usual twist, reminded again of the one time she wasn't skilled enough to help. Watching her injured friend die was the lowest moment in her life. God help her if her mother was about to create another one to better that.

"He's going to pull through, thanks to you."

Roberta shrugged. It felt wrong to accept any platitude from Nate, considering their short and recent history. If his family lived and breathed this lake and its surrounds, she didn't expect their history to improve with her temporary stay. Or with what she planned on doing.

*It better be a short stay.*

She made to walk past him on the narrow path. "Sophie's expecting me back soon. She promised me a sample of your famous scones. See you later." Her heart thundered as she passed Nate, their shoulders barely grazing. She reached up to rub the back of her neck, feeling Nate's gaze burn a hole there. *Ignore the good looks, girlfriend.* This man was nightmare territory. She'd seen another side of him, exposed at his best. With his hair messy in a hot, desirable way, he was not to be trusted. Neither was his gorgeous and tanned body which she easily pictured tangled with her own.

She bit down hard on her lip, willing all her womanly fluttery bits to calm down.

Do. Not. Go. There.

❦

Enjoying the solitude of the balcony at the teahouse, Roberta savoured each bite of the warm, fluffy scone. She'd lavishly topped it with strawberry jam and cream, oblivious to the fact that, for once, if she wasn't careful, it wouldn't take long for this deliciously wicked food to land on her hips. With a smile, she lifted her espresso for another sip. She quite liked her smooth curves. She was okay with some shape and who in their right mind didn't love sweet temptation?

A pelican swooped low before landing on the water. The view from where she sat was so incredible she couldn't help but feel grateful. It was spectacular. Serene. Relaxing. *If* she could relax. Roberta didn't know the full story yet. Why had her mother chosen the kauri pines to bury the box? The hardest goddamned place in the universe to get to without starting a riot!

Her mother's 'I've said enough for now. Find the box, and then I'll tell you more' irked her no end. Her patience levels wavered somewhere between zero and negative one hundred, so this wasn't helping. Being forced to wait, plan and devise a way of recovering the box was driving her nuts. In a national park, for God's sake. Where visitors and tourists hung around all day. She mentally swore, wrapping both her hands around her espresso for another sip. It was becoming a daily ritual to thank her mother in the not-so-kindest way. *Thanks, Mum.*

Pushing her worries aside, she glanced away from the serene lake to the busy teahouse where every table looked to be full. This would be her tomorrow. Busy, hectic and working the tables again. A rush of excitement bounced across her chest. No stress in this job and the change of scene would do her good.

Natasha promised to show her the small cottage that came with the job before she left today, but with the number of people queued for food, Roberta didn't see how this would be possible. Not unless she stayed until closing time, which wasn't ideal as she'd promised to meet up with Sally after her teaching day ended. Roberta conceded it didn't matter how tiny or cramped the cottage was. It was a means to an end. She'd cope with whatever was offered. The only requirement was a coffee machine. She'd refrained from bringing her own with her. Her car had been cramped as it was. If there wasn't one available, she'd buy one. Simple really. Roberta needed her morning dose of coffee or she didn't function. She needed to be functioning at her best to solve her current dilemma.

❧

"Oh, my God, the Surrey family. Nate Surrey. You're tangled up with them?" Sally's laughter gurgled, filling the air around them.

Sally drank her chai tea while Roberta swallowed a piece of chocolate brownie that seemed hell-bent on staying stuck in her throat. Obviously, there was something about this family she needed to know.

Sitting inside a quaint little café in the adorable village of Yungaburra, the delicious forkful of the sweet treat slid down her throat with a thud. A sip of her coffee couldn't help settle it.

"I am not tangled up with anyone. One freakish incident. That was all." Not even all the dizzying variety of coloured flowers in hanging baskets lining the streets of Yungaburra could distract her. What was she dealing with here?

"I knew of Nate. Didn't have much to do with him as he went to another school. But I remember girls would drool over him. Good looks and all that." Sally winked at her. "Then he disappeared off the face of the earth. No idea where he went or why, but clearly he's back."

*Oh, great.* Roberta hadn't shared with Sally her reasons for being in the north, and she intended to keep it that way.

"By the way, you're on the front cover of today's *Cairns Post*. No doubt the same photo is in the local *Express* paper, too."

Roberta groaned. "How bad do I look?"

Sally continued to smile and laugh in between her sips of chai. "You look great. It's Nate's expression that won't do his charming looks any good. Or his cause. Something must have happened in the past few years for him to be so worked up about environmental issues. I get his family have always been passionate about it, seeing they own the freehold on the lake. His great-grandfather played a key role in saving large areas of forest from being felled, but to go to this extent? Hmm ... interesting. What bug does he have up his backside?"

*What bug, indeed.* Once again that day, she thanked her mother for putting her in this predicament.

"Look, it's only a job to pass the time. If it doesn't work out, I'll look elsewhere. No big deal. From what I saw today, he just does the boat cruises, so we don't have to cross paths unless I'm doing the Devonshire teas on the cruises. Surrounded by visitors, I'm sure he'll be on his best behaviour."

"Yeah, this is Roberta, after all." Sally quipped with a smile. "I've never known you not to cope when around difficult men. Now, tell me the story of the man's life you saved. I wouldn't be surprised if the story turns up in tomorrow's *Cairns Post.*"

Roberta shrugged, dismissing the possibility. Why would saving a man's life make news, when it was a frequent occurrence in her normal day? She worked on finishing her massive slice of brownie, finding it was settling much better in her stomach now that she'd shared her news with Sally. As Sally reminded her, dealing with men was her strong point. Look at how she'd dealt with Antonio when she realised it wasn't an ideal life after all, despite how much money would be at her disposal. No way would Nate stand in her way and her mission. In fact, she would avoid him entirely during the day and sneak over to the cottage once her shift finished.

She could be civil for those hours. Heck, she could be whatever she needed to be. Just get the damn job done and get out. Fast!

# Chapter 8

"Y ou're working late." Nate took the only other chair in the office, sitting opposite Natasha. "You should really go home to those munchkins of yours."

Natasha replied with a weary smile. "Brad was home early enough to collect them from school. I just wanted to finish some food orders for the next week."

Natasha worked long, hard hours and was the driving energy behind returning the iconic teahouse and cruises onto the tourist map with force—refreshed and revitalised. Despite constantly harping to her to be careful of burning out, it fell on deaf ears. But still, Nate was proud of her and was ready to share the burden of the business, like family did.

"I see you're in the paper again," Natasha remarked, tidying her desk for the day by shuffling paperwork into neat piles. "At least it's a better story this time." She smirked, tilting her face towards the neatly folded *Cairns Post* perched on the end of her desk.

Splashed across its front was a picture of himself, Sophie, Roberta and the man she'd saved. He'd briefly read it during his lunch break.

"You haven't put the two together yet, have you?" He tapped his finger on the image of Roberta.

"What do you mean?" A slight frown marred Natasha's pretty face. With sandy-blonde hair not much different from his own, freckles dusted her cheeks and petite upturned nose.

"Your newest staff member is the same woman who crossed my path at the blockade."

Natasha's brows rose. Twisting the office chair around on its castors, she scrambled for yesterday's newspaper sitting on top of a pile of old newspapers behind her. "You mean Roberta?" Unfolding the newspaper, she stared at the front cover. "It's hard to tell. Did you shove her that much she fell back?"

Nate grimaced. "Trust me, it's her, and no, I didn't. She bounced off me."

Natasha giggled. "She looks like she's about to kill you."

"I thought that's what I looked like. Those thoughts *had* crossed my mind."

Natasha squinted closer, tilting the newspaper in different directions. "Nope, still can't make it out as her with her face turned that way."

"Any chance she was a total disaster today and you can ask her nicely to go back to wherever she came from?"

Natasha started laughing. Really laughing. Good, strong laughter that built momentum and spilt from her throat. Nate was not amused when tears trickled down her face. "Oh, Nate, she was amazing for someone's first day." Natasha grabbed a tissue from a box on her desk, wiping her cheeks. "Sorry, Nate, you know how short-staffed I am. Please don't ask me to do that."

Nate rubbed a hand over his stubbled chin. "I don't know what's so funny."

"Nate, she's a live wire. Full of wit and humour, and boy can she sing. She kept us entertained all day with her singing and I've never laughed so much. Come on, I've never heard of any woman getting the better of you before ... except for the last one." Looking sheepishly apologetic, she added, "She's a breath of fresh air, Nate. Might do you good to have her around."

*Do him good?* He'd given everything to Crystal. Had dutifully followed her to the ends of the earth believing they belonged together. Their beliefs aligned perfectly until he made the heart-breaking discovery he was being used for her profit gain. She wanted him for his good looks and his charismatic charm. He would look perfect in front of a camera, she'd told him as they sold their documentaries and beliefs on climate change. For Crystal, it was big money. But Nate was sceptical. Big money destroyed natural, pristine areas when overexposed.

He'd got out. Licked his wounds, taped up his broken heart and came home. At least he had some sway over what happened at Lake Barrine. But the need to protect other areas of north Queensland wouldn't leave him. Ever! It was the driving force that made up his DNA. He'd seen the best and worst of the world on his travels; it made his skin crawl when he saw nature destroyed because of money and greed.

"Does she know she's sharing the cottage with me?"

"Ah…" Natasha folded the newspaper, rolling back in her chair to return it to its spot. Facing him again, she tapped her finger against her mouth, like she did when she was thinking. "She knows she's sharing with someone. I don't think I went into specifics."

Natasha narrowed her eyes and studied him carefully. He did his best to remain neutral. "She really was awesome today, Nate."

He groaned. "Why is she up this way working tables? She's a nurse, for Christ's sake. Aren't they desperate for nurses everywhere?"

Natasha shrugged, opened a desk drawer and put her stationery away. "Sounds like she needs a break, that's all. Can't hurt her. I'm sure being a nurse is stressful. Anyway, she'll be gone before we know it, and I'll be desperate for staff again." Natasha rose, making to leave. "Why don't you go for a run around the lake? Get rid of the angst you carry around with you every day."

Nate's brow arched. Was his anguish that visible?

"Yes, my dear, wonderful brother. I see it. You're unhappy; things haven't quite gone your way. I get you thought Crystal was the one, but now she's shown you her real side, you need to move on. Please."

She stepped closer and squeezed his shoulder before leaning down to give him a sisterly peck on the cheek. "I, for one, am glad you're back where you belong. Together, we're going to rock this place."

Nate leant his elbows on his knees, rubbing both hands down his face.

"Whenever I'm in doubt," Natasha continued, hesitating before she left, "I pull out this photo of Grandad." She rifled through a stack of papers in an in-tray on the edge of her desk. "It's only a copy of the original, but take another look, Nate."

Nate looked up, knowing the photo Natasha was holding in her hand. It was of their grandfather in the prime of his young adult life. Probably the same age as Nate was now. Lake Barrine was once a mecca for water skiing enthusiasts before it was banned by national park authorities. Their grandfather was at the forefront of all the fun, the first of their family to turn their iconic attraction into a viable business. A big man, handsome, fit, healthy, and the most popular person on the lake. And boy, could he water ski.

"This is you, Nate—the exact clone of Grandad. You come with the same fire and passion he had back in the day. You're going places, and I want to be right there beside you when you do."

She ruffled his hair before hoisting her handbag on her shoulder and collecting bookwork to take home with her. "Go for that run, Nate. I'll see you tomorrow." Before she left, she paused at the door. "Be nice to her, Nate. I get that not everyone thinks the way you do, but that just makes you extra special." She gave him a sweet smile before adding, "Don't forget to lock up."

Nate sat alone in the quiet of the small office tucked behind the kitchen. Natasha kept it tidy, which clashed with his chaotic thoughts. He'd already planned on a five-kilometre run around the lake and had his joggers on. After another hectic day, he loved nothing more than inhaling the heady rainforest scents as he dodged tree roots and scrub turkeys on the run around, coupled with breathtaking views of the lake visible in disjointed visions between the trees.

As for putting up with Roberta, he stood and swore into the quiet room. How the heck was that going to happen?

Nate slowed his pace to a leisurely jog for the final one hundred metres. He'd gone hard all the way, and it felt good. His lungs burnt, and his muscles ached, just as they should. Enough to put a smile on his face as he began his warm down.

When he exited the shadows of the forest, he squinted as the late afternoon sun struck him across the face. That's what he loved about the jogging track. Complete shade all the way and, as he usually jogged before dusk, rarely was there anyone to share it with.

He bent over, hands on his knees, catching his breath. But jerked upright when loud music coming from the cottage assaulted his ears, grating along every nerve.

"Really?" he muttered. A scowl quickly replaced his smile. *People listen to music at that decibel?* Forgetting about the stretches he usually did after a run, he ploughed a hand roughly through his sweaty hair, striding to the cottage. The warning from Natasha got lost somewhere in the words Jimmy Barnes was shouting.

He wrenched the back door open and came to an abrupt halt. Roberta danced with her back to him. Sunlight streaming in from the large window bounced off her dark curls as they spilled down her back. She punched the air with her fists, swayed her hips in time to the music as though a mirror ball flickered around her and she was in some nightclub, singing every word to the song. Jimmy Barnes' 'Khe Sanh' finished and the lyrics to 'Flame Trees' filled the cabin. Classic Aussie rock, he got that, but out of place at Lake Barrine.

No matter how hard he tried, his gaze remained trapped. Roberta hugged her arms around her chest as she slowed her movements down in time to the rhythm and beat of the new song. Nate swallowed roughly, giving himself one more moment to enjoy her extraordinary voice as it filled the room, blending in with Jimmy's heart-pumping volume.

He remembered doing something similar in an Italian nightclub. The thrill of hearing an Aussie song had been a helpful balm for a boy pining for home.

He shook himself out of his reverie and worked out how she managed to project so much noise. She'd inserted a phone connection to a portable stereo left behind by some other tenant passing by. He flicked off the power switch, sending the cabin into complete quietness.

Roberta spun around. A myriad of confusion crossed her face as her chocolate-brown eyes focused on him. She stared at him in stunned silence, a fierce blush raging along her neck and cheeks. "When I didn't see a car parked outside, and nobody was around, I thought I had some time to my—"

"My vehicle is parked in the maintenance shed."

Confusion marred her pretty face, a frown puckering her forehead. Her chest still heaved after her dancing exertions, but it didn't take long for her eyes to change to tiny slits. "Why did you switch the music off?"

Nate's mouth opened, but nothing came out. Roberta's eyes returned to wide-open orbs when the truth of the situation dawned on her. "I'm sharing this place with *you*?"

Nate might've laughed out loud if these weren't his exact same thoughts.

"Bloody, flamin', bitching hell! No frickin' way. This is not happening! Not now, not today, and *not* bloody tomorrow." Roberta stomped around the cramped space that contained a table and a small brown couch, shoving at a chair, ripping out the lead attached to the portable stereo, slamming a used coffee mug on the kitchen benchtop for no reason, all the while muttering profanities he hadn't heard in a long time.

Ever mindful of Natasha's warning, he took a deep breath, needing to fix this. "Calm down, will you."

"Calm down, my arse!" She came to a halt, probably deciding there was no future in creating further havoc in the cottage, and stood ramrod straight, arms tightly crossed. She fixed him with a piercing glare, pinning him down, his breath barely able to pass through his throat.

"Whose idea of a joke is this?" She clipped each word, her jaw tight.

*Jeez*. He expelled the trapped air, wanting nothing more than to kick her out and create some semblance of order in his quiet space. The only time he'd briefly shared the cottage was soon after his return from overseas. Most staff were locals and lived close by. Dealing with noisy transient staff wasn't on his wish list. "Who even plays music that loud?"

"What?" she huffed. "What are you? Eighty or something? Bloody hell, break free. Do something a little daring. It's only music, for God's sake."

"*You* don't like the daring things I do," he barked, all the frustration over this woman crashing back into his psyche, hitting him square in the chest.

"Doing something stupid is different from daring," she scorned gruffly, hands on hips now.

"In your opinion." Nate moved one step further into the small cottage as the standoff continued for awkward seconds.

"This is not happening." Roberta picked up a small day pack he hadn't noticed and stormed out, knocking his shoulder on the way past and giving the door a fierce slam.

Nate remained rooted to the spot, relishing the quiet filling his senses. "Well, that went well," he muttered before collapsing onto one of the kitchen chairs at the solid four-seater table handmade by his grandfather. He shoved yesterday's and today's newspaper to the other side of the table, not prepared to face another reminder of Roberta. Natasha would eat him alive if she found Roberta gone the next day. He savoured the blessed quiet for one more minute, hoping it would calm him as usual. It didn't. The quiet was eerie, disturbing his normally ordered mind. Like there was something missing. Noise of some type. Loud noise. Swaying hips. A voice to kill for.

His fist hammered the years-old tabletop as he scraped the chair back, rising. Without the sound of a car starting up, he had no choice but to look for her before she did something stupid or hurt herself. It was easy enough done tripping over a tree root and spraining an ankle, especially in the growing dusk.

Grabbing his torch on the way out, he willed away the sensual reminder of those swaying hips. *Don't be so stupid*. If he was going to look again after Crystal, he wanted a woman who was at least on the same path as he was. Not some wild she-devil with a melodic voice who had already struck something inside his core.

Leaving the cottage and flashing his torch from side to side in the near dark, his shoulders drooped. Once upon a time, he thought Crystal was on his same path.

Look how well that went.

# Chapter 9

A fierce blush continued to burn her neck and cheeks. Roberta welcomed the cool dusk air as it brushed over her heated skin. Anyone else and she wouldn't have given two figs. But to be caught doing what she loved most after a busy or stressful day, by Nate, of all people—

She cringed in the encroaching darkness, swore again, and trampled her way towards the twin trees. Sharing the cottage with him? This had to be some twisted joke.

The urgency to dig for the small box and get the hell away became super important. She carried her phone and a small torch in her bag, so there was no better time than right now to determine if her plan was good to go.

At the viewing platform, she inhaled the moist air to help reduce the speed at which her heart was racing and ignored the strange sounds popping and cracking nearby. She could do this. She wasn't foolish Roberta for nothing. Fearless, brave and sometimes crazily stupid.

She smiled in the dark. This was how her friends described her. But they never complained because she always provided fun and a good time. First to jump into a freezing lake in Scandinavia. First to sample live bugs on their last holiday to Thailand. First to do a lot of things that no one ever dared to—the party always started and ended with Roberta.

She'd had the best day and thoroughly enjoyed working the tables with Natasha, Hannah and Sophie. When Roberta cottoned on that Hannah enjoyed singing too, they'd taken to hashing out singing duals, much to the amusement of guests enjoying their meals. But now she needed to forget about the café and focus on her biggest job yet.

"Okay, girl, be the first to climb over this damn rail and take a look. *Do not* think of what just happened." It was a stern and necessary reminder.

Roberta rifled in her daypack for the torch and secured it in a zipped pocket of her shorts, leaving her bag handy to collect on the way out. She didn't waste another moment overthinking her next move and swung first one, then the other leg in an undignified manner over the top of the timber rail and slid down the other side, with no idea of how far the forest floor was, but allowed her hands to slide, hoping she would touch something firm by the time her grip held the bottom horizontal rail.

Something brushed her leg and she almost screamed. *Bloody hell!* She was going to kill her mother after this. Then, her shoe connected with something firm. She breathed a sigh of relief when the forest floor appeared closer than expected.

Releasing her grip on the rail, she found her footing and freed the torch. She switched it on and swung its light from left to right. She could hear scurrying but didn't see anything move. Her mother had been specific about which tree to dig around, complete with a hand-drawn diagram. The image was so vivid it seemed permanently tattooed behind her eyelids. The left tree, around the other side, away from the path, beside one of the few tree roots jutting out.

Illuminating the base of the tree with her torchlight, Roberta quietly groaned. Three large roots jutting out. She silently cursed her mother again. How fast did a buttress root on a tree this old grow? She'd left her gloves in the daypack, and this time, she groaned louder. She needed to clear some of the leaf litter to determine which of the roots to start her digging, but she didn't want to use her bare hands. Who knew what she would touch. A shiver trickled down her spine. She muttered, threw in a few colourful words and used her foot to clear some of the leaf litter around the first root.

"Roberta, are you okay?"

She froze. *Oh fuck.* How had she not heard his footsteps? She clutched at her chest and sucked in a deep breath.

"Are you hurt?"

Torchlight sliced through the darkness, its brightness getting stronger and stronger. "I'm coming; don't move if you're hurt."

*Damn!* She had to show her face. Of course, he'd know it was her. She stupidly left her daypack on the platform. "I'm fine," she called out. "I'm coming."

She emerged from behind the tree and squinted at the bright light, her brain scrambling for a reason to justify her actions. "My ring came off my finger. I was madly cursing you; my hand was wildly waving, and it came off. I can't find it."

"You did what?" he questioned from the viewing platform, hands on his hips.

Okay, so her excuse sounded lame even to her ears. She cringed. Oh boy, she was acting like a strange version of herself.

"I'll come back tomorrow with a metal detector and look for it. I'm sorry it slipped off, but in total darkness, it's madness looking for it." Nate swept the light across the forest floor in one last ditch effort to see the non-existent ring.

*Ugh!* Why was he being so nice? From the forest floor, she stared up, her torch light reflecting off his hair, making it look like a halo. Like an angel had come to rescue her. Except she knew the very devil resided in his body. *Forget how gorgeous he is.*

"Here, give me your hand. I'll help you up."

Nate dangled his arm over the edge of the platform. "Come over to this side."

If she'd considered it earlier, it looked like a safer way to descend. She locked that piece of useful information away for her next attempt.

Licking suddenly dry lips, she raised her arm. When Nate's warm hand touched hers, an involuntary rush of goosebumps rushed over her skin. When he tightened his hold, her breath hitched in her throat.

He hoisted her back up on the platform and she stumbled over her feet. Nate used his firm hold to right her.

"Madly cursing me, were you?" He paused a beat. "That's funny because I was doing the same thing just minutes ago."

And just like that, they were back to being enemies.

"Thank you," she managed to say, even though it almost killed her. "I best be getting back. I'm hungry." Christ! Was she staying at the cottage?

Roberta picked up her bag and made to walk off. Nate halted her with his warm hand on her forearm, gently turning her around. *His hand is nothing, girl.*

"Natasha liked you a lot today. I don't want to do anything to make her life harder, so you and I need to be civil to each other if we're sharing the cottage. Or pretend to."

His unusual blue eyes were dark pools in the darkness. She shivered at his direct gaze. Was it from the threat he was making or the strength of sibling love? Everything was so mixed up that she dropped her face and nodded. "Not sure how I'll manage that."

"Hmm … makes two of us. How about we start with some dinner? I noticed you haven't stocked your half of the fridge yet, so what were your plans?"

*Oh, if only you knew.* "I … um … was going to do some shopping tomorrow. I have some bread and peanut butter. That'll do."

"Then you'll enjoy a steak and salad?" Nate's eyes locked with hers. "Unless you're vegetarian or vegan."

"None of the above. I would've thought that was more you."

"Not me. So, you'll help me. Maybe make the salad?"

Roberta scoffed. *Maybe?* She was practically born with an apron tied around her waist. Italian mother, Italian father—oops, scrap that, she had no idea who her father was. This mission was supposed to be a discovery of sorts, and cooking was something she did to soothe her nerves. She was a lover of all food, and it would one day be her downfall if her curves continued to grow. Maybe she should switch from cooking to singing. Both had the desired soothing effect.

"I'll make a salad that'll leave you panting, boyfriend," she gamely challenged, walking past Nate and leading the way out of the forest. "If your homely little cottage doesn't have everything I need, I'm raiding the teahouse kitchen. Take that as a warning."

Okay, this was beyond crazy. What on earth had prompted her to say that? Wasn't steak and salad a way better option than peanut butter sandwiches? And why was the thumping in her chest increasing with each step she took? Startled by the sound of laughter, she stopped midstep, and Nate walked straight into her back.

"Oof, sorry."

She spun around, Nate grabbing her arm to stop them both from tripping over their feet. This required more touching—hands, arms and the soft knock of their knees together. Now she was being ridiculous. Why would she care about how the hairs on his legs caused her knees to tremble at a touch? Honestly, she was here to do a job. That's all.

The muted light from their torches brightened Nate's face, revealing laughter lines crinkling at the edges of his eyes. The way his face transformed as he laughed had her stomach tumbling. Funny tummy and wobbly knees. Yep, nothing funny here!

"Did you just call me boyfriend?"

Her shoulders dropped with relief. "It's a figure of speech; I mean, imagine that scenario?"

His laughter died on his lips.

*Eyes away from his mouth, girlfriend.*

"Yeah, we'd kill each other. Couldn't possibly imagine such a thing," Nate whispered, pulling apart uncomfortably.

Roberta swallowed, draining all her energy just wrenching her eyes away from his. "The salad, bloke," she uttered, needing to make as much space between them as possible, "and you promised me a steak. Not reneging on the deal, are you?"

She stalked off, her hand gripping the torch as she swung it in front of her. She would die of further embarrassment if she tripped over a tree root.

"Now, why would I do that?" Nate said from behind her.

# Chapter 10

Nate went directly to the fridge, crouched down and opened the crisper. He lifted out the iceberg and cos lettuce he usually kept to mix together, along with a carrot, a rich-red capsicum, a cucumber and the packaged baby spinach.

"Is this enough?" he asked, balancing them in his arms.

Roberta had spotted the newspapers and was leaning over the table reading today's story. "Huh what? Natasha mentioned my front-page fame. Isn't there anything else exciting to report in this town?"

"You saved a man's life. You don't think that's worthy of some attention?"

Roberta shrugged. "It happens every day in the big smoke. What were you saying, by the way?"

"Is this enough for the salad?" Nate placed the ingredients on the kitchen sink and leant against it, casually crossing his arms. "Even the smallest gesture of kindness in our community doesn't go unnoticed. Don't be surprised if the man's family returns to thank you personally. It's how we roll in these parts."

Roberta glanced up from the paper, challenging him with a suffering sigh—city girl versus country boy—that sort of thing.

"Walnuts, mustard and cherry tomatoes."

Nate tore his gaze away, stepping towards the small pantry. "I can provide you with two of your requirements, but I'm out of cherry tomatoes."

"What about balsamic vinegar?"

"Yep, here!"

"Not good enough. Lead the way and unlock the teahouse kitchen. I know they have cherry tomatoes there."

"Honestly, they're not necessary; we'll make the salad without them."

"Not in this life, bloke. You threw out the challenge, and I'm following through with it. So, get moving and hurry up if you want to eat tonight."

For a few heart-thumping moments, they duelled with their piercing gazes. Nate capitulated first, swore quietly and led the way out of the cottage.

Roberta giggled quietly behind him. "I love a man with colourful language."

Nate harrumphed before growling, "Stay," leaving her standing on the cottage verandah. He'd forgotten the key to the teahouse and returned inside for it. This woman was turning his brain to mush. He didn't like it one bit.

On the narrow path towards the teahouse backdoor, they brushed shoulders, causing Nate to shiver in the coolish night-time air. The sooner they got past this ordeal of helping each other prepare this one meal, the sooner they could look after their own cooking arrangements. He already regretted his invitation. This salad wasn't worth the turmoil it was causing him. He also needed dinner over and done with before the crew turned up for their usual fortnightly meeting. How was he going to get rid of Roberta while they thrashed out their next move in the fight against the wind farm taking over another piece of pristine wonderland?

Would the team recognise Roberta? If they did, he would become the laughing-stock of the group. *He* couldn't believe he was in this situation.

Fumbling with the key, he berated himself for not picking up the torch or grabbing his phone on the way out. *Bloody hell!*

"Here, let me. I'm pretty good at breaking into places."

Roberta's warm hands took hold of the key attached to a piece of carved timber, causing his breath to catch in his throat. "That's reassuring. I'll be sure to let Natasha know of your bonus skills."

"Do that," Roberta casually returned, opening the door.

Nate reached over her pretty head and flicked on a switch, not missing the laughter in her eyes when they locked with his. "I'll wait here. You obviously know your way around."

She smirked and sauntered off towards the cold-room storage while Nate willed himself not to drop his gaze towards her curvy hips. *Don't do it!* He failed. They dropped at the same time he struggled to swallow the lump wedged in his throat. Why was this woman affecting him this way? Christ! She was so wrong for him. Her manner, her confidence, her everything. It criss-crossed his head, leaving him puzzled. How could being around someone when he was so exasperated with them heighten every sense in his body?

He was questioning everything when she returned and thrust the punnet of cherry tomatoes at him.

"Here, hold this."

Not giving him time to think, he took the punnet. Roberta wound her way back around the tables, stopping at the piano.

"Could I have a couple of minutes, please? It's been ages since I sat at a piano."

Pleading and asking for permission to play the instrument? All in one sentence? She didn't wait for an answer and sat down. Nate leant against the doorframe where he hadn't budged from for the entire time they'd been in the teahouse. She struck the first key, turning it into a warm-up scale. Nate moved closer, mesmerised by her supple fingers. His stupid brain imagining all sorts of things with those hands.

He willed himself to step closer. By the time he was standing beside the grand old piano, she'd moved into something so beautiful and melodic that its sound wrapped around his senses, pulling, tightening, his chest heaving, leaving him breathless and enchanted. He'd never heard anything so beautiful.

Nate dragged his eyes away from her hands. Roberta looked lost in her own world. He licked suddenly dry lips, the sensations whirling inside his head.

When Roberta stopped, the music continued to reverberate around the room.

"Wow." He wanted to say more, but that was all he could muster.

"What a beautiful, grand old thing."

When their gazes latched together, there was a softness, a vulnerability looking back at him.

Nate roughly swallowed. "My great-grandmother received it as a gift from my great-grandfather before his tragic death. That was back in 1924."

"Do you play?"

Nate shook his head. "That was really something. Does it have a name?"

Roberta chuckled. "Just a little Beethoven and his Moonlight Sonata. Not all of it of course. Come, sit here." She moved to one side of the piano stool and patted the spot beside her. "I'll teach you how to play the chopsticks."

Like a moth drawn to a bright light, he sat, immediately pulled to the warmth of the spot—spellbound.

The cherry tomatoes packet crinkled in his hand, jolting him back to reality, and he stiffened. "We can't. We need to get dinner over with. I have a meeting tonight, and I still have some prep stuff to do."

Roberta tilted her face towards an old photograph on the wall, her fingers pressing the odd key, her velvety chocolate eyes washing warmly over his skin. "With those same morons from the other day?"

And just like that, she shattered the magic.

"You need to find new friends," she declared, gently closing the lid over the piano keys.

Nate jumped up, damning his stupid self for getting caught up with this woman. Who was she? Holy hell, she could sing Jimmy Barnes at incredible decibels and then turn around and play something as emotionally sweet as Beethoven. Then irritate the heck out of him.

He envisaged an invisible net hovering over him, gently falling, dropping and wrapping around his body—trapping his arms and legs.

His breathing was laboured as if he was already ensnared. "Come and make this salad you claim you're so damn good at."

"Right behind you." Roberta slid from the piano stool and pushed it in.

She squeezed past him at the back door, allowing him to switch off the light and lock up. Despite the absence of her touch, his body burned with acute awareness. Except for their gazes—and they clashed again. Nate concentrated on his breathing, making sure it sounded normal. Not like he'd just run a lap around the lake at top speed. All the while, he cursed this woman who'd gatecrashed his life, leaving him with a sinking sensation it was going to get a whole lot worse.

# Chapter 11

Roberta unpacked her suitcase and personal belongings while voices from the living area filtered into her room. She'd made the salad a thousand times before and was oddly pleased when Nate claimed to enjoy it. Really, her staple salad growing up in a food-rich Italian family was no big deal.

They cleaned up after dinner, leaving Roberta drained after her long day. When the visitors began arriving, Roberta disappeared into her room, taking a moment to look at her new lodgings for the first time. Turning in a tight circle, the small yet quaint room came with a good-sized bed, a built-in cupboard with hanging space and shelves, a bedside table and lamp, and a comfortable-looking chair facing the massive window. It wasn't all bad.

By the morning, when the sun lifted its bright rays and spread them over another day, there would be a spectacular view of the lake. She walked over to the floor-to-ceiling window trimmed in a rich, red walnut architrave, pushed aside the light grey curtain, and slid across the top half-glass window. Breeze rushed into the room, and she inhaled deeply, feeling fortunate to be so close to this magnificent natural wonder. A whole world away from living in the Melbourne suburbs she'd called home her entire life.

Currently shrouded in darkness, she couldn't wait for the night to end so she could experience the exhilaration of waking up to the sparkle of the morning sun on the calm waters of Lake Barrine. Surrounded by a thick ring of lush tropical rainforest, she already recognised the unique rainforest fragrance as it continued to rush into the room, engulfing her senses and leaving her momentarily heady.

Roberta turned away from the window, her shoulders slumping when she eyed the door to the bathroom that joined the two bedrooms. Nate had already mentioned they would be sharing it. Sighing, she picked up her toiletry gear and opened the door. The bathroom looked like someone had recently renovated it, decorating it in whites and greys with forest green towels. She found two empty drawers in the cabinet and placed all her toiletry gear neatly away while fighting an image of a naked Nate in the shower.

*Oh, please, do not go there.*

The reminder she wasn't here to snare a man had her speeding up her actions. She unpacked in peace without having to confront anyone, but there was still work to be done that night.

With a cottage full of tree-hugging greenies, Roberta was hell-bent on returning to the giant trees for another scout. She had to forget about dazzling lake waters and World Heritage listed rainforests. They weren't for her. Get the job done, get out and return to the hum-drum of hard work and long shifts at all hours of the day and night. It was what she loved. Right?

This train of thought stopped her in her tracks, and she took a good look at herself in the bathroom mirror. Her short but satisfying fling with the super-wealthy Antonio had left her maudlin and, in some respects, damaged for life. They'd been good together until the money thing became too much. Not her style at all. It opened her eyes to other ways of life that were so different from how she was raised in Australia. There were no regrets from the experience and no turning back.

Now it was time to get things done and keep her mother off her back. She'd messaged her mum countless times already but promised her a phone call soon with an update. When she had something to report!

Time to move along. She flicked off the light switch in the bathroom and closed the door, locking it from her side. She didn't feel threatened having Nate so close, but it was probably more a symbolic gesture to save herself. Her rumbling thoughts every time she pictured a naked Nate were a concern.

Back in the tiny bedroom, she quietly groaned, reminded she would need to deal with the fallout with Natasha when the time came. It was only day one but already Roberta loved how Natasha and her team welcomed her. There was a sense of belonging, a comradery that was lacking in her usual hospital work environment. Still, there was no way she was staying here and sharing this cottage with Nate for one minute longer than necessary.

Who knew, she might even take Sally up on her offer to stay with her and continue working at the teahouse for the remainder of her holiday time. That way, she'd do her day's work and disappear after three pm. Mostly avoiding Nate.

Armed with her daypack and essential digging gear inside: trowel, torch, phone and a sharp spikey tent peg, she stood at her bedroom closed door for a moment, drawing her shoulders back. She inhaled deeply and held it in before exhaling slowly. There was no way out of the cottage without walking past everyone in the small living area. Inwardly growling, she was at least grateful Nate would be too busy to come looking for her.

Then, an idea bloomed. She'd spotted the ancient coffee machine on the island bench in the kitchen. A couple of shots of coffee would help her get through the night.

Opening her bedroom door, she made straight for it. All talking stopped as eight pairs of eyes followed her every move.

A couple of females stood out from the mostly male contingent. Roberta recognised them from the day of the protest. She didn't stop until she reached the coffee machine, placing her daypack on the kitchen floor by her legs. Separated from the living room by the island bench, Roberta faced the meeting contingent. She half smiled and half grimaced in their direction before dropping her gaze and started making a coffee.

Roberta glanced up in the awkward, quiet moments when someone let out a low-pitched whistle.

"Nate, old mate, what's going on?"

Roberta recognised the man from the other day.

"Stop it, Brent," one of the females jovially cautioned.

"She is definitely the same one from the other day," another male quipped, which led to an eruption of chatter, filling the small room, jarring Roberta's already tired head.

"Need a hand?"

She hadn't seen Nate approach. She knocked back his offer. "Nope, won't take long, then I'll leave you all in peace while I go sit outside and enjoy it."

"You don't have to."

She levelled her gaze with Nate's. Why was he being kind? The image of his naked body burnt in her mind as she imagined herself peeling away his clothes and seeing him fully exposed. Holding in a gurgle bursting to explode into laughter because of the way her brain worked, she managed a stifled smile instead. The others were beginning to crowd the coffee machine. With the water already heated in the machine, it wouldn't take long to make a drink. "I'm nearly done. I'll leave you to it."

"It's Roberta, isn't it?"

She nodded to the female who'd asked.

"I'm Nadia, and ignore these Neanderthals. I liked you from the first moment you retaliated on that blustery highway. We need someone like you on our team."

Roberta would've choked on her coffee if it had been made. "Thanks, but no thanks." She pasted on a fake smile for Nadia's benefit before whipping out the finished coffee and taking a symbolic sip to signal she was done making it. She picked up her bag with her free hand. "I'll take this outside so you can continue your meeting."

Nadia followed a few steps beside her as Roberta made for the front door. "We could use some common sense in our meetings, and I think you'd be perfect. Come on, Roberta, say you'll stay."

Now she did choke on the one small sip. As for Nate, she ignored him. If the spot burning her left cheek wasn't Nate staring at her, she'd eat worms for breakfast the next morning.

Anyway, what was it with this woman? Did Roberta really come across as someone who wanted to get tangled up in this drama? Did Nadia not remember the fuss she made at the police station?

"Maybe next time." She shrugged, hoping against all heck there wasn't a next time, and if there was, that she would be far, far away. Hopefully, clutching a small box with God knew what inside, that her mother was dumb enough to bury. In a rainforest. Beneath giant trees protected in a national park. *Good God, shoot me now?*

In her rush to be away from the gathering, she pressed closed the door a little firmer than intended, creating an eruption of more talk and probably more awkwardness for Nate.

*Oh well, he'll cope.*

She had bigger fish to fry. Without hesitating another moment, she dug out her torch, pointing it towards the twin trees. She took small sips of the strong coffee as she checked for protruding roots and anything else that might trip her up along the track. It would be her luck to hurt herself, needing Nate to save her.

She took one last quick glimpse of the star-studded night sky before the start of the path enshrouded her in dark and eerie forest noises. A shiver trembled over her back. If there was one thing she hated, it was being outdoors with unfamiliar noises that served as a reminder of another dark night when wild horses galloped towards her group of friends.

*Stop it!*

Her imagination was her worst enemy, and she forced herself to think of one man—naked.

She loosened up, the fear dislodging. Thinking of a naked Nate was bound to be the safer option that night.

# Chapter 12

R oberta leant over the timber rail, determined to finish her coffee first. Anything to bolster her reserves as she mulled over her plan. She had some idea of where she would start poking the ground. There was one tree root bigger than the others. As long as she didn't forget to dig to the left of it, her first plan of attack had a sound basis.

Her mother had harped on about it being on the left many times. Roberta dismissed the niggling concern her mother might've got it skewed over the years. Would she clearly remember which side of the damn root to dig if she'd been as upset as she claimed to have been?

Roberta grimaced. Never again would her mother be allowed to criticise *anything* Roberta did. This topped the dumb list of things to do as an irresponsible young adult—Roberta had done plenty to attract her mother's ire—and Roberta didn't even know what was in the damn box yet. She huffed, draining the last of the coffee before placing the ceramic mug down, hoping she didn't forget to collect it on the way out.

It was now or never. With her torch on high beam, she navigated the short step off the platform onto the forest floor on the far right where Nate helped her up earlier.

She stumbled a little on the uneven forest floor. Her ankle rolled slightly before she gained a better foothold by holding onto the rail and cursing for good measure. Had Nate really believed her crazy excuse for being off the platform? *Madly cursing you in every way possible. My hand wildly waving. Ring flew off.*

Her excuse sounded so lame now, she couldn't believe Nate fell for it. Surely, he was brighter than that?

She shrugged, needing to dismiss Nate from her thoughts. She was gifted the perfect opportunity to dig around the tree while Nate and his buddies discussed the next protest. Did Nadia really want her to join their mad, mixed-up lot?

*Not in this lifetime.*

She crouched beside the larger of the three tree roots unearthed earlier before unzipping her daypack for gloves and the sharp metal tent peg she'd found in the small shed her father had enjoyed spending time in. He used to dabble with the metal lathe, doing all sorts of projects with it. With a wink and a twinkle in his eye, he used to tell Roberta it was his special time to get away from Mum's nagging. Roberta's heart constricted for a moment. Whether he was her biological father or not, he was the only father she'd ever known. It hurt that her mother kept this secret all these years. A secret her father obviously knew nothing about. A secret that would never have seen the light of day if her father hadn't been tragically killed.

With renewed determination, she donned her gloves and brushed forest litter away from the tree root. *Now, to start.* She did so with a hefty thrust, surprised by how moist the dirt was. She'd imagined hacking through hard earth, but this was going to be so much easier. Overjoyed that it might be possible to get down the approximate one foot—her mum's words—she happily hummed songs played to death on the drive up from Melbourne. She made a mental note to expand her travel playlist one day.

After a few more solid stabs of the tent peg, a light sheen of sweat coated her skin, and she stopped to take stock of how she was doing. She removed a glove and raked a hand over her forehead and into her hair, making a mental note to shampoo her hair later so it looked respectable for her shift tomorrow.

Not too bad, was her verdict, as she directed the torchlight closer. It wasn't so much the packed earth that needed digging past but the tangle of other roots protruding from the main one. But she was making progress and didn't want to hack too hard, in case she broke through the small plastic box her mother assured her would fit in her palm.

Confident she was at the right spot, but not really having any idea if she was, Roberta put down the torch, angling it to get enough light on the hole. Grabbing hold of the tent peg again, she continued to loosen the dirt, pushing it out of the way with her gloved hands.

"What the bloody hell are you doing?"

Roberta froze, her arm raised for another stroke. *Bugger!* How did she not hear his footsteps? No doubt the torch resting against the thick lichen-encrusted tree was doing a brilliant job of illuminating her. How was she going to come up with a new reason for being there this time? It was obvious she was digging with the small mound of dirt beside the roots and a tent peg in her hand.

"What's going on, Roberta? And none of that bullshit about losing a ring."

Oh, okay, so he didn't fall for it. She lowered her arm in slow motion but remained on her knees.

Nate stood at the timber railing, shooting death glares at her. This was one moment she couldn't draw forth a naked Nate. It wouldn't tally up with the scowl directed at her.

"You were trouble from the start. Too much didn't add up, and to find you here working for Tash, bloody hell, I should've suspected something was off. Why are you here, Roberta?"

She sighed, put away the tent peg and picked up the torch. "Is this when you call the police or the national parks people? You might get the chance to see me in handcuffs again. Would you like that?" She didn't mean to smirk, but the slight tilt to her mouth must've irritated Nate because *his* straightened and his eyes turned into ugly slits.

In carefully clipped words, his warning came across clearly. "I suggest you remove yourself from near this tree. The tree you're tampering with is protected. You don't want to know what the hefty punishment for that is."

Roberta rose, zipping up her daypack. All meticulously done to give her some time to come up with something to say. Picking up her torch, she tramped towards the viewing deck with no idea of what to do other than tell the truth.

Extending his arm, he offered to help her back up onto the deck. For a second, she rejected it—no way was she going to give him that pleasure—until she lost her footing and realised she did, in fact, need his help. The warmth and strength of his hand buoyed her before a naked Nate flashed past her mind. She was always amazed at how her mind worked, but with certainty it was too late to be saved. She was doomed, and she still hadn't explained a thing.

Roberta focused her torch on the path, starting back towards the cottage.

"Where are you going?"

She stopped and turned around. "Walking back and giving myself time to come up with a better story than my ring flew off. Is that okay with you?"

His face relaxed for an instant, and his mouth turned up a fraction. Then again, maybe her mind was playing tricks on her. Nate was back to his stern scowl and not-so-friendly expression.

"Er ... your coffee mug."

*Oops.* Roberta chuckled, instantly regretting it. It was so not the right time to do so.

"And make it fast. I'm only seconds away from calling the police."

Roberta rolled her eyes for good measure, certain Nate would never see it when she crouched down to retrieve the mug. "Be sure to ask for Officer Molloy. He was nice."

"You won't get a choice, trust me."

Roberta grunted, turned away from the twin trees and faced the path again. "Says he who steals bulldozers, holds up traffic and God knows what else. Aren't you a model citizen?"

"Hurry up, Roberta. We don't have all night."

"Yes, we do." God, she was being obstinate and possibly a little immature. Looking for a fight. Spurring him on, determined to irritate. She used to love doing this with her younger brother, earning her parents' ire on every occasion. She guessed a leopard never changed its spots. Which was a pity because with Nate's good looks and magnificent body, in another universe, they could've had so much fun together.

In the stillness of the forest night, he growled, setting her heart singing. She was getting a reaction, and at that moment, it was all that mattered.

With the mug swinging from fingers, she reluctantly led the way out of the forest. *Come on, girl, think.* Damn it! If she had a little more information about what she was digging for, she'd feel more confident. How would her mother handle a late-night call? She could pass the phone over to Nate and let her do all the explaining.

Back at the cottage, she dropped her daypack outside the door and removed her grubby shoes. There were moist leaves and twigs stuck to the soles, and she was mindful enough not to carry it inside.

Scrunching her toes to ease the onset of what felt like cramps, she realised she'd been on her feet all day. The stress of a new job and everything happening since brought on a tidal wave of fatigue. Doubt crept into her mind, making her unsure if she'd make the distance of this new discussion. Making sense of what her mother did nearly thirty years ago was already enough to unsettle her. Attempting to explain it to someone else felt like the worst imaginable situation to be in. At least there wasn't an audience. It looked like everyone had gone home after the meeting.

With her phone needing charging, she unzipped her daypack to retrieve it before dropping it back at the front door. At the sink, she gave her mug a quick rinse, leaving it upside down to drain. Then she made for the two-seater couch and flopped onto it, aware Nate was only two steps behind.

With nowhere else to sit except beside her on the couch, Nate chose to sit on the floor beside the couch, knees raised and arms resting on top. Without lifting her gaze, she noticed all this from her periphery. Could she ignore him? Fiddling with her phone, she checked her messages first before blacking out the screen. She would put it on charge soon.

"Roberta?" Nate said gruffly, looking at her with a scowl.

*Oh, fuck!*

"My mother buried a small box there nearly thirty years ago."

Precious awkward moments passed when the only sound was that of Nate's fingers tapping his knee. "And?"

"And what?"

"What's in it, for starters?"

Roberta jumped up, aggressively slapping her thigh. She paced the small room, already knowing its cramped layout from her earlier stomping. "That's just it. I don't have a bloody clue, only that it has something to do with my biological father, whoever he is."

"And this is recent news to you?"

She stopped and spun around. "Barely a few weeks." She tensed when tears threatened to build up behind her eyes. Her hands curled by her side, her fingernails digging into her palms. As Nate's concerned gaze washed over her, she fought a wave of despair threatening to bring her down by swallowing harshly. Good Lord, she was so tired and so over this mission already. Yet somehow, she was expected to remain strong for her mum. Roberta was always strong, wasn't she? She'd handled the news surprisingly well, hadn't she?

"The news hit you hard?"

*Oh, shite!* This was the first time she'd told anyone about her mother's secret. Nate nailed it on the head, putting it into words before she could even comprehend it. The next few minutes were a blur. It happened too fast. One minute, she was mentally cursing her mother again, and the next minute, Nate had her in his arms, holding her tightly, soothing her after she burst out crying. Ugly crying.

"I'm not crying, okay? I don't do crying." She hiccupped and blubbered all over Nate's chest, her howling haunting her own ears.

"Sure," he soothed, rubbing her back. "Just a bit of moisture totally soaking through my shirt. Yep, totally not crying."

Now there was chuckling added to the messy mix, and God help her, she didn't want to think how blotchy she would look after this fiasco.

When she calmed down enough that tears only dribbled down her cheeks and the occasional hiccup escaped, she took a step back. Only as far as Nate would let her. He held her by the shoulders, his fingers lightly pressing through her shirt.

She gamely reached for *his* stretchy cotton shirt and bent towards it, using it to mop up her eyes. She reasoned if he was holding her captive, she had no choice.

When she glanced up, she latched onto his face, unable to make out what she was seeing. Compassion? Anger? A hint of understanding?

Nope, scratch that. She'd gone too far with Nate and would have to tread carefully. Tears wouldn't save her. She gulped, for once shutting her mouth and preventing the words so close to slipping out. Something about being held against her will. She quite liked where she was, and the combined smell of woody rainforest and steaming coffee made this man's aura a very attractive one.

"I'll help you find this box. In fact, you won't go anywhere near those trees unless I'm completely in charge. Am I making myself clear?"

Just like that, Nate's aura died a horrific death.

"And Roberta, if you're lying to me, so help me God, you'll regret this for the rest of your life. No more made-up stories of rings flying off fingers. Got it?"

Her lips twitched, but she made a heroic effort to remain serious. "But I *was* madly cursing you."

"Same here."

Nate dropped his serious stance and managed a chuckle. "But the threat stands, Roberta. Take this seriously because tampering with a tree in a national park is an offence I won't ignore."

His fingers gently kneaded her shoulders, and she couldn't think straight. A stress headache was hovering around the edges of her temple. Without meaning to, she slumped closer to Nate. "Can we discuss this tomorrow? I'm tired and really need to sleep."

It happened fast. A quick squeeze before he released her, giving her just enough time to suck in one last breath of everything Nate. "Are you angry with me?"

"Yep."

He didn't look it. Was he sure? She took a step towards her room. "Okay, I guess we'll keep working hard to be civil to each other. For Natasha's sake."

Nate nodded before she turned away, confusion marring her brain. She hadn't done anything that bad to warrant his anger, *and* he'd agreed to help her. Okay, she conceded, he had caught her digging.

"Don't do anything stupid behind my back, Roberta. You haven't witnessed how ugly I can get when crossed."

She stopped at her door and turned back. This responsibility thrust on her broad shoulders by her mother had been weighing her down for weeks. She was only beginning to realise how much so. She'd take another set of broad shoulders any day to help her out.

Her smile may have come across a little crooked when her facial muscles wouldn't move like normal, but she was leaving with the last word if it was the last thing she did. "I'd say crazy, Nate, not ugly. You've displayed enough already to give me a fair idea. I've been told I'm crazy too. Maybe we'll get along just fine."

"Maybe we will."

His gentle response washed over her tired body. She could've sworn his lips were turned up slightly as she closed the door and slumped against it.

Too tired to evaluate all the emotions hammering inside her chest, and the fact she didn't get the last word in after all, she heaved herself away from the door, falling face-first onto the bed.

# Chapter 13

Roberta wiped down the last of the tables in the dining room as the trading day neared its end, the sun sparkling over the lake on its western side.

Hannah was wiping down the chairs and pushing them in. "We're heading to the Yungaburra Pub later tonight for their usual Friday band night if you want to come along," Hannah called from the other side of the room.

Oh, to be eighteen again. While eighteen was a lifetime ago for her, it might do her good, and she could drag Sally along too. Roberta chuckled. "We'll see. If I don't get there tonight, I'll try next week."

Hannah accepted her response and continued working, humming a tune Roberta didn't recognise. She'd never felt her full twenty-seven years before. With Hannah showing all the exuberance and confidence of someone so young, Roberta could learn a lot from this driven young woman.

The only thing holding her back from joining Hannah and her young friends was the hope Nate would agree to dig up the box that night. They hadn't discussed a time or day, but tonight suited her. Anything to get the hell away from Lake Barrine before she dug up more than she planned. Pun not intended.

"Bye, Roberta. See you tomorrow," Hannah called, skipping down the timber staircase out of sight.

"Bye," she replied to Hannah's retreating back.

With it only just ticking over to three o'clock, buying groceries and having a proper shower were next on her list. She'd forgotten to set her alarm the night before and awoke fully clothed, smelling rank. It left her rushing to get to the teahouse in time for her shift. Their day was so busy she'd only spotted Nate twice from a distance. Word from Hannah was that Saturday and Sunday got busier again.

Closing the French doors of the teahouse and doing a last glance around to check everything was in order, Roberta made her way past the kitchen to the exit leading outside to the grass lawn. She spotted Natasha in her office and waved goodbye as she walked out.

She would give Nate no choice about digging tonight. Either he came with her, or she'd start the job alone. Not doing it behind his back but fully disclosing her intentions. She chuckled as she slipped next door to the cottage and made for her room. Grabbing her handbag and car keys, a fissure of energy zapped along her arms as she made her way up the uneven concrete steps that led to the top car parks. It would be worth it to see how ugly Nate promised he could get. God help her, she loved irritating the heck out of people who annoyed her, and Nate was presently right up there. Pity because the man had an amazingly muscular body verging on perfect. Downright sad to waste such a gorgeous-looking body.

It was his passion that really excited her, even if she didn't fully understand it. Here was a man who put everything before his own life for the safety of the environment. She'd witnessed the fire in his eyes and his protectiveness over those damn trees she wanted to dig around. Could he display the same caring for a woman? Did he have a woman in his life?

Roberta drove out of the lake's public car park, gnawing at her lip. *None of your business, girlfriend, and don't go there.* Remember your mission. Find the box, get the hell out.

"What else did you have planned?" Nate asked, back turned as he snapped closed padlocks on toolboxes.

"Is that a 'yes'?"

Nate sighed as he shooed her out, closing the door to the maintenance shed. Roberta allowed a small smile to hover at the corners of her mouth. One that Nate didn't see, even though his irritation was obvious.

She'd returned from the local supermarket in Malanda with enough groceries to fill her half of the fridge. Now showered and with washed hair, she was feeling clean and more human. Going in search of Nate to pop the question, the noise of soft banging had steered her towards the maintenance shed. It was hard to ignore the overpowering fragrances of sanded forest timbers heavily clogging the air the closer she neared the shed. There, she found Nate finishing his day amongst tools and dust. The sight of him shirtless left her drooling.

"Yes, Roberta, it's a yes to digging up this box." Nate walked off, making for the cottage.

"Tonight?"

"Unless you're too busy doing something else," he called over his shoulder.

Roberta gulped, doing her best to ignore how the afternoon sun shimmered over his toned muscles. What a waste to be gone from Lake Barrine without touching them at least once. "Well, ah ... Hannah did invite me to the pub. Some band night or something."

"They're usually pretty good. You might want to reconsider."

"No, no. I'm all up for digging. Actually, I could fit both in if we hurry up."

Nate stopped and turned around, and she collided with his chest. He grabbed her arm as they stumbled, leaving their faces millimetres apart.

Close enough for his warm breath to fan along her skin. It only lasted a split second. Enough time for his eyes to drop to her mouth before he stepped back.

Enough time for Roberta to change her mind and throw all caution to the wind, given the opportunity. Heck! Something happened in that moment, and it wasn't one sided. She dropped her gaze to Nate's neck, licking suddenly dry lips.

"Er ... sorry, but we can't do anything until it's dark when no one is about." Nate was back to the business of digging again.

"Are you sure? I was probably close to reaching it?" She was back on track too, cursing her stupid mind for going anywhere near what her body preferred.

"Yes, Roberta, I'm sure. How about a swim?"

"But—" She touched her shampooed hair.

"What?" Nate scowled, deepening a frown.

"I just washed it."

Nate tipped his head to the side, assessing her. "Would you really say no to a swim"—he pointed towards the calm waters of Lake Barrine where the afternoon sun winked and danced along its surface, waves gently lapping towards the bank—"on a hot day? To avoid washing your hair again?"

Roberta groaned. Impatient as she was to start digging, she half expected they would need to wait until darkness encroached. "Okay, we'll do it your way. I'll come for a swim."

Nate backed off, palms facing out in defence. "*The* Roberta Mintello agreeing to do something *my* way."

"Stop it!" Roberta chuckled before sobering up. "It's only a swim and ... and you know my surname?"

"I know the surname of all my staff."

"Why? I bet you cyber-stalk, too."

"Clearly I didn't check you out enough."

"That's not fair."

"What's not fair? That you're a pain in the arse and proving to be a serious problem?"

"Hey, I was going to offer to cook dinner tonight, to ... thank you for the steak last night and for giving up your Friday night. I can't be all that bad."

Nate sauntered off towards the cottage, talking back to her. "Depends. What's on the menu?"

"Pasta," Roberta replied to his back, following him.

"Do I have to make the salad?"

"Sorry, you won't have the skills."

At the cottage front door, Nate casually turned around, leaning his hips against a huge terracotta pot, where red, white and magenta impatiens blazed their glorious colours against the stark white cottage entrance. Then he laughed. Really laughed. His face transformed into a beauty of such magnitude that Roberta struggled to close her mouth when her jaw dropped at the sight. "What's so funny?" She didn't think she'd said anything too way out.

Nate did a quick job of curbing his laughter and opened the front door. "Sorry, nothing. Go get your swimmers on before the sun dips too low and it gets cold."

Nate held the door open, allowing her to enter first. She glanced warily at him, his smile dipping for a second when her shoulder brushed against his chest, and a deeper look of something passed over his face.

Only when she reached her bedroom did she expel the air she'd been holding. *Holy shite. Nothing is happening here, okay?*

Her hands shook as she scrambled for her swim tote bag inside the built-in cupboard. Yanking out her swimmers, she flung off her soft yellow cotton dress, followed by her bra and knickers. A delightful shiver passed over her skin, and a warmth trickled down to below her bellybutton. She put on her black one-piece before returning to her dress again, quietly swearing when her arms tangled in the spaghetti sleeves, making the task much longer to accomplish.

*Calm down, girl.* What was wrong with her? Anyone would think she'd never been in the presence of a good-looking man before. She found a towel and her sunnies and kicked off her shoes.

She spotted Nate waiting outside amongst the profusion of colour. Taking a closer look, she noticed that there were several terracotta pots, not just a huge one. They were all in a neat row along the front of the cottage; the explosion of vibrant colours tugged at her. Their bright mix calmed her, their beauty adding something special to the day. A memory that would be hard to forget.

She closed the front door and accepted the second inflated waterbed Nate offered her.

"Last one in's a rotten egg."

"Really?" She frowned. Was he turning this into a game?

Nate quirked an eyebrow, and a beaming smile stretched across his face before he strode purposefully towards the water's edge. "Really," he called back.

With his back to her, Roberta struggled to keep a smile off her face as she followed him. His childish manoeuvrer, in any other circumstance with any other man, would've had her shaking her head.

On second thoughts, she wanted to retract that. She *was* doing just that, but more because she was finding him such a contradiction. In the short few days she'd known him, how many sides to this man were there? Defining him using one word was an impossible task. Getting a handful of water thrown over her as she took one step into the lake ended any chance of it happening.

"Don't!" she wailed, her body shivering to the refreshingly chilly water.

"Take a few more steps, then dive in. It gets deep quickly."

Roberta stood at the edge as Nate flung the inflatable mattress out and dived in.

"Bugger," she uttered, immediately apologising to the family with small kids swimming near the bank only a couple of metres to her right.

The dad chuckled while the mum assured her the water was perfect. Roberta removed her dress, leaving it on top of her towel and sunnies on the grass. Following Nate's example, she flung the mattress as far as she could before she walked the few steps while the water was shallow and dived deep beneath its surface.

As she plunged, what she'd read about the lake came to mind. How many moons ago it formed and of its unimaginable depths. She wasn't about to hit her head on the bottom, but she levelled out, powerfully kicking her feet towards the surface.

Filling her lungs again when she broke through the surface, she took a moment to orientate herself. Nate lay afloat on his mattress only a couple of metres away, beaming, holding onto her mattress by the tow rope. She freestyle-crawled towards him.

"How was that?" Nate asked.

She chuckled. "Enough to forgive you for forcing me to wet my hair."

Nate chuckled, his laughter doing something to her. Hard to explain because they'd started off so badly on that blustery day barely a week ago, but it was a positive something.

"Here, I'll hold your mattress while you climb on, and then we'll paddle away from the bank."

Easier said than done, but with a lot of laughter and some swearing, she was lying on top of the mattress and following Nate as they paddled away.

Roberta was content to lie on her stomach, whereas Nate slipped off, diving and resurfacing a couple of times. Gradual exhaustion from the hectic day took over, her lethargic limbs refusing to move as the sun slowly set.

She closed her eyes, allowing her body to immerse in the splendour of the surroundings. If she wasn't careful, she'd fall asleep. Not such a bad idea until a slight breeze picked up and gently eddied over her back, causing goosebumps to rise on her skin. A reminder that a warm bed would probably trump this.

Her eyes jerked open when chilly water trickled over her arms. Almost lulled to sleep, she hadn't noticed Nate sidle up beside her. Caught in the trap of his azure-blue eyes, she never saw something else coming either. When the warmth of Nate's mouth touched her gently on the cheek, it burnt a hole on that spot. He drew back immediately when all she wanted to do was pull him back.

Breathlessly staring at each other, it was Nate who broke the spell with a barely audible whisper. "That was the wrong thing to do, wasn't it?"

Roberta stupidly nodded. "Very, very wrong."

"Oh, well, we all do something stupid at least once in our lives." With that parting comment and the mother of all serious faces, he flipped her mattress, and she landed in the water with a splash.

Spluttering back to the surface, Roberta fumed for reasons she didn't understand. "Nate Surrey, damn you to hell."

"What? It's only a bit of water. Surely getting wet again isn't a problem?"

"No, it's not. It's *why* you did it."

"So why did I do it?" Nate grabbed hold of her mattress to stabilise it. "No, don't bother answering; let's swim back. Pity, though, better to be damned to hell than heaven. We could have some fun down there together."

"Except I'm going to heaven, just so you know." Furiously kicking to stay upright, she grappled for the air mattress, making another effort to climb back on.

"Hah, you think?" were Nate's parting words as he grabbed hold of the tow rope on her inflatable and tugged both mattresses towards the bank with his powerful kicks.

*Oh, boy.* She would end up in hell, she was sure. Lying on her stomach, Nate did all the hard work of towing them back to shore while she enjoyed every single moment.

# Chapter 14

"So, how do you know *my* surname?" Nate meant to ask when they were swimming back to the shore, but Roberta's glare after his mischievous stunt had him zipping his mouth shut. It was bad enough he'd capitulated and kissed her.

"You, Nate Surrey, have a reputation, apparently."

"A what?" Now he wished he'd asked when she'd prepared dinner. There was plenty of time as she'd begun from raw ingredients and made the most delicious pasta he'd eaten in a long while. Nothing out of a bottle for Roberta.

"My friend Sally shared some gossip about you."

"Is this the same Sally who rescued you from the police station? I don't think I recognise her."

"Yep."

"What's her surname?"

"Sally to you, for now."

Nate growled in the torch-lit dark path as their shoulders touched, igniting a new energy throughout his body. One he hadn't experienced for a while. He was secretly excited to learn what Roberta's mum had buried all those years ago. Smart enough, though, to take great care around the old, colossal beauties. "Sally it is then, I guess."

Roberta chuckled beside him, her torch light wobbling along the path. "Sally says you disappeared for a while. Where did you go?"

His second groan in less than a minute reverberated around the forest. None of her business, he wanted to point out. Reminded again of how Crystal used him for her own agenda had his muscles tensing. He'd been young, naïve, madly in love—and duped. "I guess without Sally's surname, I can't tell you."

"Lame," was Roberta's immediate response.

They arrived at the viewing platform surrounding the two trees. Nate turned towards Roberta, working hard to keep a smile off his face. He liked her no-nonsense attitude and her lack of filters whenever she opened her mouth. It smacked of honesty, no bullshit, and was a refreshing change from the usual crowd he hung around. It was a whole universe away from the carefully articulated life he'd lived with Crystal.

The lack of light made it difficult to read Roberta's expression, but he was prepared to give as good as she gave. "I guess what I'm trying to say is it's none of your business."

She snorted. "Fair."

He raised his torch from the path to about waist height. Roberta looked at him with a smirk. The urge to cup her cheek in his hand had him curling his fingers into a fist. As relaxed as they were together, he wasn't so sure he could trust her yet. There were too many unknowns, starting with what they were about to discover.

"Um ... is it time to start digging?"

Trust Roberta to jolt him out of his trance. That damn kiss on the lake started something. Nate mumbled inane words under his breath. In her crazy way, she excited him, but it was better not to go there. After Crystal screwed him over, he lacked the confidence to try again. He shrugged in the near darkness, not prepared to let it bother him. For the time being, he was at peace with his life and too busy trying to save the world.

He carried a small shovel and crowbar in one hand which he put down before shrugging off the small backpack he carried. Crouching on one knee, he unzipped it, taking out a couple of headlamps. Offering one to Roberta, he swapped it with her torch, putting it away in the backpack. "It'll leave our hands free to dig."

He adjusted his headlamp strap around his head and secured it in place. Rising, he switched it on.

"Can you give me a hand? My strap is twisted."

"Sure." Stepping closer, Nate took back her headlamp. He received a tingle in response when their hands touched, but he ground his jaw, hoping to stem it. The Velcro strap was well and truly twisted. Probably left this way by one of the team on their last forage into the forest. As he untangled it, a potent scent assailed his senses. It was of lake water still strong from their swim, mixed with the intoxicating rainforest scent deeply ingrained in his DNA.

As it gently eddied around his nose, he detected a smidgen of something else. Whatever fragrance Roberta used reminded him of fields of wildflowers. The same scent he experienced on his travels throughout the deserts of Northern America. He'd detected it on Roberta before and was certain it was the day they were handcuffed together.

A chuckle almost broke free, but he reined it in, hoping the slight cough that escaped sounded normal. Roberta remained close but was facing the trees. His rambling thoughts only served to remind him of how they'd met. This was enough to push his crazy thoughts away and concentrate on the job.

"Here, I think I have it all sorted."

For once, Roberta was quiet when she turned back, and it unnerved him. He wasn't game enough to look directly at her but felt her gaze. Heat rushed up the back of his neck. He was glad it was too dark for Roberta to detect anything.

Tucking her long, dark curls behind her ears, he carefully strapped the headlamp in place before switching it on. He chanced a glance and regretted it the instant he did. Her large, luminous eyes looked at him, her mouth partly open and inviting as all hell.

"Oh, fuck," he muttered, his hands finding their way to her shoulders as he pulled her in closer and found her mouth. Light from their lamps blazed behind his closed eyelids as Roberta's warmth touched him in all the right places, weakening his resolve to stay the hell away from any entanglement.

The occasional click of their lamps touching wasn't enough to break the spell that had him wrapped up in this woman. When her tongue darted into his warmth, he groaned but willed the kiss to go on. She didn't seem to mind either and confirmed this by tightening her hold around his waist.

Only when common sense pervaded his senses did he step back, almost stumbling over the shovel and crowbar. His hands shook as he picked them up. "Sorry, okay?"

"Don't be sorry, Nate. You're really nice."

"Nice!" It suddenly reminded him of how he'd been just like that for Crystal. He swung the shovel in one hand as he walked to the edge of the platform. "Is that all I get? A nice?" He was tired of being the nice guy and vowed never to be that man again.

Roberta burst into laughter, disarming him completely. He stepped off the platform but sat back on it, laughing with her.

"To improve on nice, you'll have to repeat that all over again."

This was enough to sober him up, and Nate stopped laughing. "But this is all wrong. Remember how we met? I hated you on sight."

"Same here," Roberta replied, giggling. "Oh well, nice it will always remain."

This was ridiculous. Here they were, laughing, smiling and pretending nothing momentous had just happened. "Where are we digging?" He stood, needing to distance himself from this enigmatic woman. His lips still tingled, and he enjoyed it way more than he should have.

Roberta stepped off the platform, pointing to the left tree. "Behind that one, left-hand side of the largest protruding root."

"You're joking, right?" No Mr Nice Guy here.

"Nope."

"Remind me again, how many years ago was this?"

"Twenty-eight, actually."

"And you are how old?"

"I'll be twenty-eight in about nine months."

"Right." Nate dragged the word out. "So, your mother was pregnant when she buried it?"

A vulnerable look came over Roberta's face. "I guess you could say I've been here before."

Nate's heart plummeted, getting a gist of her take on the situation. Reminded of what finding this box meant to Roberta, he left the shovel and crowbar leaning against the platform and held his arms out. "Need a hug?"

"You suck; how do you know?" she argued half-heartedly, accepting his invitation.

Nate tightened his arms around her, pressing her against his chest. He dropped his face into her thick, lustrous hair and, despite her headlamp digging into his skin, caught a whiff of those wildflowers again. He filled his core with its scent. "If the box is there, we'll find it. Then you might get the answers you're searching for."

Roberta stepped back. He continued to hold her arms, his thumbs gently kneading her skin.

"Thanks, Nate. You really are a Mr Nice Guy."

"No, Roberta, I really am not."

When she finally dropped her gaze, she took another step away, breaking the connection tethering him to her.

"Ready to dig?" she asked.

Nate picked up his tools and walked to the base of the left tree. "We better." For more reasons than he could count. Once she had what she was after, Nate didn't doubt Roberta would leave. It would annoy the heck out of Tash, but she'd recover and find someone new. Roberta came to Lake Barrine for one purpose, and he got that. He was about to help her achieve it.

She was better gone, anyway. You'd think he'd learnt his lesson already. Some women were trouble, and Roberta was a red flag from the instant they met. But why was there a small ache in his chest, one he wanted to investigate further?

*Leave it be, idiot.* Easier said than done. His heart and head were two different identities, and at that moment, they weren't talking to each other.

# Chapter 15

"**I** can see where you made a start. Here, hold this."

Roberta took the medium-sized crowbar from Nate, while he used the small D-handled shovel to clear more forest debris away from the protruding root. Gently, he began digging away dirt.

Roberta held her breath, her heart thumping a little harder than usual against her ribcage. Today had been a rollercoaster of emotions. A mixture of anticipation. Heightened senses from kissing Nate. A sense of finding answers. So much hinged on finding the buried box, even though she had no idea what was inside. Her mother promised to tell her everything when she returned it. Tell her what? She already knew it had something to do with her biological father. The only snippet of information her mother let slip was that he died in a waterskiing accident. End of story. What was left to tell? He wasn't coming back.

Then there was Nate. A contradiction on so many levels. A major rollercoaster ride just on its own, without all the drama of digging up the box. An enigma when all she could think of was the next kiss. She was no shy maiden and could entice him between the sheets in an instant. But she wasn't ready to go there yet. Was in no hurry to destroy the quietly bubbling euphoria that flirting held. Powerful stuff, when taken slowly.

"Here, give me the crowbar. I'll loosen more dirt."

She handed it over, taking the shovel in return. The touch of his warm hand created a fizz along her skin, building up anticipation on so many levels.

"Okay, thanks. Shovel again."

"No, *thank you*," she pointed out, grateful for all his help.

He grabbed the shovel from her but took a moment to assess her before returning to the task. His gaze held a warmth she liked. It brushed gently over her face, his lips tipping slightly up, transforming his seriousness. *Good luck with trying to work me out*, she wanted to say. But for about the second time in her life, she zipped her mouth shut, letting him get on with the job.

"How far down, again?"

"Mum said it was a little over a ruler's length. A bit more than a foot, as it was called back in the day."

"Well, we must be nearly there if this is the right spot."

He lifted some dirt out with his bare hands and gasped. "I think I have it."

Nate dropped the shovel a little too carelessly against the rough bark of the tree while her heart now hammered wildly. Could it be this easy?

"Show me."

Her impatience thrummed. It was only a few weeks ago she'd learnt about the existence of this damn box. How skewed had her life gone off track since learning of her mother's secret?

Nate cleared a spot near the root, making room for her. She sat beside him with her knees near her chest, her heart in her throat and her emotions bubbling below the surface. Despite the magnitude of this discovery, she would not cry. Not when she was so close to learning who she really was.

She sensed Nate understood what this moment meant, the significance of it. With their shoulders touching, she drew strength from him, hoping to store some of it away. Some days she was tired of being the strong one. So, she mustered all the strength she could gather, just in case, not sure how she would use it.

Nate lifted the hem of his shirt, using it to wipe dirt off the tiny box. Her mother was correct when she said it would fit in her palm. In Nate's, it looked tiny. What could it possibly hold? Made of black sturdy plastic, being buried underground for nearly three decades had done nothing to deteriorate its condition.

When Nate was satisfied it was cleaned enough, he turned to her, his face merely inches away. "Shall we open it here?"

"Heck, yeah," she choked out before pushing a wad of anxiety back down her throat.

Nate chuckled, giving her a tight hug before dropping a kiss on top of her head. "Would you like to open it?"

She did, but she couldn't do it alone. Which wasn't the Roberta of five minutes ago. "Will you do it with me?"

"Sure."

Nate passed her the box and then wrapped her hands in his. "Look up, Roberta."

Circling them were hundreds of fireflies, their flickering lights creating an enchanting display.

"Turn off your headlamp," Nate suggested.

"But ... we're about to open the box."

"You won't regret this, I promise."

Nate let go of her hands and switched off his, then reached across to do the same to hers. Adjusting to the darkness, and with the sound of scurrying nocturnal animals in the forest close by, she feasted on the hundreds of tiny lights dancing above their heads.

"Magical, isn't it?" Nate whispered.

All she could do was nod. It was too overwhelming. She had the box and the answers to a thousand questions wrapped up in her hands. She'd made memories over the years—moments with friends and boyfriends in all sorts of places—which she stored in a happy place, drawing on them occasionally. But this was so, so different. If someone had told her a year ago that on this night, she'd be sitting beneath a 1000-year-old giant, with a gorgeous man beside her, surrounded by the dance of hundreds of fireflies, well ... she wouldn't have believed them. Surreal was a good way to describe her life that night.

She turned to face Nate with an inkling of what she would find. Nate had slipped off his headlamp, and she did the same, his mouth close enough to touch hers. Kissing again was inevitable. All the right ingredients were present, while the box and light were forgotten on her lap.

When Nate cupped her cheek, she fell into his gentle hold, losing all sense of logic. She breathed in sharply as he moved closer, reluctant to pull away. This was where she wanted to be at this juncture of her life. Didn't she? The soft touch of his tongue as it lazily slid into her mouth had her groaning, mixing with the forest sounds around them. She should be terrified of being in the dark, as she usually was, but Nate's warmth and strength surrounded her like a cloak, dismissing her fears for once.

Losing all track of time, surprised the earth didn't swallow her up for doing something so stupid, she relished the soft pressure of his mouth, meeting his tongue with hers. His lips warm and soft against hers.

She was leaving as soon as this job was done, wasn't she? So why go there? Except, her fingers ached to travel all over his muscled contours, his stubbled face, his tousled hair. It made her think of lazy Sunday mornings, rumpled sheets and sunlight pouring in through lacy, delicate curtains as they fluttered in the breeze drifting in from the direction of the magnificent lake.

When his mouth hardened on hers, a hot flush roared up her neck. She lost herself to the tingling pleasure and the throb centred between her legs. She allowed herself to enjoy it and create the memories while she could until her conscience intervened.

Eventually, she pushed back. "Nate." Her breathing was laboured. "I'm leaving soon."

Nate moved back, his chest rising and falling, before looking up to stare at the enchanted fireflies. He ploughed a hand through his hair, roughly swallowing. The fireflies descended in a swarm, hovering closer. Like they'd moved in to cocoon them while they were kissing. Their very own support party.

"I know. I get it, Roberta, and I won't hold you back. Sorry about this. It's been me every time. You've done nothing wrong. Tash will miss you."

Roberta winced. She was never meant to be here for long.

Nate chuckled wryly. "I didn't see this coming, that's all. Not my fault Tash put a beautiful, hardworking, talented woman, with a voice to kill, so close to me."

"I'm a pain in the arse, don't forget."

"Oh, I haven't forgotten. Just trying to look past it."

Roberta chuckled softly until a firefly landed on her hand. She held it up. "Look, Nate."

Other fireflies landed on them. Her breath caught in her throat. Overwhelmed with the beauty of such a moment, she gulped, needing to push her emotions back. This was not a crying moment but one to behold as a charming memory. Is this what happened to her mother? Had the rainforest and all its beauty trapped her here for a time?

"How the heck will I forget a night like this?" Nate whispered. "It's never happened before. Maybe it's you they're attracted to."

The fireflies swarmed around their warmth. Tiny, blinking green lights dazzled her, filling her core with a need she didn't understand. When she looked up at Nate, a hunger roared through her like a fire. This was too soon, too quick. This was crazy. When Nate's mouth descended for a second time, it was hot and demanding, and she greedily craved every new sensation.

It was Nate who pushed back first, his voice ragged and breathless. "I'm not going to apologise. I wanted that as much as you. Shall we ... open the box?"

Oh, boy, that opened a new can of worms. Now it wasn't only her wanting this. She fumbled with her headlamp, securing the strap. Nate did the same but took longer. With her light switched on, he looked flustered, his Velcro strapping twisted.

"Hey," she whispered, reaching out to help.

"I've got this." He put some distance between them. "Not sure how I managed to make a mess of it in less than three seconds."

Roberta grimaced but said nothing more. If he was as shaken up as she was, she understood. Her heart thumped excitedly while her skin glowed like a glorious sunset. Something happened amongst the fireflies, and even if this was all they ever shared, it would be hard to erase the memory. Forever ingrained in her psyche, it had already found a comfortable home.

"Okay, let's do this," Nate declared once his light was in place and turned on.

She picked up the box from her lap and viewed it from all angles. There was still some dirt stuck to the black plastic, but there was no visible clasp. Only two tiny holes where one might have been.

"Looks like it might be a hinged box. Should open if you prise the lid up," Nate volunteered.

"Here, you do it. I'll probably break it."

"You sure?" Nate checked.

Her hand shook as she gave it to him. She also plucked up the courage and gave Nate a quick peck on the cheek. "Yep."

Nate's voice broke into a chortle. "You'll have to stop doing that if you want this thing opened."

"Maybe we should forget the box. Probably a waste of time."

"Not in this lifetime. I'm going to open it now. Ready?"

"Guess so. Hope I don't regret this."

Nate pierced her with his gaze for a split second before returning to the box. "If the only thing you get from this experience is to be reminded of this night in fifty years, it'll be worth it. Don't forget to have a laugh over it, Roberta."

"Stop getting all emotional on me, Nate. Did you say you were an actor or an environmentalist?"

Nate chuckled good-heartedly. Thank goodness. She would have to work hard to turn the emotion off. It would make it easier when the time came to leave.

In the next instant, Nate had the box open, her light shining on a massive gemstone about the size of a five cent piece. Its bright, geometric lines pierced her eyes. She blinked rapidly, unable to drag her gaze away.

"Look, Roberta, it's in the shape of a star."

On closer inspection, she could make out its star-like shape. Unique, unlike anything she'd seen before, even from her short time with Antonio.

He'd exposed her to some amazing jewellery, including the buried jewels Connor and Liz dug up after seventy-odd years. She'd also had the privilege of viewing the Frevannini jewels they kept stored in their Roman castle vaults. It was enough to understand some things.

This stone was different. Special.

"It can't be," Nate suddenly spluttered, his fingers curling around the box.

"Can't be what?"

"Oh, my God, Roberta, how did your mother get this?"

Alarm rang along her limbs. "How do I know?"

"I know about this rock. I've heard the stories. Oh, my God, people have been wrongly accused over it."

"Nate, what are you talking about? Give it back." She jumped up, hands on her hips, glaring at Nate. "It belongs to my mother. Don't you go accusing her of anything."

"How the hell did she get it?" Nate asked gruffly as he continued to turn the box at different angles. "I'm so sure my grandfather told me this gemstone mysteriously disappeared after the man who'd found it tragically died. No one could find it. No one claimed to have it. The man's family even offered a massive reward to whoever returned the stone."

Nate snapped the box shut and got up. "I'm pretty sure I remember him saying the man's best friend was accused and might've spent some time in jail over it. Your mother had it all this time? Why the hell did she bury it?"

"Give it here. I'll deal with it, thank you very much."

"Unbloody likely," he barked, spreading the dirt back in the hole with his boot, then collecting the crowbar and shovel and stomping towards the platform.

"Nate, don't you dare go all authoritarian on me. I'll sort it out and chase up the facts with Mum. I won't be relying on old memories you might or might not have."

"*We'll* sort it out, thank you very much."

*Grrrr.* She gritted her teeth, certain Nate would never give it back. "I hate you, Nate Surrey." As childish as that sounded, it made her feel better.

"I hate you back, if that's what you want to hear. Now, let's get back to the cottage. You're going to ring your mother and get all the facts."

She wasn't sure what she wanted to hear. Clenching her jaw, she picked up the backpack, then marched off towards the cottage.

There was fat chance she was going to do as she was told. Just like that, her desire for more of Nate vanished. They were back to being enemies. Their default setting, it seemed.

# Chapter 16

Nate made one phone call to Officer Molloy but left the chat with his grandfather until the next day when he could visit him. Now in his early nineties, discussing something like this over the phone would only confuse him. Just thinking of how fast his grandfather was ageing tightened a muscle inside his chest. He would miss him when the time came. He'd played an important role in his life, sharing so much together, but the decline in his health was more noticeable each time he went to visit—and inevitable.

Roberta sat at the kitchen table, phone pressed to her ear, talking to her mother. The discovery of the white sapphire—he'd recalled what the gemstone was—resulted in the blow-up between them. Pacing up and down the small living area, he prowled like a distraught lion. He wanted to snatch the phone from Roberta and be the one talking to her mother instead. While the conversation was one-sided from Roberta's end, he couldn't believe what was coming out of her mouth.

He'd left the box on the table. Instinct told him he could trust Roberta implicitly. She held it open, moving the sapphire at different angles. The light reflected off her dark eyes, reminding him of the last kiss they'd shared. He didn't hate her. He never would.

"No, Mum, I haven't found it yet. Still looking." She held the box up, continuing to turn it this way and that.

He jerked to a sudden stop, rubbing a hand over his face. What was she going on about?

She refused to look his way, so he stood directly in front of her and raised his upturned hands in question. All she did was shrug in response.

"I'm trying to find the opportunity to dig it up, Mum. I really am. But there's this ogre here who threatens to have me jailed if I so much as tamper with anything in this forest. He's already said so in not-so-subtle terms, so I'm playing it carefully."

*Ogre?* He slid a chair back, sitting down heavily. He scowled at her from across the table, reaching out for the box. She snatched it back. He rolled his eyes heavenward. This was turning into a childish game.

"When did my father give this box to you?"

His ears pricked up. He had every intention of eavesdropping.

"The day before he was killed?" Roberta nodded at something else her mother said. "How long did you hang around? Did you wait for the funeral?" Her fingers tapped the tabletop. "Ah ... I see."

What did she see? He wanted to scratch her eyes out or at least ask her to put her phone on speaker so he could follow the conversation better.

"Okay, Mum, I better get ready for bed. I have a big day tomorrow. Yep, I promise to keep trying to find it. I won't let you down." She sent him daggers before saying goodbye and ending the call.

Nate shoved his chair back and rose, towering over her. "You lied to your mother?"

Roberta shoved her chair back, too. With her hands planted firmly on the tabletop, she glowered right back. "Damn straight I did. There's no way she's going to know I have the rock until I find out everything I need to."

"How are you going to find out anything if you don't ask her properly?" Nate shouted, frustrated she'd wasted a perfect opportunity.

"None of your business, Nate Surrey. Now leave me alone," she shouted back.

In the split second where they knifed each other with daggers across the small table, an authoritarian voice sounded from the door they left open.

"Good grief, how did you pair end up here together?"

Nate spun around. Officer Molloy stood at the door dressed in his police uniform, including a gun by his side. Nate's angst dissipated, and he grabbed hold of the back of the chair to steady himself. "I thought you said you were coming over in the morning?"

"When did you phone *him*?"

Nate ignored Roberta; instead, he invited Officer Molloy inside.

Officer Molloy took a further step in, glancing warily between them. "I couldn't wait until the morning. When new evidence surfaces on a case that started my career all those years ago, I had to come. This unsolved mystery has been a thorn in my side for a long time."

Officer Molloy warily took another step, eyes darting between the pair. "Should you two be in the same room?"

"No!" Roberta spat.

"Yes," Nate said at the same time.

A frown marred Officer Molloy's face. "Weren't you pair total strangers that day on the highway?"

Nate turned to Roberta, noting the fiery scowl she shot in his direction. He swallowed when the ridiculous thought that she looked even more beautiful crossed his mind. "It's a long story, Officer."

"Do we have time for this tonight, or would you rather I return in the morning?"

"Yes!" Roberta replied.

"No!" Nate answered at the same time.

As professional as Officer Molloy was trying to stay, his mouth tilted slightly. He looked across at Roberta, who held the box clutched against her chest. "Can I have a brief glimpse at it? I will give it back."

Roberta remained vigilant, almost as though afraid someone would snatch it from her and run out the door.

"After its disappearance," Officer Molloy continued carefully, "there was so much talk about how unique it was; my biggest regret as a newbie recruit was that I would never get the chance to see it if I didn't find it. Just so you know, this is a very special moment for me."

Nate held his breath, not sure how Roberta would react. A flurry of indecision crossed her face, but gradually, the tension in her shoulders dropped, and she offered the box to Officer Molloy.

He approached cautiously and took it from her.

"Just remember, my biological father gave this to my mother. It belongs to her, and she did nothing wrong, despite what *he* might think."

She jabbed a finger in Nate's chest, and he felt it—hard. His emotions seesawed, the tenable thread connecting him to this woman growing stronger and then weaker. He didn't want things to end badly with her. He'd been there once before, but there was something about Roberta that left him on a knife's edge.

Nate watched for Officer Molloy's reaction. He was an excellent officer and didn't betray too much, except for the way his mouth opened slightly when the magnitude of the size of the rock was finally revealed.

"What else do you know, Roberta?" Officer Molloy didn't take his eyes off the precious gemstone but turned the box in different directions to catch the reflected light.

"It was love at first sight and going on for six months." Roberta sighed. "Nothing official, just the rush of love between two young adults. The day before he was killed, he asked her to marry him. That's when he gifted her the stone. Told her he'd discovered it while fossicking with his family."

Nate couldn't drag his gaze away from Roberta, enthralled by the story. When she looked across at him, the fire and anger she'd been directing at him appeared doused. Replaced by wistfulness, maybe?

"The only thing she hasn't told me is his name. She never met his family, their short-lived affair too intense and all-consuming to share with the world. Those are her exact words. So, the day after his death, she buried the stone and returned to the man who'd been her best friend all her life and whose family assumed she'd marry one day. He was the father who raised me." Roberta's gaze dropped to the table, and she bit her bottom lip. "Recently, he was killed in a road accident. He knew nothing of what happened up here. Never knew I wasn't his biological child."

How did someone keep such a big secret? Were there any such skeletons hiding in his family's closet? It never ceased to amaze Nate how the ramifications of keeping such secrets rocked other people's lives years after the event.

"My mother only revealed the truth to me barely a month ago. My father's recent death prompted my mother to revisit this whole saga. Burying the stone was her way of burying her mistake of having two men wanting to marry her. The waterskiing accident decided for her. She returned to Melbourne and married the only father I knew. Then she spent the next twenty-eight years heartbroken over one man and relieved she still loved the other, but believing she got what she deserved."

"That's some story, Roberta. I'm sorry you were caught up in it." Officer Molloy said.

"Well, she won't tell me anymore about who my real father is until she has the stone back. But what she doesn't know is I'm not leaving the north until I find out. She won't know I have the rock until I have more information. Is that clear?"

Steely determination crossed her face, and her lips were now a straight line. Not leaving? A flicker of hope soared inside Nate's chest. He was so certain she would be gone as fast as her mother had been now they'd discovered the gemstone. And that mouth. Good grief, he wanted to soften the harshness right now. He dropped onto one of the kitchen chairs, needing to drag his thoughts away from everything Roberta. She would eventually leave. It would be wise to remember this.

"Can you help me, Officer?" Roberta asked.

Officer Molloy carefully closed the small box and handed it back. "I believe I can. Your father's best friend, Bob, was accused of stealing this stone. It caused a major rift between two big farming families. I think he's the one man who will be more than happy to help us. Maybe we should approach him first before we reveal this surprise to your biological grandparents."

"Do you know my father's name?" It came out in a whisper, like everything hinged on a name. Even Nate was holding his breath.

"I do. He was born William, but everyone knew him as Billy. Wild Billy. He was the craziest man behind a boat and knew no fear. The most amazing man to watch waterskiing. Bob was just as good. They were the best of mates until tragedy struck, rocking the very core of both families. I'll fill Bob in with what you've told me and let him decide if he wants to get involved. Are you okay with that?"

Roberta nodded while Nate gulped in more air. Seemed everything changed that day. Would things have turned out differently if Roberta's mother had never buried the rock?

# Chapter 17

C ommitted to Natasha and her job, Roberta played the patience game, which was difficult when it wasn't one of her virtues. Weekends were the busiest at Lake Barrine. With a nonstop flow of tourists to the teahouse, she ended most days more exhausted than expected. The teahouse closed on Tuesdays, and Officer Molloy had arranged a meeting with Bob that afternoon.

Nothing else consumed her as much as needing to find out more. Her nights were restless. Lack of proper sleep was showing up in all her actions and attitude, compounded by frustration. She couldn't even hide her irritableness.

She twisted her sheets around her limbs and groaned into her pillow. She had an entire day to wait before Bob arrived at the lake.

The sudden knock on her bedroom door immediately caused her to tense. It could only be Nate, so why the uncertainty? They'd tiptoed around each other since Friday night. He'd barely been around in the afternoons after the teahouse closed, eating somewhere else for the past few nights. She'd shared a couple of dinners with Sally, making up for lost time.

"Yeah?"

"I have breakfast ready. Hurry up and get dressed. We're going for a drive."

"What if I don't want to go?" Yep, that snarky reply summed her up perfectly right about now.

"You do. It'll keep your mind off things."

"Where have you been anyway?" she asked, continuing to talk through the closed door.

"With my grandfather. Now get cracking."

Roberta grimaced but reluctantly shrugged the doona off and got up. With her first day off since starting a week ago, her initial instincts were not to get up at all. This certainly put a dent in her plans to sleep, read and do absolutely nothing until Bob showed up.

Showered and dressed, she opened the door to the divine smell of cooked bacon and eggs. There was even a hint of warm toast and coffee. If she wasn't at odds with Nate, she'd give him a thank-you hug. But doing so would lead to other things, and she'd firmly pushed all that aside. They were such a bad fit, it was a joke.

"Here, sit." Nate pulled out a dining chair and gestured for her to get comfy. "We need to leave soon to make sure we're back in time."

"Where are we going?"

"For a drive in a southerly direction."

"Why?"

"Eat. Talk later."

"What makes you think I want to be back in time for anything?"

Nate skewered her with his gaze, pinning her down. "What makes you think you haven't been a frustrated, irritable and annoying mess for the past few days?"

Roberta spat out a gurgle of laughter as she sat. "Nice." She gave him a stink eye. "I'll have to remember that."

"My pleasure," Nate added with a cheery smile. "I knew you'd like that vivid description of your recent self."

Roberta groaned, picked up her knife and fork and began hoeing into the freshly cooked breakfast. "By the way, thanks for this."

Nate sat on the opposite side of the small table, his smile slipping for a moment as he contemplated her from his side. "No worries. Now relax and eat."

The way he said it had her stuck—or frozen by his probing look. Dropping her face, she used a mouthful of food as an excuse to look away. Relax? Yeah, right. She could hardly breathe after that look. As for peacefully swallowing this food, yeah, well, that was another matter altogether. She tightened her grip on the cutlery, willing her racing pulse to calm down.

Yep, still sharing a cottage. Still not going to work.

⁕

"What will I need to bring?" Roberta asked, finishing her last mouthful and getting up.

"Hat and walking shoes. I've packed a snack and water to take with us."

"Right." She debated if she should clean up the breakfast plates first, but—

"Go. I'll rinse the plates. We can wash them when we get back."

Great, he reads minds too.

In her bedroom, flustered, she rotated on the spot trying to remember where her hat was. Dragging out her joggers from inside the built-in, she grabbed the first socks she spotted and pulled them on, followed by her joggers. Her hat eluded her.

"Roberta, hurry, please."

"I can't find my hat," she admitted, rushing out of the bedroom. She halted. Nate was waiting at the front door; on his pointer finger dangled her navy hat. The one she'd picked up on the way past Townsville, with the word *Sunshine* written broadly across the front in bright yellow.

"What the?"

"Not my fault; it was lying untidily on the couch." He cocked his face, beaming at her. "Hope I see a little bit of sunshine coming from you today."

In one swift motion, she snatched it from him. "Could've told me," she growled.

Nate chuckled as he held the door open for her to pass through first. "I may regret this by the end of the day."

"I already am," she threw back as she straightened her shoulders and made for the maintenance shed where Nate kept his utility.

Inside Nate's utility, she slid a messy pile of CDs across the bench seat so she had space to sit. "Hmm ... no playlist?"

"Not in this beast. She doesn't have the technology."

"You could use your phone?"

"Why would I do that and hurt this old lady's feelings?" Nate tapped the dashboard affectionately.

While Nate reversed out and drove away from the lake, Roberta picked up the scattered CDs to see what was on offer. Nickelback, U2, Meatloaf and AC/DC were some of the artists she'd heard of. "Quite the collection. Never picked you listening to this type of music."

"They're my dad's. We've had some great singalongs with this music over the years."

Roberta pressed play to see what was already loaded. She upped the volume when Meatloaf's 'You Took the Words Right Out of My Mouth' blared back at them. Its sound echoed around the cab, making it impossible to talk. Which was a good thing. She wasn't in the mood for chitchat.

This song was followed by 'I'd Do Anything for Love'. She focused straight ahead at the rainforest whizzing by, but in her periphery, Nate's knuckles showed up whiter than normal clutched at the top of the steering wheel. It was such a powerful song, one she knew well. Who didn't? It was a classic that would never go away. Love was too powerful an emotion to ignore in this song.

It must've been the last song on the CD because when the song ended, an awkward silence filled the cab. Desperate to say something, she blurted, "Am I going to be safe where you're taking me?"

Nate glanced at her, shaking his head in exasperation. "Yes, Roberta, you will be."

"Are we protesting or something weird with your strange-ish friends?"

"They're not strange, and no, we're not. Not today anyway, so you'll be safe from handcuffs."

"Well, that's something, unless you think handcuffs are sexy."

She wasn't sure what she said to set him off, but he chuckled. A deep, rumbly chuckle that made her heart skip a beat. Try as she might to keep a smile off her face, it didn't work. There was something about being with Nate she didn't understand. They got under each other's skin so easily, tempers flaring and all that, but when the timing was right, it felt like they'd been together for a lifetime, with an eagerness to spend another lifetime together.

Which was weird. Time to stop those thoughts.

After nearly forty minutes of peaceful driving, in which Roberta restrained herself and chose not to vocalise anything, Nate indicated and pulled to a stop on the side of the road.

"What's here?" she asked, getting out once Nate had.

"Absolutely nothing."

"Hmm ... interesting."

Nate took a worn rug from out of a toolbox on the back tray, spreading it out on the small patch of cleared ground. "Except for what nature intended there to be. For a city slicker, I get you don't often get the chance to be somewhere where man hasn't destroyed yet."

"Oh, more of that." Sarcasm laced her voice. Was she in for another lecture?

"Why don't you close that pretty mouth of yours and take a moment to look and absorb? Here, I'll try not to annoy you, but sit beside me and look out at the amazing vista."

A hint of annoyance attacked her. She *was* a city slicker, so she shut her mouth just this once. She hadn't properly looked at where they'd stopped, but when she did, she devoured the natural beauty before her.

"There are many more places more spectacular than this spot, but look at how perfect the mountain range looks. Take note of its greenness, its symmetry and its perfection with the blue sky behind it. This is what nature intended. Not for us to desecrate it for something that hasn't been fully researched and tested."

"Are we back on the wind farms again?"

He ignored her jibe. "Follow the top of the mountain range. See where it takes you."

She did, and at the same time, his shoulder touched hers, sending a shiver along her neck. The mountain ridge went on to infinity, a never-ending undulating wave of mountainous rock covered in forest.

Something tumbled inside her chest. Against such grandeur, she felt so small and insignificant. The magic of the mountain worked on her, slowly making her see so much more, including the passion of the man sitting beside her. There were so many layers to him that peeling them back could take a lifetime. Pity she wasn't hanging around that long.

Nate pointed to a lone bird flying overhead. "Look, an eagle. So damn amazing."

It was. Spectacular, in fact, its wingspan an incredible length as it glided within arm's reach, or so it felt. She raised her arm as though to pat it and then laughed out into the void because that was ridiculous.

"Come." Nate stood and offered his hand to help her up.

"But where? I was beginning to relax, as you told me to do this morning."

"I must've misled you. There's another place I want you to see."

"You do?"

"I do." He tugged her to her feet before placing a warm kiss on her cheek, heating the spot, making her doubt all her good intentions about them not being the best fit.

Nate gathered up the old rug and returned it to the toolbox, and they were driving off in less than a minute.

"How far this time?" Roberta asked.

"Not far. Just a few minutes."

They drove through denser rainforest, where dappled sunlight filtered onto the road and danced along her arm closest to the window. It was a mirage of greens and browns. When they emerged from the tunnel of trees,

Nate pressed on the brakes suddenly. Forcing Roberta to lurch forward in her seat.

"Look!" Nate said. "A tree kangaroo!"

The knee-high marsupial trembled, perched frozen on the side of the road, giving Roberta the chance to get a good look. It took flight and hopped to the other side of the road, getting lost in the forest. Nate released his hold on the brakes and continued driving. The entire episode took about fifteen seconds, but it was long enough to create another memory to store away. She'd heard of the unique animal from Sally and Liz, but that was all.

"Is this your first tree kangaroo sighting?" Nate's eyes were darting across the road in case there was more to spot.

"Sure is."

"Then you're having a great day, I'd say. They're elusive as all heck."

She *was* feeling lucky. Spotting a tree kangaroo added another element to the day which she hoped would end on a high after she met with Bob.

When Nate parked alongside the road barely a minute later, Roberta got out of the vehicle, making sure to take a proper look at the landscape without being prompted. There would be a reason Nate stopped at this place. She glanced into the distance. The same mountainous range dominated the view, but now it was from a different angle.

Her mouth opened on a silent gasp.

All the pennies dropped.

Now she understood what Nate was trying to show her.

# Chapter 18

"**O**h, Nate, what a horrible blemish."

They leant back against the ute side by side, shoulders almost touching. Nate didn't pull out the old rug to sit on to enjoy the view. This section of the mountain range no longer held any appeal. An ugly scar snaked its way from one end of the project to the other, clear evidence of where the rainforest had been cleared to make way for the road.

"If we don't push to stop the state government from allowing foreign wind farm companies to simply pick where they want to set up without any proper consultation, where we parked earlier will look exactly like this by the end of next year."

Roberta lost count at fifty-two turbines. They were massive from this distance and resembled a hodgepodge of distorted crucifixes along the top of the mountain ridge.

Roberta crossed her arms, tightening their pull towards her chest. The weight of the loss settled deep in her heart. It wasn't taking much to understand how the desecration of virgin forest could hit you hard. "Tell me more, Nate."

"We're all about pushing for proper planning because currently there is none. They're not even placing these wind farms in areas which will deliver the highest energy capacity required."

"But green energy is good, right?"

"Yes, it is, but it shouldn't be at the expense of wildlife, erosion and irreversible damage to the environment."

Roberta understood how the construction of the steep road was the basis of Nate's erosion concerns.

"The next lot to go up will be some of the tallest turbines in the southern hemisphere. Taller than these, if you can picture them. These foreign companies will crash through virgin forest just to get to the area they want to demolish, not to mention the system of permanent roads they'll want to put in for maintenance. Wildlife getting caught up in the blades is bad enough, without irreversible loss of habitat full of countless species already threatened by dwindling numbers."

Nate's sigh shook Roberta to her core. *And the list will go on.*

"We lost the fight on this spot, so we're doing everything to stop the next wind farm being positioned in this area again. One is damaging enough."

She'd driven past other wind farms in Victoria, marvelling at their engineering feat. She'd never considered much more. Like so many others, she believed they were the way of the future—green energy shoved down their throats from all angles.

"They've reduced the closure date of this collection of turbines by five years. So, in twenty years' time, they will have reached the end of their life. Then what?" Nate slapped his thigh and pushed himself away from the utility. He stood staring at the ugly stain on the horizon, his shoulders tense, his hands curled into fists by his side.

"These companies putting them up are not even going to be around. Who dismantles them? Where will we put all the parts if they do? I've *seen* turbine graveyards overseas, and they're not pretty. Nothing is being done to dispose of them smartly, and no one has researched how to recycle them. They're just collected into huge piles, unable to break down."

Roberta moved closer to Nate and squeezed his arm. "Hey."

Nate turned to face her, his hardened glance softening a touch when he trapped her with his gaze. "I'm sorry, I didn't mean to land all that on you." With a wry grimace, he added, "My intention this morning was to take your mind off things for a couple of hours. That's all."

Roberta offered up a genuine smile. "I have been nervous and frustrated, all wrapped up as one." Raising her brows, she added with a chuckle, "Didn't think you'd noticed, though."

Nate's grimace changed into a lopsided smile, its beam sending flutters around her stomach.

"Bit hard not to. So, I left you alone until this morning."

"Thanks."

They continued to stare at each other; Roberta's tongue suddenly tied. At a loss with what to say next, she blurted, "Hug?" and lifted her arms.

Nate took her up on the offer. Roberta wrapped her arms around his waist, squeezing for all it was worth. Nate's arms tightened around her, and they remained fused, rocking gently, sharing a magnetic force. She closed her eyes, rested her face against his chest and inhaled everything this moment offered. The overpowering forest fragrance, the male scent that was all Nate, wishing she could bottle both up. *The power of a hug, hey.* Sometimes more powerful than the intimacy of sex.

The sun blazed on the back of her neck, a reminder her hat was sitting inside the vehicle. She pulled back, tilting her head back to Nate's gaze. "What do you hope to achieve?"

Nate dropped his arms by his side, his eyes gently brushing over her. "That they pick somewhere else or agree to the conditions we've suggested. This area already has its share of wind turbines. Choose a spot where the environmental importance has already been lost, and the forest has already been cleared."

"You won't stop fighting?"

His expression darkened, and his frown intensified. "I can't. It's worth fighting for."

Roberta agreed with Nate, even though it felt like an insurmountable goal stacked one hundred percent against him.

"Come on, let's go." Nate broke the spell blanketing them both. "There's a small creek a couple of kilometres away where we can sit in the shade and have that snack. Then we'll head back in time for your meeting."

"Do I need my joggers on?"

"For now, yes. You can take them off once we're near the creek. It's not far."

After another short drive, Roberta followed Nate onto a barely visible walking track, appreciating the hush of the forest that enshrouded them once they left the harsh midmorning sun. She wouldn't need her hat here.

After about fifty metres, Roberta heard the creek only seconds before she saw it, water trickling past small rocks and largish boulders. Mottled sunlight left shadows over the creek that barely spanned three metres, the shadows constantly moving as the breeze shifted through the overhead canopy.

"Take your shoes off and leave them here." Nate had his off already, showing her where she could leave hers. "We can sit on that large, flat rock in the middle of the creek."

Nate pointed to it, and she nodded. It would only take a few steps on selected rocks to reach it. This was another first for her as she marvelled at where she was. The spot resembled an enchanted fairy glen, with tree trunks covered in rich, lush lichen, some leaning precariously over the creek as if they decided to fall over with age but then decided against it and only fell halfway.

She half expected tiny fairies to appear, fluttering about and landing on a tree barely centimetres above the water. She grabbed onto it as she gingerly stepped from one small rock to another, the sudden chill of the water travelling up her legs with cooling delight. A couple of rocks wobbled underneath her feet. In one instance, she grabbed hold of Nate's arm to steady herself, leaving a grimy handprint of lichen from the trunk she'd held onto only a few steps earlier.

"Oops, sorry. I've just plastered your shirt with lots of green stuff."

Nate grinned. "Can't take you anywhere."

This easy banter set the mood, and Roberta was glad Nate was no longer frowning. There was much to filter through in understanding this passionate and complex man, but for now, she was hungry and glad Nate had brought snacks.

They sat on the wide, flat boulder, knees touching in the confined space. The warmth connecting them was in stark contrast to the pleasant chill of the shin-high water gently flowing past her legs.

"Here, I have some crackers and cheese prepared. Take a couple."

She did, slowly crunching so as not to disturb the surrounding quiet.

"This is so peaceful," she said once she'd finished eating. "I feel like we're the only two people in the world."

"This is what makes this area so special. You can find spots like this and not have to share it with anyone." Nate put his arm around her and hugged her closer. "Glad you like it," he added, his gaze wandering over her face.

She latched onto it as a sense of harmony settled over her. "I see how such tranquillity can grow on you."

"If you're with the right person, it can be pretty special."

"Right," she dragged out, her voice barely above a whisper. She knew exactly where this was headed—again. "You don't hate me anymore?" A hint of wariness crept in. They'd been here before—crashing and burning.

"Never." Nate's warm breath touched her cheeks only seconds before his mouth found hers. The kiss was slow and gentle, in contrast to how her pulse pumped wildly around her body. She pressed back, thankful the water swirling around her legs was keeping her body temperature in check. But oh boy, how did he manage to kiss her so tenderly when she was struggling to keep everything under control? If they weren't perched on a rock in the middle of a creek, she'd suggest other things to ease the building frustration growing heavily between her legs.

Things between them were seesawing madly. Moving way too fast on some days, taking too damn long on other days. Confusing as heck every other day.

Today was one such day.

# Chapter 19

Roberta and Bob meandered towards the cottage while Nate went to fetch the gemstone stored in the teahouse safe.

"It's been years since I've been back to the lake," Bob said, staring out towards the lake.

They'd gone for a walk to the kauri pines, Bob wanting to reacquaint himself with their grandeur and to see for himself where her mother had buried the gem.

"Thanks for allowing me another look at it. I only saw it the once when Billy first found it. He told me he was cutting and polishing it. I figured I'd eventually get to see it again when he was finished. Apparently, it was a very rare find because its size was enormous. While not a diamond, white sapphires are still regarded as one of the four precious gemstones. So, take care of it. It'll be worth quite a bit."

"I'm sorry the damn thing has caused you so much heartache over the years." Roberta caught his eye. "Why didn't anyone ever suspect my mother of having it?"

"Because not once did Billy ever suggest he would give it to her. Word had gotten out that Billy had found this huge rock, so when the family couldn't find it, they assumed someone stole it."

Roberta opened the door of the cottage and invited Bob in. "Would you like a drink?"

"Yeah, a coffee would be great."

While Roberta set the coffee machine on for their hot drinks, she motioned for Bob to sit at the small table.

"What I never understood was why anyone would accuse me of stealing from my best mate. My *dead* best mate. Did his family really think I would stoop that low?" Bob pulled out a chair and sat down, his elbows perched on the tabletop.

Roberta fiddled with the mugs on the island bench. With some trepidation, which wasn't like her at all, she finally blurted out the question she'd been holding onto since Bob arrived. "Can ... can you tell me a little about my dad?"

"Oh, Roberta, I can tell you everything. Billy and I were like this." Bob crossed his index and middle fingers. "Always getting into mischief, probably from the day we were born." He chuckled, his eyes unseeing for a moment, no doubt lost in memories of those happier days.

He straightened, sitting back when she carried their mugs to the table. When Nate walked in with the small box, a heated blush seared the back of Roberta's neck as she remembered their kiss in the creek. *Think about other things, girl.*

She went back to grab Nate's mug, putting it down on the small coffee table near the couch, the only other spare seat in the cottage, hoping Nate didn't notice her reddened cheeks or shaking hands.

"Thanks, Roberta," Nate said, a hole burning her back, certain he was following her with his gaze as she made her way back to the table.

Pushing in her chair across the table from Bob, Roberta chanced a quick glance over. Nate sat on the couch watching her every move, or so it seemed. A naked Nate flared up again in her mind, and she curled her fingers, needing to dislodge the image. Fast.

Didn't she have more important matters to deal with?

Dragging her thoughts back to Bob, she took a deep breath before releasing it slowly, resisting the urge to rub her heated neck.

Bob reached for the box Nate placed on the table, curling his fingers around the small container. Was he hesitant to open it? The damn thing had caused him so much heartache, and she didn't rush him.

"Wow." Bob let out a low whistle when he finally prised open the lid. "Billy told me he was working on a surprise. I guess the star shape was what he meant."

"It would've taken so much work." The magnitude of her father's craft suddenly occurred to Roberta.

"I'm guessing he wasn't sleeping much at the time. Needing to get it finished would've consumed him, but he did it. Oh, Billy," Bob finished wistfully, falling back in his chair.

"I'm sorry, Bob." Roberta refrained from giving his arm a squeeze. She curled her fingers instead. The urge to comfort this man, who was obviously still suffering from the pain of what had happened to him all those years ago, surprised her. They were only loosely connected through her mother, so she didn't owe him anything except for the fact that she was grateful he was helping her fill in the blanks.

"We did everything together." Bob's attention was still on the gemstone. He turned the box in different directions as she had done, light reflecting off the stone from where she sat.

"Billy's family and mine own two adjoining farms. We grow potatoes. Lots and lots of potatoes. We're still there growing lots of them," Bob added with a grimace. "We supply the biggest percentage to Australian crisp manufacturers."

"Oh, really? Like Smith's Chips?"

"Yes." Bob managed a chuckle despite his sadness. "Smith's is one of them."

Bob gently closed the small box, sliding it across the table towards her. "Thank you for showing me. It certainly sends a rush of memories back." Bob rubbed his arm like he was trying to ease shivers along his skin.

Roberta opened the box to take another look at the stone. If only it could talk. How many secrets did its shiny, polished edges hold?

"I assume you knew my mother?"

"Ah ... Lily." Bob's eyes fluttered closed momentarily, and she assumed his mind was drifting to another time and place. "Beautiful and full of life. How is she these days?"

Roberta was warming to the gentle giant who looked as Italian as she did. The similar black hair, now showing signs of grey threads, and the dark European eyes.

"She married her best friend. His name was Sam, and he was the only dad I knew. He died six months ago in a car accident. She's taken it hard."

"Oh ... I'm sorry to hear that, but ..." Bob deliberated, "I'm guessing if you're here to learn about Billy, then she left the north pregnant?"

Roberta looked up from taking a sip of her coffee to find Bob's gaze assessing her. "Yes, she was pregnant." There was a lot of Lily he would see in her features.

"Have you seen a photo of Billy?" he asked.

Roberta chuckled wryly. "I've seen nothing. Mum wouldn't even tell me his name. All she asked me to do was dig up the box and return it to her, and then she'd fill me in."

"She knows you've found it?"

"Nope, and it's staying that way until I'm ready to tell her."

"Ah ... the same spirit as Lily, I see. She was some girl back in the day." Bob gazed into the distance, lost in memories again, as they continued to sip their hot drinks in contemplative silence. Nate caught her gaze from where he sat, giving her a nod of support. She had so many conflicting emotions zapping inside her body that she pictured tiny electrons running into each other beneath her skin, squealing with delight each time they bumped into each other.

Roberta took a moment to rub her temple to ease the tension. "You wouldn't happen to have a photo, would you?" She wasn't sure if she was quite ready to see it but prepared to take the plunge. Now or never. She wasn't waiting for her mother to produce one.

Bob pulled out his phone and began tapping. "I have some old shots saved on my photo gallery. As much as Billy's family screwed me over, I've never had a best mate like Billy again. Some days I miss him so damn much."

Roberta absorbed the anguish so evident in Bob's declaration and let it settle against her chest. Again, another absurd moment where she wanted to wrap her arms around a total stranger and hug him. No amount of time would erase the pain and turmoil Bob continued to suffer.

She waited with bated breath, digging her nails into her thigh. Shouldn't she be relieved she was going to be armed with every conceivable piece of information when she returned to her mum? She was sick of the secrets and didn't trust her mother to tell her everything. If she was expected to uproot her life and deal with this shit, then she was going for broke. If syphoning everything she could from Bob was what it took, so be it. Then she would introduce herself to her grandparents next.

Bob continued to scroll past photos. "Lily leaving suddenly was what I expected she would do. She wasn't from around these parts and was only ever up this way on holiday with a girlfriend. I was one of the few people who knew what was going on between your mum and Billy. They were smitten, well I speak for Billy. I knew he was. For the first time ever, he didn't have much time for me, but I was okay with that. Not once, though, did he hint he was close to proposing or planning to give Lily the white sapphire."

"Hmm …" Roberta stored every piece of information, hoping it would tie in with what little her mother would tell her.

"Ah, here we go. I knew I had them on here, somewhere."

Roberta's breath hitched in her throat. She hadn't realised Nate had come to stand behind her until the soft kneading of his fingers on her tense shoulder warmed her.

Bob passed her the phone; an image of a young man with hazel eyes stared back at her. His hair looked to be a very light honey colour. The photo wasn't the best quality, but it was enough to show his killer good looks.

"You're an exact clone of your mum, Roberta. Sorry, but I don't think there was too much room left for any of Billy's genes."

For some stupid reason, a heavy weight lodged inside her chest, leaning heavily against her heart. She wanted one little piece of her dad. Yet here was Bob voicing her exact thoughts virtually seconds after thinking them.

All her life she'd been told she was a mini version of her mother, and she had long ago accepted it. But today, she wanted that little bit more.

She blinked furiously. Why this was making her emotional, she had no idea. The continued relaxing touch by Nate would be her undoing if she didn't get a handle on her wayward feelings. Some fresh air would work.

"Who wants to go for a walk around the lake and stretch their legs?" She swallowed back frustration as she got up out of her chair. "Then you can tell me all the stories you remember about my father."

"Great idea," Nate answered, collecting their mugs and leaving them in the sink.

When Roberta looked up, she observed a shared understanding between the two men. She shrugged. She *was* unsettled, and they both noticed. So what? Anyone would be after a day … a week … like this one.

Already dressed after that morning's outing, she marched outside, not waiting for either to catch up. She needed to draw more air in, clear her head, press reset and find clarity. Fulfilling this damn promise to her mother was proving to be harder than she first thought.

With determination, she made for the well-marked track, so familiar now. In less than a minute, Nate and Bob were on opposite sides of her on the gravel path winding around the lake.

"Roberta, are you okay?" Bob gave her shoulder a gentle, reassuring squeeze.

"Yeah, look, don't stress. Once I have this sorted out, I'll be fine. It's not like I have a father to meet."

"True, but you have grandparents and Billy's sister. She's married with a couple of kids, your cousins. A lot to take in, I get it."

"Mum told me he proposed to her and presented the white sapphire on the same night. Yet, she never met his parents."

"Like I told you, it was a very intense time. Billy worked the farm during the week, skied every competition between here and Townsville on the weekends, probably polishing that damn rock instead of sleeping, and then spent every other available minute with your mum. I think it was a case of not enough time. Then he was gone—far too soon."

"Grandad used to tell us about how legendary Billy was," Nate added, his voice tinged with nostalgia. So enshrouded in her thoughts, she'd forgotten about Nate's presence, but the sound of his voice lent her a comfort she hadn't expected.

Bob chuckled. "I believe your grandad was just as good for his age. From what I remember, Jim Surrey ruled these waters. He was always at the top of the competition ladder."

"How long ago are we talking about? I don't see any ski boats here now." It dawned on Roberta that this lake was once a mecca for waterskiing, and yet these days, it sat tranquil and still.

"Billy's death happened at the height of waterskiing on this lake. Getting a spot on the lake's edge was bedlam. People would turn up at the crack of dawn to claim their spot. It was only a matter of time before an accident happened. Billy's death *was* an accident." Bob sighed. "It was very tragic, and no one was charged. Within twelve months, the lake and its sister lake, Lake Eacham, were closed to waterskiing."

"Where did everyone go to waterski?"

"Good question, champ." Bob gave her shoulder another squeeze. "By this time, Tinaroo Dam was the place to waterski, and everyone easily transferred over to its more spacious spread of water."

As Roberta walked along the uneven gravel path, she caught fleeting glimpses of the lake through the trees. Shadows and light played havoc with her eyes as the sun filtered its way past the canopy.

Roberta stopped suddenly as an idea came to her. "Bob, can I ask you a favour?"

"Yeah," he drawled, coming to a halt beside her.

"I know you probably hate my grandparents, but would you come with me to meet them?"

"Do you think that's fair to ask him?" Nate asked from behind.

His voice startled her, and she spun around, not sure what to expect. She was ready to blast Nate and tell him to mind his own business, but a look of concern had her dropping the bitch stance.

Bob cleared his throat. "Look, I'm not sure what's happening between you pair, but—"

"Nothing!" they both said. Roberta turned back to find Bob had his head cocked to the side.

"I'll be okay, mate," he directed to Nate. Then he looked at Roberta, adding, "I had an inkling I would be seeing them soon. May as well get it over and done with."

"*Do* you hate them?"

"Ah ... Roberta, hate's a big word. It can destroy you in ways you never understand until it's too late. But heck, yeah, there's still a lot of hate sitting here." Bob rubbed his chest before curling his fingers into a tight ball by his side.

Bob looked out past the trees, lost in his thoughts, before bringing his gaze back to her. "They destroyed my life. Doing a jail term turns you into some kind of leper. No one wants a bar of you."

"I'm sorry," she offered. "How long was it for?"

"Three months before the verdict was overturned on appeal. It nearly ruined my family financially. They came close to losing the farm, and this guilt has never left me. It's the reason I hung around to help Dad on the farm instead of leaving the area like I wanted to. By then, it didn't matter what I did or where I went. I'd lost my best mate, and we now had a huge feud between both families. No amount of potato harvests was going to fix it. The sad part was the two dads always planted their crops in tandem, helping each other out. As families go, we were once very close.

"I also hated the justice system. How could they throw me in jail when I knew I was innocent? I was a mess and I can't say I've fully recovered, but heck, I can't wait to see their faces when you tell them what happened to the stone. Sometimes, a little revenge can go a long way to helping you recover."

Roberta laughed unexpectedly but quickly pulled herself together, contrite at her sudden insensitivity. "I'm sorry, Bob. I didn't mean to laugh, but you sound exactly like I would feel. I'm always up for a bit of karma when I've been wronged. So, you'll come with me?"

"You bet." Bob chuckled good-naturedly.

"When?"

"When do you want to go?"

"Tonight?"

"Heck, okay." Bob ploughed a hand through his thick hair, probably realising the enormity of what he was getting himself into.

"Are you sure, Bob? I can go on my own."

"Hell no. I've been wanting to prove them wrong forever. Damn them to hell; they probably still think I stole the sapphire. They're going to deserve what's coming their way."

"Can I just say something?" Nate interrupted.

Roberta's gaze shifted to Nate. Once again, she'd temporarily forgotten about him, and why the scowl? She and Bob waited expectantly for what he wanted to say. Neither denying him permission to speak or agreeing to it.

"While the same thought path is happening in both your minds, please don't forget these people are Roberta's biological family. Go easy, okay?"

Bob swallowed, rubbing his temple. "You're right, mate. I was getting carried away. A bit hard to dislodge the hate sometimes." Bob turned back to her. "How about I give your mother a call? Discuss this with her first and check she's doing okay?"

"This means I'll have to tell her I have the stone."

"And you don't want her to know?"

"Nope, not yet, and I'm not changing my mind. I'm going to meet my grandparents first and then decide."

Bob chuckled. "Okay, how about I ring her in a week's time? Is that long enough? It won't hurt to check on how she's doing. She could probably do with a chat from an old friend."

"Will she remember you?" Roberta asked as Nate suggested they keep walking with a nod towards the path.

They continued walking, and she could sense Bob assessing her again as he darted glances her way. If he wasn't careful, he'd trip over a tree root.

"She won't have forgotten me," Bob whispered, turning back to face the path.

Not before she spied an odd look pass over his face. What did it mean? There was enough in his expression to send a shiver along her spine, along with a hint of uncertainty. Did she really want to go there? Was she about to disturb an angry nest of wasps by introducing Bob into her mother's life again? God help her, why couldn't her mother have come on an innocent holiday to the north and just enjoyed all its tropical attractions?

How many lives had she touched and left changed forever? Her mother had so much to answer for, and Roberta was nowhere near done yet.

# Chapter 20

"**Y**ou're a loose cannon."

"I am not!" Roberta shouted back, shoving a chair out of the way and making for the front door. In the small cottage, their voices bounced off the walls and rang around her head.

Nate grabbed her by the shoulder, swinging her back to halt her progress. "Yes, you are. We stick to what we agreed to with Bob."

"I didn't agree to anything."

"Well, you didn't disagree with Bob's concerns that maybe there should be a third person around. You have no idea what to expect, and having a witness might come in handy."

It was just after dinner, and Roberta had intended to leave alone. The last thing she wanted to do was entangle Nate in her mess. Prepared with the white sapphire in a buttoned pocket of her brown cargo pants, she planned to collect Bob on the way and drive over to Billy's family farm.

"You're only thinking of yourself, Roberta. Look at it from Bob's perspective. He's already done jail time once. I doubt the memory has faded over the years. If this visit goes horribly wrong, he won't want to go through all the heartache again."

"Oh, fuck." In her quest to upstage her mother, she had to keep reminding herself how this entire saga continued to crush Bob's life. She certainly wanted no extra harm to come his way.

"Come here." Nate's voice softened, and he opened his arms to her, inviting as all heck. "You're getting all worked up. I get it."

She remained rooted to the spot. How did he read her so bloody well all the time? She *was* agitated and nervous, but they couldn't keep doing this. She was getting way too comfortable with Nate. It fogged up her brain when there was so much to filter through. Not to mention what being near Nate did to her sanity. "I can't, Nate," she whispered. By now, all the oomph had escaped her and she couldn't tear herself away from his blue-lake gaze.

"Then, I'll come to you. It's just a hug, Roberta."

She groaned at the same time his arms wrapped around her, infusing her with everything Nate. The earth, the forest and his all-male scent with the power to turn her on when she didn't have the headspace to focus on it completely. "It's never just a hug with you," she mumbled against his chest.

Nate squeezed tighter before pulling back, tucking strands of her hair behind her ear. "Tonight, it is. I've got your back, Roberta. I got you into this mess; I'll get you out."

Confused, Roberta took a step back. "You did what?"

Nate's arms dropped to his side. "I gave you permission to dig up the stone. If it was still buried, none of this would be happening."

Roberta huffed, the feel-good effect of the hug dissipating into the ether. "I did *not* need your permission. You don't *own* the forest, and I would have done it anyway."

"Are you serious?" Just like that, the dynamics between them swiftly changed. They stood facing each other like lifetime warriors about to go into battle one more time. Merely inches away was the unforgiving line of his jaw as he clenched it, clipping each word. "Not only do I run the teahouse and cruise business with my sister, but I'm also employed by National Parks. So yes, my job is to ensure the forest surrounding the lake is protected at all costs. Trust me, if I didn't think your digging around the twin trees was a good thing, there's no way you would've got anywhere near them. If you tried, it wouldn't be without a hefty fine or jail time if I believed the damage done was significant. Trust me on one thing, Roberta, I'll protect this rainforest with my life."

Roberta glared back, appalled they were back to this comfortable place they went so often—shouting at each other. She never meant any harm to *his* rainforest, but no way would she keep quiet. Not this loud-mouthed, no-filters chick.

"And you're very experienced with haggling with the law, aren't you? Treading the dark line between what's right and wrong and risking doing time yourself. You might just end up behind bars yourself one day, so don't go acting all authoritarian on me, thank you very much."

Nate's eyes turned to tiny slits, his lips forming a straight line. God, that mouth. She'd kissed it and loved it, but why was she thinking this? She groaned, breaking eye contact and walking away. "Fine!" she threw over her shoulder. "I'm taking my car, and you can drive."

Outside the cottage door, she stopped and turned, waiting for Nate to lock the door. Tripping over something in the dark was a real possibility with so many obstacles between the cottage and the top car park: steps leading up, flower beds everywhere and some uneven concrete paths. She was being sensible-Roberta for once until she was more familiar with the layout.

A sliver of moonlight flashed its luminosity over Nate, and as he turned the key, she could have sworn his mouth was curved slightly up. What the? How did he flick the switch so fast? Man, if she got riled up, she could make it last for days—and this might be one of those moments.

"What is it with you?"

Nate let out a chuckle that only served to bug her even more.

"I'm sorry, it's you, me, this—" He scrubbed a hand over his face. "I don't get it either, but I think I'm enjoying it."

Roberta's scowl tugged deeper, intensifying the threat of a headache if she didn't calm down. This was so screwed up. Just as fast, the magnetic force changed when Nate cupped her cheek in his beautifully muscled hand, turning her to mush.

"Don't Nate," she pleaded, on the verge of crumbling. Except it came out all breathy and girly, so not how she wanted it to sound.

"I can't help it. You're like the forbidden fruit, and I want it so—"

She didn't hear his last word. Was it 'badly'? She wasn't sure. Didn't care. When his warm breath fanned over her skin and the hint of earth filled her nostrils, her body came to life with a vicious roar and the real magic began at the soft touch of his lips.

Everything about the way his mouth moved over hers awoke her like a spring rain. When his tongue delved deeper, she whimpered. When his arms cradled her in their hold, pulling her in closer, she craved more. He was seeping into her bones at the same time a raw need slammed into her chest. Instead of pulling back and doing the sensible thing of walking away, she kissed him back, pressed her mouth harder against his, and enjoyed a ripple of satisfaction when his moan reverberated against her.

Until she remembered Bob was waiting. She tore herself away, panting, too afraid to look into his eyes in case she fell into them. "We need to go," she rasped.

He held out his hand.

"What?" she grumbled, shaking herself out of the trance. If she wanted to meet her grandparents, they couldn't keep going on like this. Not now! But hell, if she didn't have Bob waiting or grandparents to meet, she'd do so in a heartbeat, even at the risk of repeating her mother's history.

The reminder of her mother's mess had her cussing. How many times had she mentally berated her mother for her foolishness all those years ago? This got her moving.

"The car keys."

Oh Lord. She'd imagined a thousand other scenarios in a single beat when all he wanted was the bloody keys. *A fool, girl, that's what you are.* She almost fell back against the large terracotta pot to rest her jittery legs but didn't want to look so weak. Plucking the keys out of her pocket, she passed them over.

His warm hand enclosed hers, and he held on a fraction longer before she tugged away, pressing her fingers into her palm.

"Are you okay?"

"No, I'm not. Now can we go?" she huffed back, hating that she was losing control when her mind should be elsewhere.

Despite her angry and rude tone, Nate gently took her hand in his and interlocked their fingers. It didn't stop the avalanche of desire storming and pooling its way down below her stomach. It didn't stop the absurd desire to lay naked with this man, come hell or high water.

She must be her mother's daughter after all.

Moving to the back seat of her small Mazda after giving up the front passenger seat for Bob, she shuffled bits and pieces neatly aside. A hat, umbrella, a couple of empty takeaway coffee cups, an old road map her dad had kept in his office and a spare wet weather jacket. Not a complete neat freak, but they laid haphazardly on the backseat after her road trip.

Not that it mattered, but she never expected to be sitting in her car's backseat. If anything, it kept the roiling nerves in her stomach at bay. She scrunched her brow, worried she hadn't had time to think this through. She had no idea of how to approach her grandparents. With her frown deepening, she went there—the worst-case scenario. They were older adults, after all. If she ended up with a second heart attack case on her hands in as many weeks, well, at least she was a nurse.

Bob and Nate spoke in hushed tones in the front of the car, but she'd tuned out to work through possible introductory lines. *Hi Gramps and Grandma, it's me, your long-lost granddaughter.* Nah, that wouldn't work. *Hi Grandad and Grandma, I've come to show you what Dad gave Mum the night before he died.*

Bugger! Neither of those options sat well with her. She fiddled with the small box in the thigh pocket of her cargo pants. Anything to prevent her entire dinner from finding its way up her throat. Swallowing hard, she tried to calm down, to settle her nerves.

"You ready for this?"

Lost in her private thoughts, she hadn't noticed Nate had pulled up outside her grandparent's farmhouse. It was too dark to see a lot, but a glance outside the window showed thick trunked trees with leafy canopies looming over the gravel drive. They'd stopped short of the house where she could make out neat shrubs and garden beds.

With their arrival, the security lights flicked on, casting bright light across the driveway. When she opened her door, the distant barking of dogs filled the air.

Nate stood beside her, giving her shoulder a squeeze. "You still okay to do this?"

"I ... ah ... yeah, sure."

"I'll wait here by the car," Bob offered as he leant against the passenger door with his arms crossed.

The house's front door opened, and a tall, middle-aged man came out onto the patio. As the patio light flickered on, Roberta had a moment to take in the pretty pots and flower beds adorning it. But her gaze was drawn to the man, a striking older version of the photo of Billy she'd seen earlier that day. *Okay, so yep, he's my grandfather.*

"Can I help you?" It was a woman's voice, sounding a little uncertain.

So taken by Billy's father, Roberta hadn't seen the woman who followed him out onto the patio. Petite, yet robust, her grey hair framed a friendly face and a welcome smile when she'd spoken.

"What's the thieving bastard doing on our property?"

Her grandfather was looking past her and had spotted Bob leaning against the car. Roberta looked over and saw that Nate had come around to Bob's side, leaning against her car too.

Roberta turned back, coughing to clear her throat. "Ah ... it's Roger and Janice, right?"

Now both her grandparents scowled. Needing to act fast, Roberta blurted, "I'm Roberta, your ... ah ... granddaughter."

Roger instinctively grabbed hold of the supporting verandah post, his knuckles turning white with the strain. "What bullshit are you talking about?"

Roberta fumbled with the button on her pants. It was a miracle she didn't drop the small box when she got it out. "Billy proposed to my mother and gave her this gift the day before he died."

She snapped open the box, flashing the star-shaped glittering stone under their noses.

They gasped in unison, almost causing her to laugh out loud. That was her sadistic side coming out, which was ridiculous because the threat that her dinner would start moving up her throat became real. Frantically swallowing, her throat moved in overtime, hoping to calm everything down.

"So, did the thieving bastard come up with this story? He's had the bloody thing all this time, hasn't he?"

"Stop it, Rog," her grandmother pleaded. She latched onto his arm with a grip of steel Roberta felt from where she stood.

Roger shook away his wife's hand and stepped off the patio. "Give us back Billy's stone," he demanded.

Roberta stood mute, not computing the anger and hate this man exuded. She was their granddaughter, for God's sake, whether they liked it or not. Didn't it mean *anything* to them? Yet, he refused to move past his blind stubbornness. In less than three minutes, Roberta already had enough of this man. Family or not, she straightened her shoulders, snapped closed the box and shoved it back in her pocket, digging deep for the meanest glare she could muster. In her frame of mind, it wasn't hard to do. "Your son gifted this stone to my mother. Hell will freeze over first before I give it back to you."

She turned away with every intention of leaving but stopped short and spun back around. "And you wrongly sent a man to jail. I hope that sits well with you for the rest of your days, *Grandpa*."

She stalked off, still finding space in her confused mind to question why she'd put herself in this situation. She couldn't blame her mother, not this time, and for one moment there, she was Team Mum against this mean-spirited man.

"You're no granddaughter of ours."

The barb of her grandfather's words knifed her in the back, and she stumbled. She wasn't expecting rejection to hurt so much. Why hadn't her grandmother stepped in to soften it? Nate's muscular arms caught her in time and cradled her against his chest, her mind blanking out.

# Chapter 21

"What a complete arsehole. Fuck, nothing's changed about the old bastard. I hope he rots in hell."

It was no surprise Bob fumed the entire way back to his place. Nate said little, allowing Bob to vent on the short drive between properties. He was still going strong when Nate stopped outside the tiny farmhouse on the outskirts of the property where Bob lived alone.

"Thanks, mate, and sorry about all that. It just makes me so mad." Bob unfastened his seatbelt and opened the car door.

"That's okay. I fully understand."

Bob turned to Roberta in the back seat. "I'm not moving another inch until you give me your mother's phone number. She's got a hide sending you here alone to confront that bastard."

Roberta hadn't spoken a word since they left her grandparent's house. Granted, it was only a few minutes' drive between farms, but Nate clutched the steering wheel tighter, concerned about her.

"I was supposed to find the rock and go back home so she could explain everything. It's my own stupid fault. I can't blame Mum."

"Don't care. The number, Roberta." Bob wasn't giving up.

The light of Roberta's phone lit up the dark interior. "What's your number?"

Bob rattled it off. A few seconds later, a ping signalled the message received on his phone.

Nate was surprised Roberta gave in so easily. At the very least, he expected some fight from her. From the start, she'd been obstinate and determined not to let her mother know she had the rock until she found out everything she could. Maybe she'd reached that point.

"Thanks, Roberta. I'll let you know what happens. Now, get a good night's sleep; you're going to need it. How about dinner one night with my crowd? The oldies would love to meet you, and Mum will overfeed you as usual. You come too, Nate. The more the merrier."

Roberta didn't reply, so Nate did. "Just give her a couple of days. I'd love to come."

"I'm sorry this happened." Bob sounded genuine in his remorse, but it was still cold comfort. "I should've insisted we wait when she first suggested coming here. I knew I was hesitant for a reason. Should've had more sense than to expect the old bastard to change. Take care of her, will you?"

"I will, and don't keep beating yourself up over it. When they get over the shock, they'll come around."

After shaking hands, Bob got out of the compact car with a weary wave and a shake of the head. "I doubt it."

A pang stabbed Nate in the chest at how the night had gone. It was impossible to imagine life without his grandfather. He'd played such a significant role in his childhood that for anyone else to miss out on it, was unfathomable.

He put the car back into gear and drove off. Nate looked up at the rear-view mirror, stealing a glance at Roberta's silent form. She stared out the window with wide eyes, but he hazarded a guess she wasn't seeing anything.

Back at the lake, she got out and made for the cottage. Nate locked the car before catching up with her. The steps leading down to the teahouse were uneven in spots, and he didn't need an accident at this time of night. He took hold of her arm, exerting light pressure, enough that she could lean on him if she stumbled. She turned large, luminous eyes in his direction. From behind wispy clouds, there was sufficient light from the moon to see she was still in shock.

After fumbling with his keys, he unlocked the front door and switched on the light. "How about you get ready for bed? I'll make you a warm drink. One I make myself whenever I'm stressed."

"Like, when someone pulls a weed out of your rainforest?"

Damn this woman! The barb cut, not that he would admit it to her. Couldn't she just accept it when someone was trying to help?

He wanted to shake her until she came to her senses. Sometimes, she was so funny and comical that it made him laugh like he hadn't for a long time. But other times, like now, she made him so angry he could scratch her eyes out. "Maybe you don't need it. You seem to be back to normal. I guess you can take care of yourself from here."

Nate stalked off. The niggle of the promise made to Bob would eat at him, but he'd be damned if he took one more insult from her. Shutting himself in his room, he flung off his clothes and flopped onto his bed. Having showered earlier, all that was left to do was brush his teeth. But he couldn't move to do so. Her waspish tongue infuriated him, and he was damned as to why he cared.

One of his miracle herbal drinks would help him calm down, but his stupid mind kept seeing her beautiful curves. Her sparkling dark European eyes and how they danced whenever she laughed. He hadn't heard her voice in song for a few days, but he brought it back to mind, recalling the few times he had or the remembered moments over the past week when he'd been close enough to the teahouse to catch Roberta and Hannah singing in tandem.

Just as he was slowly nodding off, there was a soft knock on his door. Not bothering for a reply, his eyes flicked wide open when the door handle turned and Roberta strolled in.

Splashes of moonlight struck her distraught face. "I'm so sorry, Nate. That was so rude of me and—"

She burst into tears. Nate was up and over to her in seconds. Sucker that he was for this woman, and getting worse by the minute, he put his arms around her and led her to his bed. Holding her close, she rained tears all over his bare chest, soaking into his skin and warming the spot around his heart. Odd he should feel this way. Had any woman ever driven him to be so caring in one moment and then want to tear his hair out the next?

As this dictated the caring Nate take over, he tightened his hold and kissed the top of her head. Repeatedly. Tucked beneath his chin, he felt every vibration. From the racking sobs of earlier to the small whimpers and sniffles of her nose against his chest hairs. He didn't need a soothing drink. His eyes closed of their own accord as his body began shutting down for the night.

"Oh my God!" Roberta pushed away, putting space between them. "You're naked!"

The curtains lifted with the breeze above his head. A chillness slid across his bare skin, raising goosebumps and another part of his body.

"You're the one who barged into my room," he whispered, suddenly wide awake.

Her eyes shone from her recent crying, but the paltry moonlight sneaking in from the open window showed more than just shock.

"And you sleep like this?" she whisper-hissed as though it was necessary to lower her voice in the dead of night because others might hear even though no one was around.

"Sometimes, and yes, none of your business how I sleep." His traitorous finger led a dangerous trail from her brow, down her cheek, to her mouth, which was still gaping. Why were they such a good fit when they could be so snarky to each other? Weirdly, he enjoyed it.

"Can I?" There was a hint of mischief in Roberta's voice, a slight quirk on her lips.

"What?"

"Touch you like this?"

He swallowed when she reached down between them—touching his arousal, causing him to choke on his next words. "*If* you stay fully clothed, or you need to leave. Now!"

"Scaredy-cat," she taunted, enough to break the tension between them as she broke into a fit of giggles.

He laughed with her, his once-hard cock losing its hardness as they held onto each other. But it didn't matter. No way was he taking advantage of a woman who was upset. There were other means to calm her down. Finding her mouth, he sealed it with his own, allowing the delicious ride to go on.

They must've eventually fallen asleep because Nate remembered pulling up the doona and cocooning them beneath its warmth while a fire burnt deeply where any patches of bare skin touched.

He awoke once during the night, got up to brush his teeth and dressed in his pyjamas. When he returned to bed and the warmth of Roberta in his arms, it came as a shock that he'd never slept with a woman where sex wasn't involved. Was this even possible when presented with such a sensual woman? Why was Roberta different in every single way?

Was there a smile on his face when he thought this? Scrub that, there was definitely a smile on his face, and only Roberta had the power to instantly transform it into a frown or a scowl at a moment's notice.

He was okay with that. They clashed on so many topics. Next week would be interesting. The state's premier was arriving in Cairns for a cabinet meeting. They were organising a protest at the airport first and then later at the council chambers where the meetings would be held. They were desperate for a meeting with the premier, and it was Nate's task to do everything possible to make it happen. Should he invite Roberta to come along?

With his eyes already closed and his nose nuzzling the top of her hair, he breathed in the heady scents of her warm skin, deciding to leave tomorrow's problems for another day.

# Chapter 22

"Holy crap! What have I done?"

The full impact of the night before hit Roberta hard, and she sucked in a breath.

Nate's eyelids shot open, his arm snaking out to stop her from getting out of the bed. "Wait a second."

"Yeah, nah. Not this little duck."

*Faaark!* Crying girl falls into the arms of a man. She cringed—how stereotypical—making another attempt to get out of the bed and the mess she was sinking deeper into. Half asleep only moments earlier, she would never admit she'd lain drowsily half-awake, taking her fill of a sleeping Nate.

Nate loosened his hold. A pleading 'stay in bed' look won out, and she collapsed back down, making no effort to look away. In fact, she continued to feast, wanting nothing more than to emit a guttural groan and touch him in all the right places. Curled up beside her, his sleeping body was taking a little extra time to catch up with his wide-open eyes.

"One morning hug, okay?" Nate asked.

Roberta snorted, on standby with red flashing lights. It would be so easy to succumb to sex with this man. So what if they fought like cats and dogs? Imagine the extra buzz they could create. She could already envisage their first time. Hot and fierce.

"I don't bite this early in the morning," Nate said with a delicious, lazy grin.

Now she groaned. In frustration, in confusion. Why? *Just do it. Get it over and done with, then get on with the rest of your life.* "Yeah," her words struggled to come out when her brain was already on the path of touching his flesh, "you start biting by about three."

Nate chuckled, his warm breath whispering through her hair as he gathered her under his chin.

This only served to remind her of where she'd touched him last night. God help her. There was no saving her. His tousled bed hair had her licking suddenly dry lips, and disappointment was a real thing. There would be no naked Nate in daylight. When had he got dressed?

"Relax, Roberta. You're all tense. I just want to check you're okay after last night."

Roberta sat up, with every intention of getting out this time. "Yep, all good this side of the bed."

"I didn't ask how well you slept."

"What do you mean?"

"A stubborn old bastard refused to acknowledge you as his granddaughter last night. That will be hurting."

"Actually, not really."

Nate put a finger across her mouth to stop her talking. *Good luck with that.*

"It may not hurt today, but it might down the track. This is your biological family we're talking about, and it will impact the rest of your life. Please, give yourself five minutes so we can talk this through."

"I have to get ready for work."

"So do I." Nate twisted around to check the digital clock on his bedside table. "We have plenty of time." He turned back. "Five minutes. Okay?"

Roberta lost all the tension and snuggled back against her pillow, looking anywhere except at Nate. Five minutes to reflect might do her good.

Nate took her gently by the shoulder until they were lying face to face, taking his fill of her. The rush, the heat of just this exchange had her wanting to run a mile. Because if she stayed and experienced what was building between them, how would she be able to leave? Imagine the havoc she could cause this man.

*No good ever came from sleeping with the wrong man.* While these were wise words from her mother, in Roberta's life, they'd never been proven. She'd slept with men before purely for a good time and was yet to regret any of it. Why the hesitancy now?

This was different. Nate was so far off her spectrum for what she looked for in a man that enjoying his kisses made her want to turn herself in and throw away the key. She was a danger to him.

When he smiled, it was slow and warm, like the sun rising right now outside their window. When he smiled at *her*, it was those same rays of sun sparkling over the lake's surface. Glistening diamonds in a magical world. Hmm. Just having some fun with this man would feel like a violation of some kind. He was the stayer, the long-termer, the forever man if you were lucky enough to snare him. *But* you'd have to have some things in common, she hazarded a guess.

She closed her eyes, forcing her mind elsewhere. Following Nate's lead, she took a moment to reflect on the meeting with her grandparents. It *had* hurt. A lot. Damn them to hell! She didn't need them in her life. While she no longer had other grandparents alive, she did have her Aunt Fiorina. Roberta was nearly due for another visit to Falerna, the tiny out-of-the-way village in southern Italy where Aunt Fiorina lived and Roberta visited every few years.

The heart-wrenching realisation that one day she would have to tell her aunt she was not a blood relative was relegated to the back of her mind. A problem for another day. As far as she was concerned, her aunt would always be special to her. Not just the sister of the man who'd raised her as his own.

Chewing on her thumbnail, she stopped when Nate reached over and tucked her hair behind her ear. Her eyes fluttered open, and a turbulent rush of heat rippled through her. This was so tempting. So easy to entice a man. So damn easy. With superhuman effort, she pushed all such thoughts away.

"He must be such a miserable old man. Look how he treated Bob and the hate he still carries. It's like a grudge he can't let go. I mean, I can hold onto a grudge too when I'm riled up enough—I'm his granddaughter, after all—but I wane after a few days, and then I can't be bothered."

Nate chuckled. "I'll have to remember that."

"Won't matter. I won't be here forever. All good things usually come to an end. I mean, who gets to live in such a beautiful and magical place like this, complete with thousand-year-old trees?"

"I do," Nate whispered, his mouth awfully close to her temple.

"I'm annoying. You'd get tired of me quickly."

"When have you ever annoyed me?"

Roberta laughed softly in the early dawn, and Nate joined her.

"I think you've already forgotten how I barged in here last night. Hijacked your bed, took all your covers, and had one of the best sleeps where I can't remember a single minute of it."

"Bummer, hey?" Nate drew her closer. Stealth like.

And there it was. The huge reason she needed to stay clear. As worlds apart as they were in many aspects, this man had the capacity to care. About her, about the environment and probably a host of other things. Something she wasn't used to when choosing a partner to have sex with.

"I'm more concerned about Bob's welfare." The kind-hearted man who'd already suffered so much over that damn rock had taken more backlash from Billy's family. Hard to imagine Billy was once his best mate. Probably felt like another lifetime for Bob.

"I am, too," Nate said. "We're supposed to be having dinner with his family. I'll check on him then. In the meantime—"

Roberta noted the charged, electric air between them. The ease with which Nate closed the discussion on Bob with a very satisfactory resolution. The way he gently traced a path down her face, his lips warm and soft against her skin. Her eyes gently closed, and she leant into his touch. What the heck. She was going to enjoy this and do her best to ignore the unashamed hunger raging through her like a bushfire. Her legs tangled around his, and she pressed up against his full length. There was no Einstein required to explain the physics behind the chemistry building up and pressing against her stomach.

So tempting. She pressed her mouth harder against his. Touched her tongue to his and let slip a whimper. Allowed desire to seep into her bones and ooze out like honey.

God help her, she wanted everything but pushed back, tearing her mouth away from his. "I have to start work soon."

Blue flames of desire smouldered in his eyes. "Me too. Got carried away there. I'm sorry."

She was relieved the earth didn't swallow her up and then toss her out. She did not deserve such a caring man. To leave or not to leave. Before or after. This time, Nate let her go easily. They were both due on the job soon, and there was a whole day to think everything over. The message was crystal clear. If she found herself in his bed again, she'd be begging for handcuffs. There would be no stopping either of them, of that she was certain because for once in her life, she didn't want to rush into this, but she wouldn't be able to help herself.

# Chapter 23

"Enjoy the rest of your stay."

"Come again another day."

"So glad you enjoyed the cruise."

Nate cheerfully wished the cruise passengers a goodbye and a terrific stay. With a smile plastered on his face, he was struggling to concentrate fully, hoping nobody noticed. He and Roberta were moving towards something, and that was living centre stage in his mind.

Halfway around the lake, he remembered his grandparents were coming for lunch at the teahouse. That he'd forgotten was a trigger. Not a good one.

It was his grandad's eighty-ninth birthday next week. While this lake was once the mainstay of his grandfather's life, these days, due to his age he rarely came, so each visit was special and treated as such. Nate's parents would collect his grandparents on the way, and they would have a memorable morning. Stories shared—again, jokes told and delicious teahouse food consumed. His family were a close unit and always had a way of bolstering him when he needed it. A reminder that someone always had his back.

"Ah ... Nate, the um ... esky is ready."

Nate switched his attention to Sophie who approached him on the gangplank.

"The last visitor disembarked a few moments ago. Everything okay?"

"Sorry, Sophe, thanks." Heat rushed up his neck. Sophie had caught him daydreaming, but hopefully, nothing was noticeable past the stubbled cheeks he didn't have time to shave that morning. "I've got it, thanks. See you up at the teahouse soon. The family is arriving for Grandad's birthday. I better hurry."

Lugging the esky up the hill to the back kitchen door, he set it down to a flurry of activity and noise from the staff, indicating good numbers in the teahouse. Nothing unusual.

Tash whipped past him. "Nate, Mum and Dad have arrived. Hope you're feeling okay?"

"What do you mean?" Had Sophie said something?

"Not sure how it happened, but there's a plus one out there with the fam."

"But Brad was always coming with the kids. Didn't you say you were taking them out of school for a couple of hours?"

"Yeah, they're all here. It's the other plus one no one warned us about. Not sure how it happened but good luck, Bro."

Probably one of Grandad's crusty old mates ready to cause a stir. Probably still thought he'd been a better skier back in the day. Rivalry, it seemed, hung around for years. Nate would have to intervene and go into damage control so Grandad enjoyed his family time.

"Where have you set up the table?"

"Usual spot with the best view. Don't want Grandad to miss a single moment of his lake." Tash's compassion and generosity put a smile on his face, and he promptly forgot about the plus one.

Tash had already rushed off. There was plenty for her to do before she sat down and relaxed with the family. If at all.

As he rarely hung around the teahouse during the day—more likely to be completing the million and one maintenance chores that required his attention—he took a tumble in his stomach as a good sign. He'd be around Roberta. With any luck, she and Hannah would strike up a singing duo he could enjoy as an excuse to look at her and take his fill. Yep, this woman was worming her way into his heart even with the list of incompatibles between them longer than his arm.

But nothing could wipe the lazy grin beginning to be the norm whenever Roberta entered his thoughts, despite the concerns he had for her. He worried about the fallout from meeting her biological family. He didn't understand dysfunctional families. Didn't understand how grandparents rejecting a grandchild thought it was okay. He shook his head. Life certainly had a way of making him rethink many things.

Now to wash his hands before joining the family.

⁕

"Uncle Nate!" his niece and nephew bellowed in unison from across the teahouse.

Nate's heart swelled. Being an uncle to these two monsters was the best part of coming home. He crouched down as Sammy and Chase barrelled into him, always fighting for more of his attention. Nate wrapped his arms around them, giving them a big squeeze until they squealed with delight. "How are my two munchkins this morning? Who gets to miss school for a couple of hours?"

"Me!" they chorused.

"Mum said that being with great-great-great grandad was important too." Sammy, the older of the two at seven, piped up.

Nate smiled at the number of greats she added in. She was such a clone of Tash, with her cute freckles already a highlight of her facial features. Nate could only wish for a daughter as adorable. "As long as you always work hard at school, but yes, family is important too." Nate was the fun uncle, but he was always aware every word he spoke to these two rascals was absorbed and stored somewhere, so every word had to count.

"What about you, Chase?" Nate ruffled the five-year-old's darkish hair, an obvious trait from his dad, Brad.

"I wanna go on the boat with you, Unca Nate."

Nate could already picture the robust young man Chase would become. It was uncanny, but his obvious joy every time he came for a ride was infectious. If this young fellow didn't carry the Surrey family genes when it came to water and boats, then shoot him right there. He didn't doubt one day it would be Chase doing his job when he no longer could.

"Hello, Nate."

That voice. Nate jerked upright, almost sending Sammy and Chase across the floor. He stumbled, righting himself and the two children too. No one was harmed.

"Crystal?" he choked, his throat clamping tight.

"So wonderful to see you again." She stepped in and wrapped her arms around his neck, hugging him and leaving a lingering kiss on his cheek. "Ooh, that stubble. Always so rough on my skin. Did you forget to shave this morning?" She tutted quietly by his ear.

An image of Roberta flared up, and he nearly burst out laughing. Should he tell her whose fault it was? He checked his thoughts, biting his tongue.

"I dropped by your mum's place this morning. She generously invited me here today."

Nate looked past Crystal at his mum. Two tables were set behind him for their private use, overlooking the glorious lake. He didn't miss the small shrug and the unspoken words all over her face. Crystal had a way that was difficult to refuse. He remembered it well. How easy it had been to fall under her spell when she took command of his weaknesses—his love for her and the protection of the environment.

Until the day he fully awoke, realising how toxic she was in so many ways. He would be extra cautious today. There would be no falling under her spell. She'd done it to him many times over. Until the day he couldn't take it anymore and left.

"Sure," he muttered under his breath, not wanting to cause a scene. He disentangled her arms from around his neck at the same time Roberta approached their table.

It happened quickly. Roberta hesitated for a fraction of time, her eyes opening marginally wider for a split second before the shutters came down and she plastered on a fake smile.

Nate wasn't fooled by Roberta's smile. With it went any good family vibes coming from him for his grandad's birthday.

"Good morning, everyone. I believe we have a special birthday happening today," Roberta announced, standing at Grandad's side.

Grandad was a sucker for a pretty face and a wide smile. Roberta went overboard with her efforts to make Grandad comfortable. She opened his napkin, placed it on his lap and wished him a happy birthday. Then she began taking everyone's tea or coffee orders and promised a table full of delicious food would follow shortly.

Nate watched with alarm when Crystal raised her hand and clicked her fingers. "Excuse me, waitress."

Roberta stopped taking orders and rose to her full height. Nowhere near the willowy height Crystal carried, with her strawberry blonde hair and killer beautiful face. Or so he thought. What easily turned him on and captured his attention for so many years, the benefit of wisdom now showed an entirely different person.

He waited with bated breath, almost fearing for Crystal. Roberta was a rival in every single way. Crystal was unknowingly confronting Roberta with no idea of this.

"Yes, how can I help?"

To everyone else, Roberta was doing her job. To Nate, her tone was clipped, and her tight smile didn't fool him.

"Could I possibly have a chai tea brewed from soya milk and topped with a dribble of your delicious local honey? I remember it well," Crystal added, recalling fond memories from her infrequent visits to the north.

Nate didn't miss the slight arch to Roberta's brows.

'Look at me,' he wanted to shout at Roberta above the general babble of the family surrounding them. Crystal's appearance from across the border didn't seem to faze the family too much—except maybe his mum and

Tash—even though Nate made it clear when he returned home that it was over between them.

Roberta refused to look his way. This mattered to him—a lot.

It was only when Crystal's detailed order was taken, and everyone else's too—including frothy, milky Milos for Sammy and Chase—that Roberta took a moment to write his order down without once meeting his eyes.

Nate willed her to look at him. He touched her thigh below table level, making it look like an accident should anyone notice. No one did. No one suspected anything between them, but the split-second look she shot his way was filled with disdain and contempt. Like he'd kept a secret from her. Was playing the field with two women.

Crystal's arm shot up again, her fingers clicking once more. "Waitress, dear, could I please order a glass of water too?"

What followed was a torturous morning of Crystal talking over everyone. Describing her future plans, and how terrific they aligned with the philosophy Lake Barrine and their team instilled. How she had a perfect project she wanted Nate to help her with.

Roberta, in charge of their family gathering, walked back and forth from the kitchen, ensuring everything was smooth and everyone happy with her impeccable service.

Nate spoke very little. Not even Sammy and Chase could hold his attention.

As the lunchtime rush slowly subsided, he looked up to see Roberta—with her tiny black apron now removed—approach the piano. His body tensed. No one else was watching. Why would they? They were with friends or family, possibly on a long-awaited holiday. Everyone was too busy chatting and finishing their food and drinks.

The breeze wafting in from the open deck filled him with warmth and strong, moist rainforest, while the sunlight glinting on the water's surface sent a quiver rustling along his skin. The weather was so damn perfect; Nate blinked back a tiny prick of moisture, reminding him of how special his home was. And with Roberta at the piano, why did he suspect the unexpected when no one else had any idea?

The first touch of a piano key had some heads turning. Not too many. Nate's breath jammed in his throat. Instinct told him he should pay attention.

Roberta enclosed herself in her bubble, playing and singing the emotionally charged song 'You Are The Reason' by Calum Scott. He didn't doubt every single word was sent in his direction, hitting him in the chest like you would with a dozen rocks. All her previous songs he'd had the fortune to hear were lighthearted and fun, played in the background to enliven the atmosphere at the teahouse. Guests would listen but still chatter and eat.

This was different, snagging something inside him. Her words twisted and coiled the sinewy muscles holding him together. When she sang the lines telling everyone she'd climb every mountain and swim every ocean, his heart squeezed so tight he feared he might not release the next breath. When she sang the line that her hands were shaking, he clamped his knee tighter to stop his own from shaking.

By the time she finished the last words in tacet, without any music, promising to fix what she'd broken, every face was turned towards her. For a couple of beats, not a single sound could be heard. Even Tash and her crew stood in the doorway leading to the kitchen.

Nate had no control over what happened next. He would look back one day and never understand it. He rose abruptly; at the same time, the teahouse erupted in applause. His chair screeched over the polished timber floor, but only those closest to him heard it, averting their stunned gazes from Roberta to him for an instant before looking back at Roberta to continue their applause.

He turned to Crystal beside him. She'd touched him frequently like she had the right to. She would've probably done a whole lot more if he hadn't sat throughout the morning like a statue. His family would hear his words, but hopefully none of the patrons would over the cheering. "You need to leave *now*, Crystal," he hissed between drawn lips. "You are no longer welcome here."

"But, I was—"

"Now!" His tone brooked no argument while he controlled the urge to grab her by the arm and lead her out himself. He hoped his penetrating stare would be enough. She'd gatecrashed this party. God only knew what her agenda was. Their relationship was over. Thank goodness he was no longer paralysed by her beauty and manipulative ways. Relief washed over him knowing there was no risk he would fall for her wiles again.

He could finally hold his head up with a clear conscience. Over was over. He'd made it perfectly clear before they'd parted. Had explained his reasons. There was never any going back, no matter how many times he'd struggled with his decision.

Nate patiently waited until Crystal rose and made her goodbyes to his family. She approached Nate. He suspected she wanted to hug him goodbye or desperately whisper some last-minute plea in his ear. Before she was given the opportunity, he turned on his heel and walked out, leaving Crystal to make her way to the car park. There was no need for any further parting words. He'd said everything needing to be said. He even ignored Roberta, who, in his periphery, rose from the piano. She was getting congratulations from many of the visitors, demanding she play some more.

Her words kept ringing in his head. Around and around. He made for the walking track and his secret hidden path. It'd been a long while since he'd gone searching for it. It led to an ancient tree with gnarled tree roots that had cradled his teenage body from time to time. Whenever he needed to disappear and think things through, unwind, it was this place he visited.

That Crystal could turn up and continue to twist his insides, when they had been so spectacularly wrong together, gnawed at him. This was his issue. He and Crystal spent some memorable times together before her real guise infiltrated their relationship. To go there again with someone new had to, in his mind, be a forever kind of thing.

But nothing was forever. Right? He rubbed at his eyes, the overwhelming emotion that had filled him while Roberta sang washing over him all over again.

When did a person know if they'd found the forever thing?

# Chapter 24

Roberta could sing. It was no secret in her family. Busking and pub gigs with a couple of schoolmates back in the day had driven her natural talent and given her confidence. What she'd performed at the teahouse was nothing new, except everything about it was. It was the first time she used her vocal skills to vent, directing every single word to only one person.

Was she the jealous type? Heck yeah! Was Nate in bed with her only that morning? Hell yeah. So, who the bloody hell was the super attractive woman who'd fawned all over him? Tall and beautiful with fairytale coiffured honey-blonde hair falling in faultless waves halfway down her back. And boy, did she have a knack for clicking those long fingers with perfectly manicured nails.

Roberta glimpsed her nails as she gripped the steering wheel tighter. They weren't chipped or anything, but they were uneven and work worn. It'd been a few months since she'd been bothered to colour them.

She switched her attention back to the road. Her stomach had roiled during her entire work shift, with nausea a genuine threat. It was still suffering as queasiness continued to churn. How she didn't trip and spill the soya chai tea, *with* the dribble of local honey, all over the woman's gorgeous pantsuit was a testament to how loyal she was becoming to Tash and her team. The lovely beige chai would have gone well on her white pants after aiming to spill it over her lilac blouse first.

She'd seen Nate leave first but missed where the woman had gone. It was none of her business, and she couldn't get out fast enough either. Only after the promise of one more song, an old favourite of Delta Goodrem's—'Born To Try'—was she able to finish her shift and get the hell away from the stifling and conflicting thoughts strangling her.

She forced her foot off the accelerator when her speed verged on the ridiculous. That was all she needed, an accident in her frame of mind. But why was she all bothered? Didn't this work perfectly with her plans? She'd found the rock—now leave!

She blinked, moisture clouding her vision. Roberta didn't cry over men. She hadn't even been teary when things ended with Antonio. So, why all the girly emotions now?

With her bottom lip gridlocked between her teeth, she steadied her speed which crept up again. She was only minutes away from Sally's home, and she hoped like crazy Sally would be back from work. Otherwise, she'd have to go back to the cottage, and she wasn't ready for that.

Blinking rapidly, she drove around the last corner of the quaint street in Malanda, where its width might have fit another sixteen houses if it were in Melbourne. Sally lived in an older street where the block sizes were enormous and the houses, mostly from the late eighties, came with well-established yards.

Roberta jammed on the brakes when she overshot Sally's driveway, nearly ramming into another car parked on the street.

Her heart hammered uncontrollably as she turned off the ignition. Then she made a point of engaging the handbrake so the car didn't roll down the slight decline and sat back to give herself a minute. *Come on, girl, get a grip!* This wasn't end of the earth stuff, so why all the drama?

Large shrubs bordered the council footpath hiding her view of the front of Sally's house, but she spotted Sally's car parked in the driveway. Relief washed over her, and she opened her door to allow a cooling breeze to wash over her heated skin. Parked under the shade of an unusually tall golden penda, she gulped, swallowing a backlog of emotion dying to get out. *Okay, I've got this.* She just needed another minute.

Roberta was knocking on the open door and walking through before she registered people talking and that Sally had visitors. Once past the short hallway, it led to the large lounge room filled with a couple of comfy couches, walls dotted with framed family photos, a bookshelf stuffed to the rafters, a couple of healthy, vibrant pot plants, and a welcoming vibe which Roberta always envied. She gasped when she saw who the visitors were.

Sally jumped up off the couch. "Roberta? What are you doing here?" A frown dug into her brow. "What's wrong?"

"Surprise!" the visitors announced.

"Liz! Connor!" Roberta promptly burst into tears.

Sally was all over her in an instant, too. "Roberta, what the heck. What's going on?"

Nothing she said could explain why she was showcasing her rare crying skills. If anything, her tears intensified, and this only served to bring Liz into the fray as they demonstrated what a group hug could look like, if that was the intended purpose.

She took the tissues Connor held out for her, relishing the idea of crying some more because it was making her feel so much better. But, she decided, if she was crying over a man, it was time to bloody well stop.

"How come I didn't know about you two being here?" she blubbered, trying to stem the flow of tears streaming down her cheeks.

"If *the* Roberta is crying actual tears, then I think we made it just in time." Connor offered her the box of tissues this time, a jovial glint showing on his face.

"Shh, stop it, Connor," Liz admonished him, eyeing Roberta with concern.

"This was the surprise I mentioned I might have for you," Sally said. "We didn't expect you to turn up here this afternoon. The plan was to surprise you at the teahouse tomorrow for lunch." Sally squeezed her shoulder, pressing her closer.

"Roberta doesn't just arrive. She barges in," Connor added, enjoying himself.

"You still haven't forgiven me, have you?" Roberta shot back, Connor's words going a long way to stopping this shitshow they'd never seen from her before.

"Connor, please." Liz was starting to sound impatient, which was not how this couple worked.

Connor's hands shot up in defence. "All I'm saying is that for Roberta to be so upset, it must be over a man she actually cares about."

Both Liz and Sally groaned in unison. Connor was spot-on and Roberta broke out into blubbery, sad laughter. Both women looked at her in alarm.

"See, I told you."

Before Roberta had a moment to assess all their reactions, Connor was before her, his arms outstretched. Well, one real, the other prosthetic. "Here, let me give you a hug, Roberta. Trust me, you were forgiven a long time ago."

He put his arms around her, drawing her into his warmth and security. "Without your interfering ways, I would have never found my way back to Liz. So, thank you if I haven't already said so because I owe you everything." He pulled back from the hug and gave her a piercing stare. "Now, who's upsetting you?"

She loved this man for many reasons. He made Liz so happy.

So much had changed between them, considering where they had come from. It began with distrust and dislike from the first time they met him in that tiny Italian village. She thought he'd wronged Liz and fled the scene. It eventually became guilt on her part when she learnt how wrong she'd been about Connor and made it her priority to ensure Connor and Liz came together again.

Since those days after Connor and Liz reconciled, whenever she was in his company, they riled each other perfectly. Laughing and bantering good-heartedly. There wasn't a mean bone in Connor, and Roberta considered him one of her best friends.

"If you tell us your news, we'll tell you ours," Connor continued with a cheeky grin.

Roberta wasn't completely brainwashed from the morning not to pick up on Connor's hint. She turned to Liz with her mouth open wide. "You're not, are you?"

"I am," Liz replied with a shy smile, her hand resting gently on her flat stomach.

"You are?"

Liz nodded

"Oh my God, such good news. Congrats to you." Roberta wrapped Liz up in a bear hug, inviting Sally to join them too. Remembering Connor, she turned his way, extending an arm. "You too, since this is all your doing."

She jiggled up and down, her heart swelling with love for these people. Such a rare find in a world so big, it was hard to believe how fate put her in Liz's path a couple of years earlier. Now, here they were, talking about babies. She pulled back a fraction, unable to stop the tears from starting up again. "You guys are going to be the best parents, and I'm going to be the greatest godmother."

They all burst out laughing. Roberta was putting her hand up first for the job, whether it was official or not, which only brought on more tears.

"Okay, enough of this. Where's the real Roberta?" Connor took a step back and eyed her suspiciously.

Roberta slouched as the group hug disassembled. She looked at Sally, crushing her lips between her teeth, deciding how best to start this. She had to spill. There was too much building up inside, and she needed to share it with someone. Those someones were staring her in the face, and she loved them all for many reasons. Withholding information wasn't her way. She was blab-mouth Roberta, never holding back on anything. More likely to tell them way too much. She took a deep breath before releasing it and letting it spill. "I haven't told you everything, Sal."

"What do you mean?" A frown continued to mar Sally's pretty and usually carefree brow.

"Uh oh, I knew something was off," Connor added, taking Liz in his arm and kissing the top of her head.

"Shh, Connor, let her talk." Liz directed a frown Connor's way before planting a light kiss on his cheek.

Ugh! This pair. Nothing but the perfect love story. She despaired of ever finding what they had. Here she was in the perfect mess, with every single man in sight taken, it seemed.

"Can we sit, and I'll tell you my real reason for being in Malanda?"

"I think this requires alcohol." Connor extricated himself from Liz and made for the kitchen. "I'll put the kettle on, too, and find another box of tissues and something strong to add to your coffee."

Roberta managed a lopsided, teary smile as she settled onto the couch and hugged a cushion to her lap.

"Are you okay, though?" Liz slid her arm around her once more.

Roberta's smile slipped as her eyes filled with moisture again. "I'm not sure. Hear me out, and then you can tell me."

# Chapter 25

It was nearing eight pm when Roberta finally left, leaving Liz and Connor to get some much-needed sleep to recover from jetlag.

It felt good to talk, to unburden herself. Starting from the day her mother dropped her bombshell, her growing attraction to Nate, the rejection from her newly discovered grandparents only yesterday and finishing with the mysterious woman who'd turned up at the teahouse for the birthday gathering.

Roberta held nothing back. They all wanted to know if she was feeling better after. *Hmm.* She tapped the steering wheel, still uncertain if she was. Too much too soon. She almost craved boring and predictable.

Mixed with tears, hugs and lots of coffee, Roberta expressed her confusion and guilt over her mother's secret. That her mum kept it from the dad who'd raised her made her question many things. Why reveal it now when she'd never get to meet her biological father? As for her mean-spirited grandparents, who needed them?

Connor's occasional quip made her laugh or cry, alternatively, throughout the afternoon until they all pitched in and prepared a simple dinner of pesto pasta and salad.

"And no sex with Nate yet?"

Roberta had chuckled over Connor's question. As much as she was the no-filters chick, they all groaned whenever she was telling them too much. Connor, in his unique way, had a knack for asking the hard questions or the sensible ones. It depended on whether you were in the firing line or not. She had yet to decide, but he had a point. Sex usually determined if it left her with a glow of love or a big black hole of nothing.

They all knew she wasn't the blessed virgin, indulging in sex before, purely for the enjoyment of it. She believed for a short time she had experienced that glow with Antonio, but in the end, it evaded her again. It was the sum of all those previous experiences making her wary of taking that step with Nate. Why? She wasn't so sure.

Overall, she worked hard to reassure them she would feel better soon. It would just take some time.

They were all coming to the lake the next day for lunch after a morning boat cruise. Top on the must-see list was the gemstone. Next were the kauri pines. Sally boldly added they'd take their fill of Nate while on the cruise.

Roberta mulled over this as she negotiated the right-hand turn leading into Lake Barrine. She wasn't sure how she felt about that. Ogling and assessing Nate without her there had her stomach churning. God alone knew what mischief they would get up to. No doubt Connor would bombard Nate with nonstop questions. Connor had already warned her he would assess for himself whether Nate was good enough for her or not.

At this point in the conversation, they'd hoed into their delicious meal, stuffing their faces with aromatic garlic bread. Roberta was past the point of crying and had begun laughing more.

Finally pulling into her usual spot in the top car park, she turned the ignition off and got out, filling her core with the sweet, potent air of the rainforest. She held onto it for a moment, rallying the soldiers inside her head before she sent them out to fight. She was mentally tired. Telling her story to her friends exhausted her more than she thought.

It felt good to be clear of her secret. Overlooking the teahouse, cottage and the shadowy lake from this higher vantage point, all that was visible was a sliver of moonlight making a show on the water. For a second, she wondered if she was all alone. A shiver of apprehension shimmied around her chest. She wasn't sure how she felt about being the only person in the car park at this time of night. There was always that fear of a herd of galloping brumbies coming out of nowhere, which was ridiculous in this place. If she wasn't careful, her imagination would conjure up a snake pit of tropical pythons she'd fall into or a collection of drop bears walking out of the rainforest and stalking her.

She shook her head, smiling. *Get to bed and get a good night's sleep*, she admonished herself before looking down towards the maintenance shed. It was in total darkness, too. Beside it, though, was another dark shape. A smaller shed she'd seen in that spot with no idea what was behind its doors. Thin beams of light shone along one side, spilling out of what looked to be a door slightly ajar. She shrugged, shutting the car door. She might go check whether someone accidentally left the light on.

Making for the steps, she took one last look at the shadowy waters of the lake. Even at night, its beauty never ceased to amaze her. How had she never heard of this place? Why did some parts of the world get to experience such incredible natural beauty while others contended with harsh, dry climates with no relief from the burning sun?

Which switched her thoughts back to Nate and his determination to protect it all with everything he could muster. She didn't doubt Nate would choose death over life for his cause. On nights like this, when she saw it through his eyes, she understood his driving passion, which did nothing to diminish her newly discovered feelings for him. Or her hesitancy as to what to do next. She had a job waiting for her in her concrete jungle. Was she at a juncture in her life where a decision had to be made?

A man with such powerful ambitions was hard to ignore. So, who was the woman draped all over him today? Roberta didn't doubt there was a shared history there. But it was none of her business. She had the gemstone. She'd learnt more than she needed to. It was time to ring her mother, tell her she was coming home and demand the entire story the second she did. There were many gaps for her mother to fill in.

For now, it was time to call it a day.

She resigned herself to the fact she would leave the north changed somewhat. Probably no different from how her mother's visit all those years ago had left her changed, too.

She pondered this as she carefully made her way down the uneven concrete steps to the cottage. A shower would go a long way to making her feel human. She was still grimy from her work shift. Greasy from the delicious pasta dish. Full to the brim with the extra garlic bread.

With that plan made, she entered the eerily quiet cottage, making straight for the shower. There was no sign of Nate, and for once, she was grateful. She could sing to her heart's content in time with the needle pricks of scalding water on her skin. Hot was on the menu that night. If she came out rosy skinned, there was no one to remark on it.

But then again, this was something her younger brother would often remark on and now she missed his brotherly bantering, his bad jokes and his messy, unkept hair only a tradie could perfect. The thought of telling him they were only half siblings filled her with dread because, deep down, she wanted nothing to change between them. This news would.

Once finished, she stepped out of the shower and slipped on her worn and comfy Snoopy shirt and pyjama shorts. Only then did she remember the light in the mystery shed. Damn!

Natasha's number one rule when closing up was to switch off all unnecessary lights. She scrummaged around in her daypack for her torch and slipped her feet into comfortable slip-ons. It should take her two minutes. She was already dreaming of bed.

Leaving the cottage, she walked along the lake's edge towards the sheds. The quiet ripple of water was a balm to her tired mind. The gentle breeze wrapped itself around her bare legs while it eddied the water towards the edge in soft wrinkles.

The gravel path crunched under her shoes, dimming any other sound. As she looked ahead, there was no mistaking a light was on. As she got closer, there was a whooshing sound. Her brow scrunched up. Was someone there? Was it Nate? Before her heart could pound any faster and before she thought too much about her actions—just in case she was putting her life at risk—in usual Roberta style, she swung the door open wide and stepped inside. The squeak of the old hinges reverberated around the small shed space.

Nate.

He froze at the intrusion. His arms mid-action, sanding an upturned timber rowing boat.

Robotically, he straightened, revealing his bare chest. The paltry yellow light glistened on the sheen of sweat coating his torso and his light-coloured hair along his chest. Her eyes followed it all the way down to the neat vee near his belly button.

She swallowed, mouth suddenly dry, her gaze moving to the hard knots of muscles in his arms until she looked up and their eyes connected. Her breath caught inside her throat.

The aging bulb gave him a honey-glow effect as millions of dust particles from sanding the timber floated and drifted around them. She inhaled the smell of the fresh shavings. Toxic to the point she wanted to keep inhaling its strong timber smell.

Her traitorous body began a song of its own. Pulsing at different points and tingling all over her skin. This was so unfair. Reminded of the old Snoopy shirt she wore, a fierce blush scorched her skin, racing uncontrollably up her neck and over her face.

"Roberta." Her name came out croaky. He cleared his throat. "What are you doing here?"

"I came to check if someone had left the light on. You know how Natasha goes on about that."

He nodded once, then stilled. Awkwardness hung in the air as they continued to stare at each other, growing more uncomfortable with each passing moment. "Are you okay?" he finally asked.

She licked her lips, tasting the timber particles. Was he referring to now or earlier at the teahouse? "I wasn't."

"And now?" He reached back for something off the old, dusty workbench beside the upturned boat.

She shrugged. "I went to Sally's. Liz and Connor were there."

"Liz and Connor?" Nate motioned for her to come closer; his only offering was a sheet of sandpaper.

She braved a couple of steps, the confined space in the shed closing in around them. Accepting his offer, she took the sheet of coarse sandpaper, pressing its rough grit against the soft skin of her palm. He picked up another sheet and showed her what to do. Back and forth. Back and forth. Hypnotic.

She started talking. It was what she did best. Beginning with the day she met Liz on a train in southern Italy. The jewels, how Connor came into the picture, his amputation, Antonio. How the glow of that relationship shone for a few months, until it didn't. Until the pressures of too much money and always being in the public eye got too much. She delved into the past too and talked about the night of the brumbies and how their friend was killed. The reason she became a nurse so she could save lives instead of feeling helpless. All the while, in tandem, they swept the sandpaper over the hull of the upturned rowboat. Soothing. Cathartic. Sensual.

As she spoke, Nate listened attentively, interjecting with sporadic questions. Occasionally, their fingers touched. Other times, their arms brushed. But still, Roberta chattered, building up the anticipation of what a friendship between them could be like. A situation where their tempers weren't flaring and unkind words weren't being said. Until she exhausted her story. Had no idea of the time. Was no longer that tired.

She straightened her back, her spine knuckles slipping back into place one by one. Nate was on the same side of the hull, and he did the same. So much for her shower. Timber dust lightly covered her, creating a static sensation as she ran a finger along her skin.

"That's some story."

Feeling braver than she should, or stupid, she stretched up and gave his cheek a lingering kiss, tasting sweat and dust. He smelt so good it made her giddy. The strong fragrance of the aged timber filled her senses, and she momentarily swayed. He reached out to steady her.

"Will you tell me yours?" she whispered, her heart beginning to beat faster. Did she want to know? Was there unfinished business with the other woman? Enough to kill whatever was building up between them?

When he didn't answer straight away, she stepped back, her thigh colliding with the edge of the rowing boat. She rubbed at the spot for something to do with her hand. She was overstepping and should walk out and go to bed.

"There's nothing to tell."

"Who was the woman?" Bugger. Her and her big mouth. Why did she never shut it when it was absolutely necessary to? Nate owed her nothing. Especially not an explanation.

The way he glanced towards the door suggested he wanted to escape, too. His fingers, she noticed, were curled inwards, scrunching up the sheet of sandpaper he held.

He released a guttural sound that came from deep within and, with a rough jerk, switched his attention back to the rowboat, sweeping it harshly with the gritty sandpaper crumpled from his fierce hold.

Roberta's heart thumped. This was a new version of Nate. Angry, emotional, grim.

"Her name is Crystal," he spat between lips drawn together, "and she had no right to be here today."

# Chapter 26

Nate stopped sanding, the used sheet of sandpaper dropping to the ground. He ran his hand over the smooth section he'd just worked all his angst on, feeling much better for it. Relief washed over him, pleased he had the opportunity to explain Crystal's presence today. "And that's that. The full Crystal story. I don't want to think about her anymore today."

"Hmm … that's also some story, Nate. Sorry it ended the way it did for you. She meant something to you once."

"Yeah, well, sorry I didn't have time to explain it to you today."

Roberta ran a finger along the smooth-sanded base of the hull. "How about you tell me a little about this old beauty?"

Nate chuckled wryly. "My great-grandfather crafted it by hand as a birthday gift for the girl he wanted to marry."

"Did he end up marrying her?"

"He sure did."

"He's the man who died tragically, isn't he?"

"Yeah."

"What are your plans for it?"

"I want to bring it back to bare timber so I can reseal it with a two-pack epoxy. Give it a new lease of life. It's been gathering dust in the boatshed forever. I thought it was time to clean it up and bring it out."

"Maybe for the woman you want to marry one day?" Roberta quirked a brow and chuckled, causing a jolt to shimmy inside his chest. Nate tried to smile, but it might've looked like a grimace combined with a groan. He wasn't rushing into anything after Crystal's reappearance. "I'm a long way from anything, so I probably won't wait that long."

Roberta continued to smooth her hand along the hull, hypnotising him with her elegant piano-playing fingers.

"She's very beautiful." Her fingers halted for a moment.

"The boat?"

"Yes. No. Actually, I meant Crystal."

When Roberta looked up, he latched onto her gaze. There was a stirring in his shorts. It only required one step to be close enough to touch her. He cradled her cheek, gently massaging her chin with his thumb. "Don't be fooled by it."

"It's hard not to."

Frowning, Nate dropped his hand. "Let's go. It's getting late, and we both have work tomorrow."

Nate went about shutting the small windows facing the lake, ignoring what he thought might have been disappointment on her face. She was leaving soon, wasn't she? That had been made clear in the many arguments they'd had.

He needed a cold shower to help him calm down. He'd vented too much to Roberta. Revealed too much. There was a good chance he would regret it the next day. Yet, he felt better for it. Unburdened, laying the truth on the table.

"How do you manage any boat building in this tiny space?" Roberta waited at the front door. With the windows shut, he quickly tidied some tools, placing them back on the designated hooks and stacking them on shelves.

"You'd be surprised. Nowadays, the boats are built offsite and transported here, but Grandad would tell me stories of how a bunch of his mates would all crowd in here, drinking a few beers, building the latest."

"There's just so much *in* here. Almost like a mini museum."

"That's what happens when you've been in one place forever. One day, I might take the time to sort it all out. Who knows what I'll find." With enough tidy up done, before he switched the light off, he asked, "Have you got the torch handy?"

Roberta fished it from her pocket and switched it on, providing enough light to close the old shed door and secure the padlock. Their hands met, and he laced his fingers with hers. More to ensure she didn't trip on the uneven gravel path, but it also felt like the right thing to do. Her presence eased the anxiety hovering over him since Crystal's arrival.

When she gripped his hand, it made him bolder. Less than ten metres away from the shed, he stopped, pulling her to a halt too. "I'm going to take a quick dip and rid myself of all the dust; otherwise, I'll spread it throughout the cottage. I'm sure my hair is coated in it too. You can do the same if you want."

"Er ... that's a no from me. It'll be freezing."

He laughed out loud, stripped down to his boxers, and left his soiled clothes and worn joggers in a pile on the path. "Chicken."

She laughed back. "Happy to be a chicken all by myself here. Just don't be too long. I'm seeing dark and murky from here."

Like a weight had been removed from his shoulders, Nate continued to laugh, stepping into the shallow edge before diving deep and disappearing underwater. Yes, the water was a tad chilly on his skin, but boy, did he need it. It was hard to ignore Roberta, all gorgeous and sexy, wearing Snoopy with all the grace of a catwalk model. So hard to ignore those womanly curves!

He emerged from the deep and sucked in some air before turning back to the shore again. He hadn't expected Roberta to be standing in the ankle-deep water. When had she stepped in? Heck, it was too tempting. He dived under again, aiming directly for her legs, emerging where she stood, bringing enough water with him to drench her completely.

The sound of her shriek cut through the still night. "Nate, what the?"

"Come on, it's beautiful once you get in." He tugged gently on her hand. When she didn't resist, her high-pitched melodic laughter filled the night only seconds before she dived under the water with him, completely clothed with Snoopy.

When they emerged, Nate grabbed her hand. "Float on your back." They gently eddied with the soft current of the lake, holding hands, shoulders tapping occasionally.

"Oh, this is so relaxing. Wake me up if I fall asleep."

"I know, right?" Nate said before adding, "And I will."

"Have you ever done this before, with … er … Crystal?"

His hold on her fingers tightened. "No! Can you picture it? She was never a spontaneous woman."

Roberta giggled. "Look at all the fun she missed out on." She rolled off her back, paddling upright as she shivered beside him. "This really is cold. I need to get out."

Nate didn't hesitate. Still on his back, he used his powerful kicks to get them quicker to the edge. Once out of the lake, and not a towel in sight to dry off with, he grabbed his pile of dusty clothes and joggers while Roberta picked up the torch and slipped her feet into her shoes. "How fast can you get back? You use the shower first."

"I'm running, Nate. Geez, you're as crazy as me, and I've done some foolish things in my time."

Laughing and slippery on his bare feet, they burst into the cottage, and Nate shut the door behind them. "Off you go."

She did, and for one second, he would've liked to join her. See where it led. But Crystal still lingered annoyingly in his mind. He'd have to rid the images of her presence first before he considered anyone else. But Roberta was fun. She made him laugh—a lot—when she wasn't infuriating him. He needed that therapy right now.

When Nate emerged from his shower, toasty warm again, he found Roberta wearing what looked like a worn and comfortable tracksuit, her knees raised on the couch. She cradled a mug, its distinct aroma floating in the air when he sat down beside her. She pointed to another on the coffee table. "I made you a hot Milo, too."

"Thanks. That'll go down nicely."

Nate tucked himself in the opposite corner, eyeing Roberta as they quietly drank. It was getting close to ten pm, and the strain of the day was wearing him down. No doubt Roberta was feeling the same way. He should let her go to bed, but the compulsion to remain awake all night and be this close to her wouldn't go away.

Roberta's eyes were fixed straight ahead, but she stole glances his way every couple of sips. She was probably zoned out from exhaustion. It'd been that kind of day. It was a comfortable silence though. Neither rushed to finish their drinks.

When he finished, he put the mug on the floor, allowing that compulsion to raise its sorry head. He opened his arms in invitation, and Roberta didn't hesitate. She placed her mug on the table and shimmied over to his side. He wrapped them around her and tightened them comfortably, her scent reminding him again of wildflowers.

"I should let you get some sleep."

"I know. I'm dead on my feet. A late-night dip certainly has a way of tampering with your body's core heat. I'm only beginning to warm up now."

Nate slid down a little, tucking her beneath his chin and partially lying down. He pulled on the rug that lived on the couch and covered them both. "I'll try and help some more."

She giggled, snuggling in closer. "You, Nate, are doing nothing of the sort. But thanks anyway. If I fall asleep here, I'm sorry."

"There are worse things."

Nate could easily close his eyes and dream big on the wildflower scent filling his nostrils. But he wanted to be the responsible one for a little longer. "Have you phoned your mother yet?"

"Wow!" She tried to sit up, but he held on tight. "Way to spoil the moment."

"Shoosh. You know exactly what I mean. You've found the box, revealed what's inside and learnt all about it. It doesn't take a genius to understand you've fulfilled your mission of coming to Lake Barrine. You never intended to stay for long, did you?"

This time, when she tried to sit up, Nate didn't stop her. "Natasha is going to kill me, isn't she?"

"Tash likes you a lot. As she says, you're a breath of fresh air. Was your mother's request the only reason you applied for the job?"

Roberta nodded, and stupid sentimental hope crashed to his feet.

"I haven't phoned her yet. I'm waiting for Bob to ring her first. If he has, then I should expect a call from her first thing in the morning."

"What are you going to tell her?"

"Mission accomplished. I'm coming home. You better tell me the full story when I get there. That sort of thing."

"You didn't want to come up in the first place, did you?"

Roberta twisted her fingers in her lap. "Nope. Couldn't believe the far-out story she told me. Didn't for one minute believe I'd find the box."

"But clever Roberta did. You're not one to give up easily, are you?"

She chuckled. "I had to fight this environmental warrior to get there, though."

Nate welcomed her back to her earlier position and held her tight against his chest, loving how she warmed that part of him.

"When were you going to leave?" Nate asked. The answer signalled an end to whatever was happening between them.

"I have six months before I have to return to work."

"Six months! Then you can stay longer?"

"Oh, Nate." She twisted around and looked up at him, her soft smile turning his bones to jelly. "You're so tempting, even with your weird ways."

Nate scowled. "Weird?"

"Yep. I've never met anyone like you before, but I kind of like it."

Nate's breath hitched in his throat, waiting for her next move.

"But can we like not rush this between us? Because tonight I'm exhausted, and I don't want to do anything I might regret in the morning."

"Yup, straight out tell me exactly how it is. That's the Roberta I'm getting to know."

This put a delicious smile on her face, and she snuggled up a little more.

"I'm in the same boat, okay?" Nate dragged his fingers down her spine. "I'm still having nightmares over today. If you're going to invade my head space, I don't want to share it with anyone else."

"So, we're on the same page?" she asked.

"Totally," Nate agreed. "As long as I can do this any time." He tilted her face up, manoeuvred his body into a better position and placed his mouth on hers. Slow. Sensuous. Delicious Milo-tasting kissing. No tongues and no hands. Just in sync, relaxing, eyes shut, body tuned out.

Nate couldn't recall when they might've fallen asleep. It was one of those nights when he'd woken a few times, grimaced at the cricks all over his body and then closed his eyes again. It was the worst place to sleep, but somehow, they did.

In the early hours of the morning, he came fully awake with a numb arm reminding him that his bed was a necessity. With a sleeping Roberta in his arms, he stood and took her to her bed. After tucking her in and taking his fill of her for a moment, he retired to his bed, where he must've slept like the dead until his alarm jolted him awake.

# Chapter 27

"I don't believe I'm doing this," Roberta wailed.

"Look at you. Having the time of your life." Nadia jostled beside her, placard in hand. She was holding it above her head, ensuring it was clearly visible for the local television crews set up across the lawn in front of the Cairns council chambers.

Nate squeezed her shoulder, a silent sign of reassurance. "Smile, Roberta, so at least you can laugh over it when you watch the news tonight," before distracting her with a quick kiss on the cheek behind her placard.

A heated blush crept across her face, and she failed to smile. How did she ever think this would be a good idea?

So much had happened in the past week since the night she and Nate had stumbled on some kind of truce and fallen asleep on that goddamned tiny couch.

"Did your mother ring again this morning?" Nate asked quietly, gently nudging her with his shoulder. Roberta recognised the signs of concern on his face. The same ones directed to her after all her mother's daily phone calls. Last night, he'd stayed in Cairns to prepare for this event, so she hadn't been able to fill him in yet.

Roberta grimaced. "I'm sure she's just checking to make sure I haven't given the rock away or sold it for a pretty penny."

"Hmm ... there must be something else bothering her," Nate said. "I wonder if Bob knows what?"

What her mother was doing *was* unusual. She'd called every day since speaking with Bob. Asking how she was. What her plans were. Was the rock safe?

Bob came across as a man of his word. She must've copped a good serving from Bob to elicit this kind of response from her. But now it was getting beyond ridiculous and tedious.

It was this morning's phone call that decided it for Roberta. She was going to stay at the lake and keep working for Natasha until her leave ended. It would be easy to lie and convince herself it had nothing to do with Nate. But in a matter of days, they'd established an easy, relaxed friendship that would be hard to walk away from. Who would've thought it was possible without a single mention of sex.

Connor would be proud of her. After their visit to the lake, he and Liz went to Brisbane for a few weeks to conduct business, taking Sally with them as it was the third-term teaching holidays. Roberta would catch up with them again before Connor and Liz departed for Canada. What would they think of the new Roberta?

Brent's chant via a megaphone pulled her from her reverie, and she turned her gaze towards him.

"Meet with us, Premier. When do we want it? We want it now!"

The entire protest group repeated for the benefit of the cameras, leaving Roberta with the urge to shrink and disappear. This was so not her scene.

With all the protesters joining in with the chant, Roberta stopped using her placard and slunk behind it, hiding from the gathering crowd. She was getting a little bored with it all and allowed her mind to wander.

What would it be like to have sex with Nate? She'd already imagined it plenty of times. Had fallen asleep thinking just those thoughts. Something was building between them. Strong, unbreakable. They were making memories: swimming, hiking, sanding the rowboat and talking, sharing ideas, opinions and fears. It's what Roberta did best, and Nate had shaken his head aplenty over how she spoke freely without censorship.

The best moments were when she made him laugh, and it was a lot. It was good for her and him, she suspected. Sometimes she sang. This always snagged Nate. It only took a couple of words strung together, and it reeled him in, entwining them closer together.

She'd never experienced this with Antonio. Her repertoire of Italian music was limited and failed to convey the same emotion. It was a powerful strength she had, often leaving Nate choked with emotion.

Agreeing to come and help support the protesters was an easy decision to make. But she threatened all sorts of unimaginable things if there was one instance of blocked roads or everyday people hassled by their actions.

Nate had smiled and kissed her plenty over that. She secretly smiled at the memory before raising her placard a little higher as pulse points sent her zappy messages beneath her skin.

"Are we still on for tonight?" she asked Nate as the chanting quietened down and he sidled up beside her.

"Yep. Bob has confirmed his mother is cooking up a storm. Apparently, the entire clan is turning up."

"Huh? Why? To gawk at *me*?"

"I doubt it. You know how it is. Big Italian families, gathering and eating great food any day of the week. Surely, you're familiar with this?"

"Yeah, I am. To be honest, I've missed decent Italian food. If I don't cook it around here, it doesn't exist."

"I, for one, can vouch that you're a brilliant cook." Nate shifted his placard, swooping in for a kiss. She was enjoying this banter way too much.

"Jeez, you pair. We have important business going on here."

Roberta stepped away from Nate when Brent appeared beside them. She hated being caught this way. As showy and loud as she could be, she much preferred it when they were alone at the cottage or jogging around the lake. This week of laughter, jokes, singing and cooking, believe it or not, was flirting at its best. Would they take the next step and make that commitment?

"Have we got word yet?" Nate stepped back too but couldn't wipe the smile off his face.

"We sure have," Brent beamed. "Our meeting is scheduled, Bro. We go in next."

"Really? She agreed to meet with us?" Nate's smile matched that of Brent's. "Oh, man. I had a good feeling about this. We've lobbied, protested, put up our valid arguments. There was no way she could refuse coming to the party." Nate fist-pumped the air, his excitement palpable.

"Don't get too far ahead of yourself. Just make sure you bring in the Nate we need. Not the sappy someone with eyes for only one person." Brent scowled like he'd lost a best friend.

Nate playfully slapped Brent on the back. "I'm here, mate, with all guns firing. If I get the premier's ear, she won't get a chance to back out. We're prepared, ready for this."

Roberta had witnessed firsthand how this cause dominated Nate's days and nights. Contrary to what Brent believed, despite how much time they'd spent together, Nate had diligently worked late every night of the past week writing up this report to present to the premier and her ministers. He'd worked overtime for just this moment, and finally having some success made Roberta happy. A private meeting with the premier and her cabinet was no mean feat. As a collective group, they'd done it.

For an instant, she wished she could be part of all this group's successes. As she watched on, she witnessed the connection between them as they shared hugs and patted each other on the back. She didn't belong. To do so, she would have to commit to staying in the north past her six months of leave. Commit to more than just hanging off Nate. Believe in this cause.

But to give up her life in Melbourne? Move away from her family? Stop nursing?

What if everything was great between them, and then one day it went pear-shaped? She was a risk-taker most days, but she didn't think she had it in her to crash and burn again so soon after Antonio.

And the warning signs were all there. Bells clanging nice and loud. They clashed on so many topics. Something as simple as pineapple on pizza caused a riot during the week. It was fun and with lots of laughter, but it highlighted the enormous gap pervading their thought processes.

This sombre reminder had the muscles around her chest tightening. She might have to settle for sex alone. She'd done it before. Have some fun, enjoy conversations, not get hurt. Was Nate the man for casual sex?

She sighed as Nate meandered his way back to her. She lowered her placard. "I might head off and do some shopping before I drive home."

Nate put his arm around her, giving her a gentle squeeze. He was grinning, disbelief still written all over his face. "There's a shopping centre down along that street." He pointed out the direction. "This meeting could take a couple of hours. I'll be back in plenty of time for dinner with Bob's family."

"Okay, sounds like a plan." She made to walk off, but Nate tugged on her hand, halting her amongst the crowd.

"You're addictive," was all she heard when he wrapped his arms around her waist and found her mouth. A kiss full of energy, excitement and the buzz of success for all the hard work this environmental warrior had done. The kiss was possessive, like he was claiming his stake on her too, no different from the land he was trying to save.

As he let go, Roberta couldn't help but smile, savouring the lingering touch of his hand before she turned and walked off. *Holy heck.* Apart from floating a couple of inches off the ground, this was so out of her normal. When it came to men, she was always in control. But Nate, with his climate activist ways, was probably more extreme than bringing home a professional boxer for the parents to meet. Or an Italian prince, for that matter. She'd never brought Antonio home to meet the family.

Her heart thumped erratically. The problem was that she wanted Nate to meet the family. All of them. The cousins, the uncles, the aunties. Even her mum, if she ever came clean on what was really happening.

# Chapter 28

*W*here are you?

**On the pontoon.**

Roberta smiled as she pocketed her phone after sending a reply to Nate. She'd seen him arrive and garage his vehicle in the maintenance shed, the same way he would've noticed her parked car and known she'd be somewhere at the lake.

She dangled her legs over the side of the pontoon, splashing her feet in the cool afternoon water. The boat's shadow shaded her as the rubber fenders protecting its side softly tapped against the pontoon, the lines holding it in place straining with the gentle current.

The click of the cottage door closing carried on the soft breeze. Nate was coming to look for her. Her heart thrummed, picked up pace and refused to settle.

A few families remained at the lake this late in the day, including a group of young children laughing and splashing along the edge directly in front of the closed teahouse.

Roberta shivered when the breeze picked up and swirled along the water's surface. She looked up as Nate approached, his sunny smile matching the bright afternoon's last rays. This bode well, didn't it?

Nate plonked himself beside her, his arm instantly enveloping her, pulling her tight against his side.

Adrenaline was pulsating from his body. It discharged from every pore, covering his aura and spreading to her. She chuckled. "So, the meeting went well?"

"She listened and liked what we said. Promised to seriously consider our recommendations. This is good."

He was jumpy, and she wasn't surprised when he got to his feet, tugging on her hand to help her rise. "Want to see something?"

"Maybe," she boldly backchatted in the face of his excitement. Moving across to the other side of the pontoon, she climbed onto the rail and spread her arms out in the classic *Titanic* movie scene with her back to Nate.

"What the heck? What are you doing?" Nate asked in a tone that was half growl and half amusement.

She turned around to scowl but gave him the sweetest smile instead. Precariously perched on the tubular rail, she began singing some lines from the *Titanic* theme song 'My Heart Will Go On'. It had aired on the local radio station on the drive up the range from Cairns, and its lyrics remained stuck in her head. She hated it when a song did that. The only way to lose it was to belt out more of its words or wait for another song to come along and kick it out of the queue.

With this one firmly stuck, she sang to Nate that love could touch you one time and last a lifetime. When she added some clever falsetto, it tripled the emotion she conveyed. Nate remained frozen where he stood as though her voice and words paralysed him.

A sudden knee wobble had her jumping down from the rail back onto the pontoon before adding another line telling him that whether he was near or far, the heart would always go on. When she sashayed back, Nate's mouth was slightly open, his gaze fiercely penetrating hers.

"Where were we going?" Roberta asked, squeezing his hand to break him out of the trance.

His Adam's apple bobbed up and down. Looking so endearing and lost, Roberta reached up to brush her lips against his cheek. "Come on, Nate, it's only a song. It was playing on the radio this afternoon and it won't leave me."

"Keep singing like that, and *I* won't be responsible."

She chuckled, finally getting Nate to ditch the serious look for a more relaxed one.

"Look, I'm all yours. Take me wherever."

Hand in hand, they strolled off the pontoon. When they reached the end, Nate pulled her close and whispered, "I want to show you somewhere private and special." Nate glanced towards the visitors still swimming before admitting with a cheeky grin, "Some days, I hate sharing this place."

Roberta burst out laughing as they made for the same path leading to the kauri pines. His infectious energy was back, and she bounded alongside him as they entered the shadow of the forest, darting to the left of the path as some late visitors returned to the car park.

"Tell me more," she said once the path was clear.

"About what?"

"The changes you want the government to make."

"Oh, okay. I will. Soon. There's a bit to sort out, including a report I must send before the end of the week."

"Is this place you want to show me far?"

"Nope."

They were fast approaching the twin giants but didn't stop there, continuing to walk past the viewing platform. "Not much further." Nate gave her a cheeky wink.

"I'm glad; otherwise, we'll never get back in time for dinner with Bob's family."

Nate came to a sudden halt on the path and faced her. He looked into her eyes solemnly. "I've never taken anyone here before. I don't even remember how I found it as a kid. Promise me you'll keep it a secret," he pleaded like he might already be regretting his decision to show her.

"Huh? I can't do that. I don't know what you're about to show me."

Nate harrumphed. "I should've guessed you'd never grant me this one wish. See this tree?" He pointed to one on the edge of the path and its odd-shaped trunk. It resembled a woman's torso with breasts in the right place. "Turn off the path here. It's only about six metres in, and you'll see why it's so special."

"Why do I need to know how to get here?"

"You never know when you might need some private space."

"Well then, hurry up." Roberta giggled, clutching his hand tighter as she followed Nate on an invisible path, inviting laughter to spill from his lips.

When she saw the tree, she came to a sudden stop, and Nate did the same. Although it was only a tree, its roots were bigger than any others she'd seen, leaving her in awe. Two massive buttress roots rose to resemble a comfortable and inviting lounge chair, complete with mossy, lichen-encrusted armrests. "This is it?"

Nate nodded, looking uncertain.

"What do you do here?"

"I come here when I don't want to be found. When I need to think things through."

"Have you been here lately?"

"I have."

In the slowly darkening forest, Roberta faced Nate. His thumb gently stroked her cheek, starting a hum along her skin. The enormity of him sharing this place with her hit her fair in the chest. He was making it harder for her to leave. She wet her dry lips before biting down on it. "The day Crystal was here?"

"Yes." His voice came out husky. His usually light blue eyes were now a darker shade, drawing her in like a moth to light.

"Would you care to share my space?" He lowered between the two tree roots, the space big enough for two adults. She followed his lead, laying against his reclined length, cradled on either side by the roots and feeling protected all round.

Her eyes fluttered closed as she rested her head on his chest and melded against him. The soft beating of his heart pulsed against her cheek as a rich, earthy smell infiltrated her senses. She breathed deeply, filling her well with goodness and relaxation.

"What do you think?" Nate whispered the words against the top of her hair. She reached up to cup his cheek, the gentle prickle of his afternoon stubble sending a shiver of awareness along her skin.

She looked up, wanting to see his face in the fading light. "It's as though the tree has a vibe. I can feel it hum. Can you?"

"Hum, hey."

Nate wriggled her up a little higher and began working his lips along her brow, down her cheek, his mouth edging closer to hers while he gently kneaded her arms.

"I thought you said you came here to think." Lulled by his kissing, she closed her drowsy eyes. At least she was comfortable against his body. As for Nate's comfort, she wasn't so sure.

"I am thinking. My mind is working out how to best kiss you right now."

Roberta chuckled softly, tilting her head back so Nate could reach her. Her fingernails scraped against the wet, moist lichen for leverage, and with her eyes open again, she saw them filled with green muck. She held her hand up to the light. "This could get messy."

"I wasn't going to suggest we go that far. It's not that cosy."

The more they laughed, the more their mixed meanings tangled with their lips.

"Are you sure this isn't killing your back?"

"Yep." Nate gathered both sides of her face and drew her closer.

She stretched along his length. Not the securest of places considering Nate lay on top of a system of tree roots that might've looked snuggly, but which she doubted was.

The tranquil surroundings well and truly made up for any discomfort. She closed her eyes and sank into Nate's touch. Their tongues duelled and lured contentedly until the kiss moved into intense territory, her soul unravelling just that little bit more. She quivered in his arms, recognising the shameless urgency to take the next step. It was enough to elicit a groan of appreciation from Nate when she began rubbing against him.

With his strong, secure hands, he wrapped her closer, and desire flamed at every pore. It was a kiss to steal her soul. His arms tightened further, and she feared he'd cut off her breath. Then her stomach let out a loud rumble, causing the perfect moment to shatter. Roberta pulled back. "We should probably get ready for dinner. We're going to be so late."

Nate chuckled, releasing his hold a tad. "Has anyone ever told you there's a time for talking and a time for other stuff? Can we just get this done?"

They laughed some more, kissed again, tried to find the intensity again, but the moment was lost. Gone was the mood, moment and sensation. The harder Roberta tried to concentrate, the harder it was to stop laughing. She wriggled around, needing to untangle her legs and rise. She grabbed hold of the top of the buttress root and groaned when she came away with a handful of icky, moist lichen. "Nate, are you sure these roots aren't digging into your back? There's no way you're comfortable."

"Ahh … Roberta. Stop your fussing. Let me worry about that."

When he tugged on her sticky hand, she ended up in the warmth of his arms, and she loved it. It felt like home. There was no hiding the bulge pulsing between them and the threat of how she could easily escalate this to so much more. But they were running out of time. Damn!

For once, Nate persisted. Dragging her thoughts away from what they should be doing and steering them towards what they could be doing. The moment she stopped worrying, his kiss continued its magic. The insistent touch of tongues, the sharing of warm breath, the delicious current zapping between them, the more urgent their kiss built up again. Sharp pleasure jabbed at every point on her body, leaving her intoxicatingly warm.

She no longer sang the *Titanic* theme song on repeat. It was long gone. What did take up space in her thoughts was that Nate took her to his private place and wanted to share it with her. This was powerful. That two was better than one crossed her mind. No matter what the circumstances or the place, and regardless of the setting, when two people clicked, there was no turning it off.

"Ah, finally. I have the Roberta I've been craving all day." Nate nuzzled against her cheek, teasing her there, allowing her to gulp some air.

She mumbled indecipherable words; she was sinking. Deep into the unknown. A place she'd never been before. It terrified the hell out of her, leaving her unbalanced and unsure of what to do next. When she retreated, the forest was almost too dark to decipher Nate's face.

"I know, I know. We're going to be so late," Nate admitted as he shuffled out from underneath her and helped her up.

Drowsy and floppy, she disentangled herself and rose; her body, though, was still craving his closeness. "I tried to warn you earlier," she managed to say over the tightness in her throat. Her next problem was calming the rapid flutter, the hammering of her heart. She caught his gaze in the near dark and merriment looked back at her.

"You did. So sorry I didn't listen. Come on, let's go."

Nate grabbed hold of her hand in a good, firm grip. Leading her out of the forest, neither spoke, but her veins throbbed. The very air surrounding them vibrated. How was she expected to behave and act normal surrounded by a cheerful Italian family and a mountain of food?

She groaned, tripping slightly on a tree root, only to have Nate steady her again.

It was going to be a long night. Already she was wishing they were alone and doing other things.

# Chapter 29

Roberta hugged Bob's mother goodbye and thanked her for the tenth time. "Thank you for inviting me to your home and for such a delicious meal."

"You're welcome. Come any time. You fit in with this noisy crowd too easily."

Roberta felt at home around Bob's family. They shared the same food culture and joy for life as her extended family. Lots of eating, talking and laughing. To be heard over everyone else, you learnt from a young age to speak louder. This was a skill Roberta had fine-tuned over the years.

She turned to Bob, who'd remained surprisingly quiet during the meal. Occasionally, she caught him glancing her way. Usually with a lopsided smile or a shake of the head, depending on what his nieces and nephews were talking or laughing about. "Thank you, Bob. Your family are lovely." She gave him a brief hug too, liking this gentle giant of a man. Reminded of the cruel streak of bad luck that had followed him for most of his life, Roberta found a special spot in her heart for him.

"You'll have to come over again someday. Mum will insist."

Roberta chuckled, liking the friendly smile always pasted on Bob's face. "With your mum's cooking, don't be surprised if I turn up every night."

Bob shrugged. "Happens all the time, so she wouldn't even bat an eyelid. I'm sure Mum feeds half the neighbourhood. If it's not the homemade salami everyone wants to sample, it's her legendary bolognaise sauce to die for."

"I'm not surprised, so thank you again. Now, we better leave so you can all go home, since tomorrow is a workday. See you around, Bob. Oh, and thanks for ringing Mum. Or not." Roberta grimaced. "She's been ringing me daily to check I'm okay."

"She's probably missing you."

"Nah, I'm a troublemaker. She's probably enjoying the peace and quiet. Actually, I think she's just worried I'll lose the sapphire before she gets to see it again."

"Then tell her to come and fetch it for herself. Melbourne's not that far away."

Roberta laughed. "I should. Okay, goodbye again." Roberta gave another little wave to Bob and his parents, making her way over to Nate, who was chatting with some of Bob's nephews about water skiing.

"Finally ready to leave?" Nate grinned, taking hold of her hand.

"Did Nanna give you a doggy bag?" one of the grandsons joked. "She'll be worried you won't be feeding yourself properly."

Roberta chuckled along with Bob's nephews. "She did ask, but I kindly refused her offer." She understood exactly where they were coming from. Bob's parents weren't so different from her aunties and uncles. "It was lovely to meet you all." Roberta thanked the young adults before adding, "Sounds like I'll be back again before too long."

"Yep, Nanna's homemade pasta is hard to refuse."

Roberta waved goodbye and walked off with Nate. Bob's family continued to chat on the driveway. They could easily still be there in half an hour saying goodbye. She smiled, understanding how it worked.

Nate squeezed her fingers, leading her to her car. "Are you right to drive back?"

"Yeah, I held back on the wine."

The drive back to the lake was in comparative silence, broken only by the occasional sigh and the purr of the motor. Only as Roberta turned off the main highway into the road leading to the lake did Nate reach over and place his hand over hers on the gearstick.

Comforting, secure, strong, and with enough warmth to put to rest any thoughts of curling up for a long sleep. His hand dropped away as she sliced down the gears and traversed the speed bumps forcing her to slow down as they approached the car park.

When she parked overlooking the lake, the moon had decided to turn a fabulous night into an enchanting one. Its undistorted reflection rippled gently on the surface of the water, ending in front of the teahouse. The moonlight glinted off countless mirrorlike facets in the small waves and ripples.

"Wow!" Roberta exclaimed.

"I know. Can be special some nights." Nate opened his door and got out.

Roberta did the same before locking the car and pocketing the key in the back pocket of her jeans.

Nate came up behind her, wrapping his arms around her. "Thanks for being so much fun this week."

"Same." She snuggled in closer to his chest, liking how it warmed her back.

Nate touched her neck with his mouth and a shiver travelled along her arms.

"Cold?"

"I doubt it."

Nate chuckled softly against her skin. "It's been hard keeping my hands off you."

Roberta blushed, grateful the night was hiding it. When it turned into an outright fire, the muscles in her stomach clenched. "We're adults. Do we have to ask anyone for permission?"

Nate groaned as he explored more of her neck with his mouth. "I want you to be certain, that's all. I'm a crazy, stupid person. When I fall for someone, I always assume it'll last forever. But I've learnt the hard way it doesn't work that way."

"Shh, I've already figured that out about you." She turned around and cradled his face in her hands, drawing him closer to her. "I've been foolish in the past, too, when it comes to this stuff. Always rushing in too early, but I got that vibe from you very early on. If tonight you'd kissed me goodnight and wished me a good night's sleep, I wouldn't have questioned it. I would've hated it, but there's no way I was making the first move."

"What? Roberta a chicken?" Nate teased, running his hands up and down her arm, making her hyper sensitive everywhere he touched.

"Stop it," she admonished, grabbing his hands and entwining their fingers.

"Sorry," he hummed, closing the space between them and deliciously warming the spot where they touched. "It's not knowing that'll kill me in the end if I don't take the risk."

Nate wrapped his arms around her waist, holding her closer still. They were touching from chest to knees. It was hard to ignore all the signs between them. The perfect lake night, the soft meandering breeze, the burning sensation on every patch of bare skin Nate touched.

"I don't want to wait for another day," Nate added, nuzzling her neck and sending tingles to every pore.

"I can't promise you anything long-term because I suck at it," she whispered, "but the time feels right."

If Nate needed permission, this was it. They stumbled down the uneven steps leading to the cottage, not a word needing to be spoken. Heat radiated from her body doing all its usual preparations for what lay ahead. She wasn't new to this, but she *was* in unknown territory. Nate was not a man she could discard easily. It frightened her how there were so many uncertainties between them. For God's sake, she was only temporarily here, but tonight, she was ready for this. *They* wanted this. Preparing to risk it all, she held onto the hope that one day, their paths would align.

Nate shut the cottage door behind him and led her to his bedroom. Once there, he began stripping off his clothes. This was going to be fast and furious. Roberta didn't hesitate to remove her jeans, shirt, bra and knickers.

Nate pulled the doona out of the way only seconds before they fell together on his bed. With senses heightened from the drive home, they fell onto each other, mouths burning, hands rubbing along scorched skin, tongues fighting for supremacy.

"Let me get ready. Give me a second." Nate fumbled in a bedside drawer, coming up with a condom. Roberta took it from him, tore it open and handed it back.

"Get it on fast, Nate. Please," she begged.

Nate sheathed himself and rolled her onto her back. Roberta raised her knees, opening up to him and groaned. "Now, Nate, please."

Nate fell to his knees and took a moment to get his breath working again, his chest rippling in time with hers. It was his eyes. Shaded and dark with a reflection of the moonlight coming through the window that pierced hers for an intense moment. "Please don't regret this."

"I won't," she whispered.

With that promise, he slid inside, opening her up the same way he opened new possibilities between them. Then began a rhythmic thrust lasting only minutes. They were too hyped up. Too aroused for this to drag on for long. The same moment Roberta shattered, Nate moaned in unison with her groans, the earth cracking open where they lay and Roberta falling into its blissful abyss.

When the earth closed again and the room righted itself, Nate flopped down over her. She relished his weight. Could stay this way forever. Never wanted to move.

Nate was the first to do so, leaving her snug on his pillow while he went to the bathroom. When he returned, she gladly allowed him to spoon her, holding her close, holding her heart in his hands. She was all his now.

She might've dozed off but couldn't be sure. The night air carried a cooler chill the later it got, and she snuggled closer, Nate's hands secured around her waist.

When Nate whispered in her ear, "Would you like to do that all over again, but a lot slower?" her eyes fluttered open, and her heart picked up speed.

"Yes, please," she whispered back, now certain she had slept. So they did. With infinite care and attention. More time spent on touching. Hushed moans in the dark room. When Nate's hand idled down and his fingers found the entry, she pushed against them, instigating a rhythmic pulse, wanting so much more.

"Do I need to rummage in your drawer?" she asked, receiving a rumbling laugh in return.

"Nope, took it out earlier before slipping back into bed."

Roberta chuckled. "So, you were planning this already?"

"You bet. The first time totally blew my mind. I wanted to experience it at least once more tonight."

"This is nuts, Nate. How can I need this again so soon?"

"I know, right. Is this how it should be?"

"I hope so." There, all dialogue ended. Nate rolled on another condom, took control of her mouth, and began their second ride. It would remain etched in her mind forever. All previous attempts had been practice runs for the real thing. And this *was* real because it involved their minds, hearts and bodies. When the earth opened again and swallowed them whole, it left Roberta believing they were the only two humans left on Earth.

If only.

# Chapter 30

Nate slowed his jog, getting ready to warm down as he returned to where he started by the boat shed. School holidays made for hectic days at the lake with visitor numbers higher than usual. Today was one of them. As he exited the shadow of the forest and made his way towards the cottage, blaring music assaulted his ears. Unlike the first time this happened, Nate shook his head and couldn't help but smile.

He stopped short of entering the cottage, doing some stretches instead on the front porch to ease and release his muscles while memories of the previous night bombarded his thoughts.

Adrenaline had powered his run around the lake, drunk on Roberta. An entire week of being drunk on her. Night after night. He wanted to keep sipping from that glass and refill it forever. Had it been like this with Crystal? He thought it had, but now he wasn't so sure.

Before entering the cottage, he lifted his shirt to mop the sheen of sweat coating his face. He didn't recognise the music. Roberta's playlist consisted of music going back years, way before they were born.

She turned the moment he entered, motioning for him to come towards her as a new song began. It was a slower number. She swayed with the music, holding him captive with the emotion in her voice and the action of her hands as they slid down her curves. Mesmerised by her hands, they followed her body from the sides of her breasts down to her hips. She beckoned him closer, still with words about swaying rooms as the music started. Something about strangers making the most of the dark. How two by two, their bodies could become one.

He wasn't a great one for dancing. Didn't believe he had any natural rhythm. Roberta took hold of one reluctant hand, placing it on her waist. The other she entwined with her own, urging him to follow her moves. Music filled the room as her words blazed around his head, the heat between them turning up a notch.

His dancing wasn't exceptional, just small, simple moves in any direction. It was how Roberta moulded her hands over his body that turned him on tenfold. He'd have to remember to breathe at some stage because the words she now sang expressed that she was crazy for him. If he touched her once, he'd know it was true. That she never wanted anyone like this and could he feel it in her kiss.

Nate gulped as Roberta tantalised his arms with her fingertips. She heightened every sense in his body, her emotion-filled words reminding him she was trying her hardest to control her heart. But eye to eye, they needed no words at all.

She encouraged him to keep moving so that with every breath, she was deeper into him until they were standing still in time.

While Roberta continued to sing, the volume of the music seeped into his bones, both his hands now resting on the top of her butt as they moved as one.

He kissed along her neck. Up her cheek. Across her brow. No way was he touching her mouth while words were coming out in song. Her voice vibrated along his skin, inflaming the tingle taunting him at every move. He wanted her now. Again. When the song finally ended, he could wait no longer. He found her mouth, his arms tightening as he pulled her against his chest, throbbing between them. There was no way she could miss what she was doing to him.

While his tongue lashed against hers and his heart pumped harder, he recognised the next song on her playlist. The Goo Goo Doll's famous song 'Iris'. Its slower verses calmed him. Enough to slow down on the rough kissing and begin kneading her waist as he held her tighter.

In between a two-second spell in the music, he thought he heard knocking on the door. The loud music moved on, and he ignored it.

Roberta pulled back. "Someone's knocking."

Nate remained frozen, unable to drag his gaze away from her swollen lips. As though he hadn't heard a word, he moved to claim them again.

Roberta stepped back and went to her phone on the table, tapping the screen. The music stopped. "Someone is at the door."

He heard it again and scrubbed a hand over his face, making a herculean effort to calm down.

"Are you right for me to open the door?" Roberta whispered, eyeing his crotch. She turned away before he could mobilise himself. "God, what a waste," she mumbled, the sound of the doorknob turning finally enough to break him out of the stupor.

Roberta pulled the door open. "Officer Molloy, how nice to see you again."

Officer Molloy looked anywhere but at either of them. Was it written all over their faces? "Er ... did I disturb something?"

Roberta chuckled with a wry smile. "Not at all. We were just getting ready to prepare dinner."

When Roberta looked back at Nate, they both knew where they would've ended up if Office Molloy hadn't knocked.

Nate grimaced, ploughing a hand roughly through his sweaty hair. "Is there something we can help you with?" Getting his fill of Roberta would have to wait. How fast could they deal with what Officer Molloy wanted and get him out? Roberta was addictive, and he was desperate to fill up on her drug again and again.

"Ah ... I have some disturbing news to explain."

A jolt of fear shimmied over his skin. "Is everyone okay?"

Officer Molloy took a couple of steps into the small cottage, dwarfing it with the full regalia of the uniform he wore. "Yes, there's nothing wrong with any of your family. My reason for being here has to do with the white sapphire."

"Huh?" Roberta said, a confused frown beginning to show on her brow.

"A couple of days ago, we received a report that the grandson of a landowner on a cattle property west of Mount Garnet discovered that the sizeable white sapphire he should've inherited with his grandfather's collection was missing."

"But no one knows I've found it," Roberta insisted, "and I didn't steal it."

Nate went to stand behind Roberta, gently massaging her shoulders. "Shh, let him finish."

"No, you didn't," Officer Molloy carefully continued, "but someone did about thirty years ago. While the grandfather was alive, the family didn't keep the collection locked up, but after his passing, the family stored it securely away, hoping to get back to it one day and catalogue everything. Recently they did this, only to realise the giant white sapphire was missing all this time."

"How do you know it's the same one?" Roberta asked, her shoulders tensing under his hands.

"We don't, but we know Billy did a stint of work on this property at about the same time the stone could've gone missing, or taken, without anyone being aware of it."

"Are you suggesting my father stole it?"

"I'm not suggesting anything, Roberta, just stating facts. I'm here to collect it for verification."

Roberta shrugged Nate's hands off, taking a step away. "That stone belongs to my mother. As much as I begrudged having to come up here and find it, she was given that stone, and she has every right to keep it. I'm sorry, but I'm not giving you anything. You need better proof than that."

Roberta's voice had risen a notch, and Nate was worried the slight flush to her skin meant she was getting riled up. It was time he stepped in to pacify her.

"Roberta," Nate began carefully, "how about I go fetch it for Officer Molloy? Give them a chance to check it isn't the same stone." Nate reached closer to take her arm, but she waved his hand off and took another step away as though his touch might singe her skin.

"My mother told me this morning she might come up for a few days. You're not getting anything until she sees it," Roberta stated. "Prove it first. This is bullshit. Word has gotten out, and not from me, and now every scammer has come out from under every rock with plenty of good stories to try and take it off us. I'm not fooled that easily." She crossed her arms, not prepared to budge an inch.

Now she was showing all the signs of being peeved. "Roberta, you're going about this the wrong way." Nate tried to make his voice sound calm and reassuring.

She spun away from Officer Molloy and glared at him. "Are you that stupid you can't see what is happening here?"

That stung. So much for trying to cool the conversation.

"And don't do anything without me agreeing to it," she threw at him.

"Roberta," Office Molloy tried to placate, "it's only until we can verify facts."

"Facts my arse. It'll end up in your coffers until God knows when. That stone belongs to my mother. Hell will freeze over first before I give it to anyone else."

"Roberta"—Officer Molloy pulled out an envelope and attempted to give it to her—"this is a signed warrant for it. You've given me no other option."

Roberta ignored it, her arms remaining firmly crossed, so Nate took it. Opening the envelope would inflame Roberta further, but the law was the law.

Taking a moment, he scanned the warrant. "I'll go get it out of the safe."

"Don't, Nate," she persisted.

"You don't have a choice. Can't you see that?" He waved the piece of paper in front of her. "This is a court issued warrant. It's legit, and you need to hand it over. Here, take a look."

She faced him again, ignoring the letter and scowling with her arms crossed. "I can't see anything other than a planned scam here by someone who's reporting an alleged stolen rock that might've happened thirty years ago and decides only *now* to report it. Are you all so stupid you can't see this, too?"

"I'm going to get it now, Roberta. Try and calm down."

"Calm down?" she hissed, fisting her hands by her side.

Christ, she wasn't getting off her high horse any time soon, but Nate had to be the responsible one. Do the right thing. Being a hothead wasn't going to help anyone. "The stone is on my property, Roberta. I'm sorry but I don't have a choice."

"Don't have a choice? Are you kidding me?" Complete and utter fury was directed at him. "This is my father we're talking about. We're accusing a dead man of being a thief!"

Nate tried to pacify her by taking her in his arms, but she pummelled his chest, pushing him away.

Officer Molloy approached, and suddenly, he was beside them, swiftly securing her wrists in handcuffs from the front.

"What the hell! Get these off me." Roberta twisted and turned, trying to release her hands.

Fuck! She would never forgive him for this.

Now she pushed into his chest with manacled hands, the metal bolts digging into his skin through his shirt. Nate fisted her hands in his to try and stop her.

"Roberta, what *is* going on?"

Nate looked up at the open front door as a woman and Bob stood on the threshold.

Roberta stopped thrashing, her arms dropping to her front, her chest heaving with spent energy. "Mum!"

# Chapter 31

Roberta gulped; deathly silence followed her mother's arrival. She shrugged off Nate's attempt to soothe her, brushing off his arm. "Don't touch me."

It was uncalled for, but his attempt to override her wishes about giving up the rock without a fight still bruised her. She should care about the warrant being law, but she couldn't get rid of the thought that this was a scam.

Nate grimaced beside her but turned to Officer Molloy. "Please remove the handcuffs."

Officer Molloy quirked a brow and looked directly at her. She raised her arms to chest height. "I'll behave from now on. Please remove them."

Once the cuffs were off, she rubbed her bruised wrists and glared at her mother. "Why didn't you tell me the truth this morning? I take it you already had your flight organised?"

Lily glanced briefly at Bob. "Mostly, yes. I wanted to surprise you."

*Grrr.* Everything about this ate at her. Her mother's secrecy only added to it. Why now? Why would someone claim after thirty years that a gemstone had been taken from a collection? It made no sense. After all the effort she'd gone through to dig it up, why now? God! She wanted to fling her arms up in the air and wash her hands of this entire mess. Then walk out the door and never come back again. Except …

"Bob, why are you here?" She was determined to ask questions to keep her mind off Nate and what they should've been doing that afternoon. Someone would wear the brunt of her frustration.

"What is going on?" Roberta spat. I assume you're here for the same reason he is? She pointed in Officer Molloy's direction.

"I have been questioned about it." Bob fiddled with the hem of his T-shirt before glancing nervously at Lily.

"Well, did my dad steal the stone?"

Bob coughed to clear his throat, struggling to speak, but finally said, "I was able to confirm to the police that Billy worked a stint at the station in question. I was there at the same time, but I can neither confirm nor deny if he took the stone. We all knew the old fellow did a spot of prospecting and was proud of his collection. We lived in the station accommodation and had no reason to be near the main homestead. It was only a once-off summer vacation break that took us out there, and I really enjoyed it, but it wasn't forever. We both had working family farms to return to."

"So, my father was a thief?"

"I didn't say that. If he stole the rock, I never saw it happen."

"But he's not here to defend himself. It's no longer the rough stone. How will they tell if it's the same one? And why did its disappearance conveniently come up now?"

Roberta turned towards Officer Molloy when he spoke.

"The old man collector was quite the expert and recorded details about each gemstone he found. Things like its clarity, colour and whether it contained any imperfections. His grandson has now inherited the collection and recently went through all the paperwork matching it to each stone. This was how he found this significant gemstone was missing. Exceptionally large, it had attracted the news back then but was largely forgotten after the old man passed on. But there's proof of its existence, and now we need it in our possession so an expert can examine it. Regardless of whether it's been faceted or not, they'll be able to tell. If it isn't the stolen gemstone, you get it back. No questions asked."

Roberta turned on her mother. "Did you know anything about this?"

"No!" Lily exclaimed. "Why would I?"

"But they're claiming the man you loved was a criminal. Are you okay with that?"

"Oh, Roberta," Lily moaned. When Bob put his arm around her mother's waist, Roberta frowned. Bob's actions made no sense.

"Billy," Lily wavered, uncertainly all over her face. "Oh, I did love Billy, but—"

"Huh? But what? You either loved him or not. If you didn't, why this wild goose chase?"

Tears trickled down Lily's face. "I did. Very much. We were inseparable. Then ... then one night, he hit me. Oh, I can't remember why we argued. We were both so emotional and hotheaded; it just happened. But the slap was a huge shock, one I wasn't expecting. It was late at night, and I took off. I can't even remember why I drove to Bob's place, but he was always so kind and gentle. I had to talk to someone. At the time, he was the only person I could think of who was in close driving distance."

Bob tightened his hold around Lily when she struggled to halt her tears. "Shh, it's okay."

"What's okay?" Roberta wanted to know.

"It happened," Lily continued but couldn't carry on, a sob catching in her throat.

"What happened?" Roberta impatiently demanded.

"Surrounded by Bob's kindness, it just happened."

"What happened?" Roberta suspected what her mother was working towards, but no way would she say it first.

"We ... we slept together and immediately knew it was the wrong thing to do."

"You had sex with your boyfriend's best friend?" Again, she shrugged off any attempt by Nate to placate her when he came to her side again. "Oh, this is good. This is so, so good." Her voice sounded like a wail to her ears. After years of being reprimanded by her mother for her bad behaviour, this topped it off. Who cared about the rock? *What rock?* she wanted to shout.

"Roberta, stop it," Bob pleaded. "Let your mother finish saying what she has to."

"No, you stop it. All of you. I don't want to hear any more. All I've gotten from this conversation is that I was asked to dig up a rock my father gave you because *he* loved you. We can't be sure you felt the same way because you had sex with his best friend. But that's not the best part. Oh no, my father was also a criminal and an abusive one too. You know what? I don't want to hear anymore. Ever! Period! Go back to Melbourne and leave me alone … forever, thank you very much." She sped past her distraught mother and out the door.

⁕

Nate grimaced when the front door slammed shut behind Roberta. She was hurting, and he should be the one trying to console her, but he knew better. Roberta needed a cooling-off period. He'd look for her soon. Without her car keys, she wouldn't be driving anywhere. That was a good thing. But how to clean this mess that started many years ago? It could so easily screw Roberta up and their relationship, and he didn't want that. He was in damage control on their behalf, but first things first. As for what he was about to do, he hoped like blazes he wouldn't regret it for the rest of his life.

He turned to Officer Molloy, leaving Bob and Roberta's mother to console each other for now. "I guess we don't have a choice about the gemstone. It's in the safe. I'll go get it for you."

"Much appreciated, Nate. I'm sorry about all this. I wish we could've done things differently, but I don't have a choice."

"All good. I'll go now." Nate grabbed the bulky teahouse key tag off its hook, asked Bob and Lily to take a seat on the couch and left. It wasn't all good. Nate understood what he was doing would never pass muster with Roberta. He was risking everything they'd shared. Would she forgive him?

He glanced in all directions but didn't see Roberta outside the teahouse. When he returned to the cottage, Roberta's mother approached him. "It's Nate, isn't it?"

Nate nodded.

"I'm Lily. Roberta has talked about you."

Grimacing, Nate didn't respond. He didn't want to think about some of the things Roberta might've told her mother. Their short rollercoaster of a relationship had probably landed him in verbal hot water many times during phone conversations.

"Thank you for taking care of her. Sometimes we've struggled as mother and daughter, and it feels like we've been at loggerheads for years, unable to agree on anything."

"I'm sure she'll come around. You know Roberta, she just needs a bit of time to think things through."

"I'm not so sure. There's more I haven't told her. I'm scared it might break her this time." She hesitated, her hands knotting and her knuckles showing their whites. Her eyes filled with longing as she gazed wistfully at the small box he held. "Can I look at the stone, please, before you hand it over? I was such a terrified mess the day I buried it, with no idea what the future held or if I was doing the right thing."

Nate looked to Office Molloy, who had taken a seat at the small table and was checking his phone. When he glanced up, Nate asked, "Is that okay?"

Office Molloy nodded, so Nate opened the box and gave it to Lily.

Lily remained transfixed as she looked at the gemstone. Tears trickled down her cheeks again. She used her sleeve to wipe them away. "I wasn't imagining it over the years. I remember it being so large. I thought maybe I made it bigger than what it really was." She turned the box in different angles, giving Bob the opportunity to view it too. Lily glanced up and met Bob's gaze. "Do you think Billy stole this?"

Bob took the box from Lily and turned it to the light. "I wish I knew, Lily. I really wish I did." Bob gave it back to her, enclosing Lily's hand in his large one. "I guess it's time to find out. I hope he didn't. He's been my idol since the day he died. It'll be a blow to learn he did the wrong thing."

Lily nodded as though she understood what Bob meant. Nate didn't doubt that if Billy had stolen the rough gemstone, it would damage these two in ways he couldn't be sure of and bring more bitterness to Billy's parents, who already carried enough of it as it was.

Lily approached Officer Molloy. "Thank you for being so understanding with my daughter. She's had a big upheaval in her life, and this will only fuel her anger. But I have no regrets. From the very first day I held her in my arms, I have fiercely loved my daughter, believing that burying the rock and forgetting everything that happened up here was the best decision at the time. I still feel this way."

She passed the small box to Office Molloy, then took Bob's hands in her own and faced him. "I wish your life had turned out better."

Bob's reaction to Lily's words stirred something in Nate. Bob's Adam's apple bobbed, evidence of how emotional a moment this was for him. Nate understood this better after Lily's revelation earlier.

Officer Molloy stood and slid the chair under the table. "I'll be on my way. I apologise for the upheaval my turning up has caused, and I hope Roberta is okay."

Nate extended his hand and Officer Molloy shook it. "All good, mate. I'll go find her now."

When Officer Molloy left, Nate turned to Lily. "Have you organised somewhere to stay?"

"Bob has arranged it," Lily said.

"Okay, great. I'll go look for Roberta. Check she's okay."

"Thank you, Nate. Will you let me know?"

"Of course."

When Lily and Bob left, Nate remained rooted to the spot. There were things going on that he couldn't quite grasp. Either way, it would affect Roberta, and she would need all the support she could get.

With a sigh, Nate picked up a torch and left the cottage. Why did he suspect it would require Roberta crashing first and him picking up the pieces?

# Chapter 32

Nate wasn't sure what compelled him to walk towards his special thinking spot. Roberta could be anywhere along the walking track. It was still daylight, probably half an hour left. He couldn't see her anywhere near the water's edge or on the pontoon. He checked in case she was sitting in the shadow of the cruise boat. He also ducked into the boatshed to check and instantly regretted it. They'd spent so many hours cooped up inside, sanding the old rowboat, talking, laughing and enjoying each other's company.

Tourists mingled close to the edge of the lake as he made his way to the track leading to the kauri pines. A group of young adults laughed and chatted as they sat atop paddle boats. They were calling it a day and paddling in towards the bank. Nate had done just that on countless afternoons with friends. It lent a good vibe about his carefree younger days, and the nostalgia of those memories continued to surface. He sighed wistfully.

As the sun shimmied the last of its happy rays over the lake and its guests, Nate wasn't feeling it. A premonition jarred his view of the world. After such an intensely sweet couple of weeks, would it all disappear? Was his life destined to be a continuous rollercoaster of highs and lows, where he never found that happy medium?

Once in the rainforest's shadow, it wasn't long before he passed the platform beside the giant trees with barely a glance in their direction. Reaching the odd-shaped tree, he veered off the path onto the hidden track. He wouldn't put it past Roberta to remember how to get there. She was a strong, resilient, intelligent woman and would've noted every detail ... and she had a lot of thinking to do.

It wasn't long before he spotted her sitting amongst the tree roots. As he approached, she raised her gaze to meet his. Despite the rapidly dwindling sunset, there was just enough light to see her face was puffy and blotchy. He wanted nothing more than to take her in his arms and console her. She was receiving shock after shock. A tiny part of him damned Lily for all she was putting Roberta through. But getting to the bottom of family drama and history meant hearts would hurt along the way.

He sat cross-legged at the foot of the tangled root system, waiting for Roberta to talk. This was how she rolled. She wouldn't be able to help herself. He just had to be patient.

"Hey," she whispered. The crackle of undergrowth by a small forest wallaby sounded nearby. "I'm feeling a bit messed up. I'm sorry."

"Don't be." He longed to reach out and touch her, but she sat crouched in the far corner of the root system with her untidy tangle of hair resting against the highest part of the buttress, not caring if it came away full of moist lichen. Sitting on the lower end of the buttress, he absentmindedly picked up a stray twig, rolling it between his fingers, playing with the forest litter around his feet.

Awkward silence blanketed them. If necessary, he'd sit there until eternity, until she was ready to talk. Then the oddest question popped into his head. "What song were you singing when I came back from my jog?"

One, two, three seconds passed.

"I don't want to talk."

"I know. I'm curious, that's all. Some songs you sing I've never heard of."

Nate stole a quick, sidelong glance at her. She hadn't moved from her crouched position.

It took a few more quiet moments before she answered. "It's an old Madonna song. It goes back to her early days. It's called 'Crazy For You'. It's one of Mum's favourites. She used to play it often."

"Will you sing it again to me one day?"

Another glance and she straightened slightly. "Stop it, Nate. I was always leaving, you know that."

"Were you?"

"I have to." She tapped her head with knuckles. "I'm too messed up here."

"Understandably."

"Stop being the nice guy, Nate. I'll destroy you like Crystal did. Let me go without any fuss so you can get on with your life."

"You're nothing like Crystal."

"No, I'm worse."

Nate's heart plummeted. He'd found something so special in Roberta, and his premonition was coming true. He would lose her fast. Way faster than the time it had taken to disentangle himself from Crystal. This fall would be catastrophic. He was older, wiser, and understood what he was losing. There were things about Roberta that wouldn't leave him. Ever. Her incredible voice, her sassiness, her forthright honesty, her take-no-bullshit attitude. Her desire to live life in the present and make everyone around her happy.

He shuffled his joggers amongst the forest litter, building little piles, the shadows lengthening as the day slowly turned to night. He needed to tell her he'd handed in the white sapphire. He wanted to savour every moment she was still talking to him, regardless of what she said and how hurtful it was. Because when she stopped talking, he would miss it like crazy.

As soon as she started humming, he looked up, watching her face transform into something peaceful, calm. Her voice vibrated in the hollow where they sat, and he shivered.

She sang of words, telling him that the day was long and the night was his alone. That if you'd had enough of this life, to hang on and not let yourself go. When her next words told him everybody cried, he recognised the song as REMs 'Everybody Hurts'.

If she kept singing, her voice would destroy his soul. Each word pierced a hole the size of a crater in his chest. He didn't want to hear her sing the words that sometimes everything was wrong but to hold on. That if he ever thought he'd had too much of this life, to hold on, hang on. To take comfort in his friends because everyone hurt—sometimes. And everybody cried.

By the time she finished the last of the words that would echo around his head forever, Roberta was a dark outline. He swallowed back hurt tearing at the back of his throat and blinked rapidly. The words of the song were too close to home.

"You gave the sapphire up, didn't you?"

He nodded. She wouldn't see his pain, but she'd see his head moving.

"It wasn't yours to give away."

"It wasn't yours either."

"Yes, it was," she cried. "My father touched that stone. He put his soul into creating it. Regardless of how he got it, it was the only tangible thing I had from him. Now I have nothing. Not even a single memory."

Her words crushed him further, and he didn't have to see her face to know tears were falling down her cheeks. He fished inside his pocket for the torch, switching it on. The light dazzled him momentarily, and in the space of time it took for the light to spread around him, Roberta had risen and was negotiating the tricky step off the buttress onto the forest floor.

"Now I have nothing," she repeated, staring him down.

He handed her the torch, its glow illuminating the narrow path as she walked away. He would use his phone to guide him out. She would get through this. Roberta's strength would do it, with some help and support from him. He owed it to her. He gave up the gemstone knowing it would backfire—and it had.

Total blackness descended around him, crushing him. On any other night, he loved the darkness, was fascinated by everything that came alive. But this kind of darkness spoke of loneliness, hurt and pain. He'd glimpsed light and dazzling sun over the past weeks and greedily wanted it back. Would this be his destiny forever? To always feel this way?

And then, just like the words to the song still echoing around his head, he cried. Silent tears that coursed down his face.

Because everybody hurt—sometimes.

# Chapter 33

Roberta dumped another load of dirty dishes beside the kitchen dishwasher before washing her hands.

There was another meal waiting to be brought out for her section of tables. With her mind focused on one task at a time, this was next up.

"You okay, Roberta? You've been quiet today."

Roberta acknowledged Natasha with a shrug and a forced smile as she picked up the prepared meals and walked out onto the deck. She couldn't be trusted to talk because, at any moment, she would break down. Now wasn't the time or place.

She squinted into the bright lunchtime sun. Usually, an astonishingly beautiful day like this one would have her at least humming. Had she sung her last song?

She shook the fuzziness from her head. She hadn't eaten the night before and missed breakfast, too. Running on adrenaline only was bound to trip her up any moment. She concentrated on getting the meals placed correctly in front of the diners and smiling at the right moments.

Soon she would have to tell Natasha she was leaving the teahouse. She knew where Sally kept her spare key and would crash there for a couple of days before making her way back to Melbourne. She racked her brain trying to remember when Sally was due back, but in her fatigued state, it was beyond her.

Nate had appeared in her periphery a few times that morning while she worked her shift, but so far, she'd been able to avoid him. She needed to.

In her sleep-deprived state, losing the white sapphire was a big deal. Why she was making such a ruckus over it, she didn't understand. She'd never known Billy. Why should she care? But somewhere in the deep recesses of her brain, she did. If Billy stole the rock, this reflected badly on her. The revelation that her mother had sex with Bob didn't help. Her life was a lie. Was she the result of a loving relationship or the byproduct of a violent one? Not knowing the whole story irked her. This time, the blame was solely hers. If she'd stuck around, instead of running away, her mother might've told her everything.

As the afternoon wore on, she continued to clear tables and deliver meals. Robotically doing her job while Sophie and Hannah eyed her cautiously, aware she wasn't her usual self.

Back at the cottage the previous night, she'd showered and crashed, crying most of the night, sleeping fitfully. Then there was Nate. Good, kind, loving Nate. Her environmental warrior. He would go to the ends of the earth to protect every single leaf on a tree if he could. Would protect her with his last breath if she allowed it.

This was the same man who insisted Officer Molloy remove the handcuffs after she attacked him. He'd done everything right until he gave up the stone. She'd wanted more evidence. More time. The happy ending. Returning the rock signalled the end of her stay. How could Nate want her if her father was a thief? If her mother slept around? It was better that she left and didn't taint Nate and his beautiful family.

Gradually, the rush subsided, and the clock rolled over to three pm. Roberta made her escape, needing to work out when and how to tell Natasha she was leaving. Right now, her priority was to get away from the lake and all the memories until she could think clearly again. She rushed towards the cottage intending to collect her car keys and a change of clothes, but when she took a step inside, Nate was in the kitchen. She stopped short. Nate would usually be in the maintenance shed at this time of the day. Not standing in the kitchen looking all ruffled and to die for.

"I made you a sandwich. Come and eat it."

"I'm not hungry." Her stomach rumbled loudly, mocking her.

Nate arched his brows. "Doesn't sound like it. Now sit, and I'll make you a coffee too."

"I'm not hungry," she repeated, which was ridiculous considering Nate heard her traitorous stomach. "And I was about to leave."

"Sit!" Nate carried a plate with two thick slices of bread filled with what looked like delicious ham and a mountain of salad. Her stomach rumbled louder, causing Nate to frown as he set the plate down. "Your mum and Bob are due here soon. They want to talk to you."

"How do you know?"

"Because she rang and told me she'd be here this afternoon."

"Why would she do that?"

"Why would you run away?"

"What's that supposed to mean?"

"We have something happening between us and you're willing to give it all up?"

"You don't understand."

"Damn right I don't. I want your mother to clear the air first with whatever it is she has to say so I can then deal with the daughter and this fallout we're having. I'm not ready to give up yet, even though you're prepared to do just that."

"What fallout?"

"Eat, will you. You're going to need something in your stomach."

"I don't know what the heck you're talking about."

Nate came from behind, gently guiding her to sit down. "Your coffee is nearly ready, and don't tell me you're not hungry because I know you haven't eaten."

"Have you been watching me all day?"

"No, but Tash has. You haven't spoken a word to anyone, so I was wondering when you were going to tell Tash you were running away."

"Stop it, I'm not running away."

"You're not? You weren't planning on going somewhere just now."

Roberta dropped her face, eyeing the sandwich which was calling her faster than the need to drive away was. Was she that much of an open book?

Her shoulders dropped as she picked up one half of the sandwich. "I was coming back to tell Natasha. I just wasn't sure when. I just needed a break from her, the lake … you."

Nate put a mug of steaming coffee before her and sat down with a hot drink of his own. "Look, it's okay to be mad at me, your mum and the world in general."

When she didn't reply and wouldn't look up, Nate said, "Look at me, Roberta."

She was having trouble swallowing the mouthful of sandwich she'd chewed off. Couldn't process the taste. Refused to look up because any moment now, she would break down. She wasn't sure of the reasons anymore.

She gulped once, allowing the food to pass by her throat and slowly shifted her gaze up. Nate looked at her with a worried frown. Her heart was breaking with his concern. "I've never given a damn about anything in my life. I was raised happy and loved by parents I thought I knew. Normal, happy, boring. The stuff dreams are made of. No questions asked. But—" One sob escaped, and she dropped the sandwich back onto the plate. Gritting her teeth, she clenched her jaw, determined not to end up blubbery. "My whole life has been a lie. Do you get that, Nate? Do you understand where I'm coming from? My younger brother is only my half-brother, and I'll have to tell him soon. My Aunt Fiorina in Italy, who is Dad's sister, has adored me my entire life. We're no longer blood related. Who do I belong to, Nate? Billy's parents don't even want a bar of me."

Nate took her hand, covering it with his warmth. "I understand this has been a shock to you, but I'm here, Roberta. I'll help you every step of the way."

"But do you? You have the perfect family. What do you really understand?"

"Now you're being obstinate, and I don't deserve that."

Roberta tried to take her hand back, but Nate held on tight. "Are you going to let me eat?"

Nate reluctantly freed her. "So you can run away sooner?"

"I'm not running away, okay? I just need to get away for a few days. To breathe, think things through."

"Where will you go?"

"To Sally's place." Feeling like the threat of tears had subsided, Roberta picked up her discarded sandwich again.

"I thought she was away."

"She is, but I know where she keeps her spare key. She won't mind."

"And you want to be alone during this time?"

Roberta took another bite and looked across at Nate. Pain reflected back, sharp and piercing. Her stomach muscles clenched and knotted. At this rate, she'd never get another mouthful down. It wasn't meant to be like this. "Nate, I'm—"

"Don't say it!"

The bulky emotion was back, hovering, ready to spill over.

"Don't you dare say you're sorry for what happened between us. Don't you dare walk out of here believing I'm sorry one bit." Nate's chair scraped back as he got up. He ploughed a hand through his hair as a knock sounded on the door.

Nate stood motionless, his body tense like he dreaded opening the door. It was her mother. Hadn't he already told her this?

When the knock sounded again, it was Roberta who called out, "Come in."

The door opened, and her mother and Bob tentatively entered. Again, the niggle that something was happening at lightning speed between these two. Didn't they bury her father only a handful of months ago, and already Lily was moving on? Roberta wanted to shout that this was all wrong, but she kept her mouth shut. Lily looked nervous. Her hands were twisting in front of her, fingers knotted tightly together. Bob didn't look any better.

An awkward silence descended over the room. Roberta's heart thumped erratically. Was something wrong? "What's going on?" she asked Lily.

Bob had his arm around Lily's shoulder and was kneading it.

"Roberta, your biological dad isn't Billy, it's—"

Again, awkward silence.

"It's who?" she demanded.

"I'm your biological dad, Roberta," Bob finished for Lily.

# Chapter 34

R oberta couldn't breathe. The muscles requiring this to happen failed to work. Her chest was filled with pain and she swayed, dangerously close to fainting as she took shaky breaths. Strong arms held her steady. She needed to concentrate on processing one word at a time.

*Bob. Is. My. Biological. Dad.*

A volcano bubbled below the surface, and within seconds, it erupted. All her anger was vented towards her mother. Every event in her life led to this moment. Every difficult moment between them. Each time her mother looked at her with *that look* Roberta could never decipher. Now, it all came rushing back. "You knew this?" she spat, her voice filled with disbelief.

"I ... I've suspected it." Lily's voice wobbled.

"Suspected it! What, since the day I was born?"

Lily offered a slight nod, her fingers a cruelly knotted mess in front of her stomach. "When Bob first phoned me, I couldn't hold it in anymore. He suggested I get hair samples DNA tested, along with his. It's ... it's a match. But I ... I already knew it would be."

Roberta sucked in more air, her chest hurting as she struggled to speak. She was vaguely aware of Nate's continued, reassuring grip on her arms. Otherwise, she might've collapsed by now. "You sent me up here for what? You told me nothing, leaving that small bit of information out. Why? I knew there was more I needed to know, but why let me believe Billy was my father? Why not tell me the truth before all the bullshit I went through?"

Lily fought back, growling. "You were supposed to find the sapphire and come back home. But oh no, not stubborn and headstrong Roberta. You had to open the hornet's nest behind my back, go it alone, get it all wrong right from the start. Upset everyone."

Roberta's eyes widened in utter disbelief, unable to comprehend what she was hearing. "You're saying this is all my fault? Like somehow, I was involved in this deception?"

Her mother swayed, but Bob held her tight. The scowl dropped, changing to forlorn and sad. "Oh, Roberta, I have held onto this forever. It's torn at me every single day, but there was no way I would ever hurt Sam."

"Sam! Dad! He loved me like his own daughter," Roberta wailed. "I loved him, but you've lived a lie your entire married life. How could you?"

"Don't you think I know that? Don't you think I haven't mulled over my actions every single day since you were born? I made a mistake. Hell, I made many mistakes, but not once did I ever regret you coming into my life."

Roberta sagged back against Nate, her body exhausted. "But we were always at odds, like I was the bad kid."

"I didn't want you making the same mistakes I did. You were always so wild. Some days, I doubted myself and wondered if you really were Billy's child."

"But you knew, didn't you? The minute I was born and didn't have the blonde hair and blue eyes, you knew I was never Billy's child?"

Tears trickled down Lily's cheeks, and her face fell sombre. "It made it so much easier for the world to view you as Sam's child. For some absurd reason, God looked down on me with pity instead of anger and gave you Bob's features, which easily passed as Sam's. But now I realise it was only a temporary reprieve. One day, I would have to pay for the secret. I can't lose you, Roberta, you've got to know that. You're my everything, and I'm so proud of you. I love you. That will never change."

Roberta wasn't game enough to look at Bob, couldn't look at her mother. Couldn't process anything past the anger still simmering towards her. What she once considered to be a perfect childhood, a haven, her backdrop, her family security, was now a mishmash of confusion and uncertainty. Like the earth had been stripped from underneath her. Who was she?

"How about we all sit down?"

Nate's sensible suggestion grated. Nate with his perfect, loving family. She was so out of place in his life she almost burst out laughing. She needed something to break the trance she was in.

Lily came closer and tried to wrap her arms around Roberta, but she shrugged her away. She wasn't ready for that. Nate tried to guide her to the table, but she fought back standing firm. She wasn't budging an inch. Only when she was ready. An awkward silence filled the small room, but the buzzing inside her head grew louder. Until it reached bursting point. Until it shot through the top like molten lava and she stumbled a step back. "I have to leave. Can't be here, in this room with all of you."

Lily and Nate exchanged a knowing look. One that spoke of trying to stop her. She wasn't having a bar of it. With a sense of urgency, she raced to her room for her handbag and spun around to leave but halted. Having second thoughts, she rummaged inside the built-in cupboard for the duffel bag she came with and shoved everything, including the few pairs of shoes, inside it.

Lily followed her in and stood in the doorway. "Don't do this, Roberta."

She ignored her mother and picked up a discarded shopping bag. From the bathroom, she grabbed her toothbrush and other items, piling them messily on top of each other. "Go away!"

"Please don't drive in this condition."

"What condition? You've been lying to me my entire life. If being pissed off is a condition, then yes, I have it."

Roberta slung her handbag and duffel bag over her shoulder and stormed out of the bedroom, only to slam into Nate. He not so gently grabbed her by the arm to halt her. "Roberta, please don't go anywhere. Let's talk this through together."

"I'm done with talking." Evading his hold, she stormed out the front door. She was smart enough not to make a scene outside the cottage because visitors would still be at the lake, and she wasn't that sort of person. She zipped her mouth, aware Nate followed her every step as she made her way to the top car park.

"Roberta, please don't drive like this."

She ignored him until she got to her car, then she spun around, her chest hurting with the exertion of climbing the steps.

"Forget about me, Nate. I'm a mess. I'm no good for you and your perfect family."

"Perfect family!" he hissed between drawn lips. "Who cares about my perfect family? What about us? You're going to walk away?"

A low growl escaped, starting deep within her and moving up her throat. "The news didn't come as a shock to you? Like dirty laundry being hung out to dry for all the world to see?" She kept her voice low, but so much emotion bubbled inside her that she struggled to speak without her voice breaking.

"Only when she asked to come over did I begin to have the slightest niggle."

"You kept it from me, too?" Her voice rose a notch, but she gritted her teeth to keep from yelling.

"I kept nothing from you. If I did know, it wasn't my place to tell you." Nate spoke in a clipped whisper, struggling to keep his voice down too. A family walking past them looked in their direction.

"You'll regret getting tangled up with me. Go live your life free of all this drama. I'm leaving. I was always leaving. There's no reason for me to stay now."

"Don't go, please. Give us a chance to talk this through."

Roberta brushed his common sense aside, a barrage of longing only just hanging in there. "It'll never work, Nate. It's better if I leave now. I'm such a bloody mess. The last person you want anywhere near you is me. Go live your life. You're better off without me." If she didn't get away now, it would all come rushing out. God knows what she'd do then.

She yanked the car door open, threw her collection of bags onto the front passenger seat and settled in the driver's seat. Nate loosely held the door from closing. He was so damn fucking nice he would never stand in her way. The realisation he was giving up on her too easily struck hard. Why wasn't he fighting for her to stay when she needed someone forceful to do just that? And why was she letting her stupid stubbornness get in the way and ruin everything between them? Would she ever learn?

"Roberta, I won't stop you from leaving, but I wish I could. We had something between us. You leaving is going to hurt. Take care—" His voice broke, and he took a moment before adding in a whisper she barely caught, "I'll miss you."

She closed the door on those final heartfelt words and started the engine. The regret of running away from a good man would haunt her for the rest of her life.

In her periphery, Nate didn't move as she erratically reversed before changing the gears to drive forwards. Only when she was facing away from Nate did heaving sobs tear at her throat as she negotiated the exit from the lake onto the main highway. She was headed for Sally's place, away from the lake. Away from Nate, her mother and her biological father. Her foot pressed a little harder on the accelerator, the need to find sanctuary for a couple of days before starting the drive back to Melbourne taking up all the space in her head.

Through the blurriness of her tears, she didn't see the truck that turned onto the highway and was slowly building up speed. Was sure she'd applied the brakes in time. Her scream grazed her throat only seconds before the impact. The sickening sound of crunching metal was the last sound she heard.

# Chapter 35

*F*our Weeks Later

Roberta flicked through the TV channels with the remote; daytime soapies and infomercials weren't her thing. She stopped at a news segment. It was probably the most stimulating channel so far, but she wasn't interested in any news outside her hospital room. She lowered the volume, allowing the noise to drone in the background.

The physio was due to arrive any moment, and a hint of annoyance hovered. Lily and Bob turned up for every physio session. All she wanted was to be left alone. To wallow in her self-pity. Getting into her car and driving away in the state she was in that day had been irresponsible. She was an adult and should've known better. She'd never forgive herself for this stupidity and thanked her lucky stars she was the only one who'd suffered injuries.

An induced coma for four days to monitor any possible head injuries. A fractured ankle, a couple of broken ribs and lots of bruises. She was alive, but some days she didn't think she deserved to be. The reminder of Nate's last words only served to stab her chest with more self-loathing. His absence was hurting.

"Good morning, Roberta." Bob entered her room, his usual cheerfulness on full display. She got that he'd gained a daughter he never thought he'd have, but she didn't share his joy yet.

"Where's Mum?"

"She's too busy for her daughter today."

This was said with a smile, a chuckle and a little fragment of humming.

"That figures," came her sullen reply.

"Thought you'd feel that way. She's getting my spare room ready for you. You're coming to stay with me until you fully recover."

"Can't wait," she added with an eye roll.

"Then, when you're good to drive again, you can return to Melbourne."

She twitched when a flash of metal hitting metal reared its ugly head in her mind. She'd have to learn how to drive all over again. The accident had shaken her up more than she cared to admit to anyone. For now, it was easier to be a real bitch. It was the only way she could move past the horror of the accident. The endless possibilities of what could've happened constantly bombarded her.

She could talk, move and soon be walking again. Her situation could've been so much worse, but she wasn't at the grateful stage yet. She may also never recover from pushing Nate away. There was never any going back to apologise after Nate and Lily begged her not to drive away upset. She cringed. She deserved nothing less than unhappiness for the rest of her life.

Nothing could buoy her spirits, the same way nothing could dampen the joy radiating from Bob's demeanour every time he was in the room with her. It was like he'd won the lottery of a happy life since discovering he had a daughter. Her happy vibes were unlikely to pop up any time soon.

A familiar voice came from outside her room, and her heart lurched inside her ribcage. Her brother Daniel arrived two weeks ago. He brought all the noise and banter she'd so desperately missed and entered her room with his usual fanfare of loud general chitchat.

"Look who's here. Your favourite brother." Bob stepped forward and patted him on the back like they were long-lost mates.

"Half-brother, remember." Roberta reminded them both.

Daniel ruffled her bed hair around her pillow before leaning closer to give her his usual brotherly hug. "Thank God for that. I knew I was never as bad as you. You are the worst, Sis. I'm just lucky I got genes from a better father." He turned towards a smiling Bob. "Sorry, mate, it had to be said. Officially, she's all yours now. See if you can make something good out of her."

Bob and Daniel continued to chuckle and joke. Daniel had received the news so good-heartedly, why couldn't she accept it too? Why was she still so hotheaded and sour about it after all these weeks?

Janelle, the physio, entered a few moments later, crowding the room. "Ah, looks like we have the extra helper here again today. Not sure why." This was said with a shy, yet bold smile towards Daniel.

It'd been a slow work in progress, but Roberta secretly smiled at what was happening between her physio and brother. The flirting started on the first day Daniel arrived. Recently freed from his last possessive girlfriend, he was free to look again and wasn't wasting a single minute.

Daniel comically puffed out his chest which almost elicited a smile from Janelle. God, how she loved her brother. Tall, dark and so indecently good-looking, he normally had women hanging off him in minutes. Kudos to Janelle who wasn't falling for Daniel's charm as fast as he would like.

"Without my help here yesterday, you would've struggled," an affronted Daniel replied.

Janelle scoffed but moved the only chair in the hospital room. "Here, can you hold this chair straight while I get Roberta down from the bed?"

"Hold a chair down with four legs of its own? Wouldn't you prefer it if I helped Roberta down from the bed?"

"Oh, I think she can do it on her own now."

Daniel joked further with the pretty physio. A light blush touched Janelle's cheek, and Roberta didn't miss the shrug Bob sent her way at the jokey banter.

Janelle maintained a professional approach, though, as she began the exercises designed to prevent her ankle from freezing up as the fracture healed. Daniel would help later when she did some walking. A moon boot would be fitted next in readiness for her discharge from hospital.

A small part of Roberta appreciated having others around as much as she wouldn't admit it. She wasn't a solo person; instead, she always needed a horde of people surrounding her, making lots of noise. She wouldn't have minded one other person around, and craved those days of just her and Nate alone, but, yeah, she wasn't letting her mind go there. It had tried countless times over the past weeks but shut it down quick smart.

"Okay, time for the moon boot, Roberta," Janelle announced after one last massage of her calf muscle.

Yesterday when she'd walked with the moon boot on, the pain wasn't so bad. The sooner she got the hang of walking, even with the aid of crutches, the better. She wanted to feel the brush of fresh breeze on her skin, the sun glistening and dimpling on a lake's surface, and the thick cloying smell of moist tropical rainforest. Except she wasn't going back to Lake Barrine.

Not any time soon.

Her shoulders sagged as she sat down on the edge of the bed, struggling to fit the moon boot and secure it in place. She was mentally drained, and her body language might be confusing Janelle. During the past few weeks as she lay mending in this room, all the whys and what-the-fucks circled her head nonstop. Not a single mention of Nate by anyone. Not by Natasha when she made a mad dash down the winding hill to visit her on a day when the teahouse was closed. Nothing from Sally either who drove down every weekend to spend time with her.

"You should be ready to leave in a couple of days, Roberta."

Janelle was by her side as she walked unaided down the hospital corridor and outside into the small garden for patients.

Dark, heavy clouds filled the sky that day, perfectly matching her mood. She shrugged at Janelle's assessment.

"I think she'll need much more physio work once she's out, don't you, Bob?" Daniel casually elbowed Bob as they stood outside waiting for Roberta to enjoy a few more minutes of fresh air.

Janelle smiled politely at the implied suggestion, and Roberta finally managed a chuckle. She couldn't hold it in any longer. She was beginning to feel sorry for Daniel.

"Hey Janelle, can I request you do my final sessions up on the Tablelands after I'm discharged?" Roberta asked cheekily, hoping to give Daniel and Janelle more time together.

Janelle started to say something, stuttered once and then sighed. "If I don't agree to at least one coffee with this damn brother of yours, he's going to be hellish to live with. That won't be good for my patient's recovery."

Janelle's outburst was so out of character for the prim, proper and professional person she displayed whenever she was with Roberta, and they all burst out laughing.

"I couldn't have said it better," Daniel replied, nose pointed in the air and his hands joined behind his back. "Lead the way, Sis; it's time to get you back to your room."

Roberta steadily walked back along the corridor, oblivious to what Bob, Daniel and Janelle were chatting about. All she was concentrating on was walking and minimising the pain.

Inside her room again, the television continued to drone on. Another news segment was starting, but something the newsreader was saying snagged her attention. She stopped, frozen halfway to her bed.

*Local man Nate Surrey and his band of willing helpers find themselves on the wrong side of the law again as they protest the proposed Liverpool Range Wind Farm located between the townships of Coolah and Cassilis in central-west New South Wales.*

He was in New South Wales?

*"Nate, can you tell us why you travelled so far from home to be here today?"*

*"Thank you for giving us some airtime. These renewable companies keep proposing ridiculous projects. We've applied enough pressure that they are changing the number of turbines from 267 to 220, but this will still make it one of Australia's largest wind farms. One of their concessions is that they want to increase the maximum blade height above ground level to 250 metres. They initially proposed a height of 165 metres."*

*"What are your concerns here?"*

*"The risk to flying wildlife will be catastrophic, not to mention the area of natural forest which will need to be destroyed for this number of turbines to be erected. This many turbines will create a maze of windmills that no wildlife will be able to fly past without risk of ... "*

Roberta remained glued to Nate's image on the screen, but his words rambled on in the background as she lost the thread of what he was saying.

Bob coughed in the background. "Are you okay, Roberta?"

At least she knew where Nate was. Who was skippering the boat in his absence? His dad? A small knot tightened inside her chest. She missed this lunatic so much, yet—

She shrugged. "What did those morons do this time to get the attention of the media?"

"They've been protesting for nearly a week on the steps of the Opera House. They refused to budge from their post until the NSW government listened to their concerns. Finally, yesterday, they agreed to do so."

"How do you know this? I've had this channel on every day and haven't heard anything."

"There's been a bit of stuff on the local social media pages."

That figured. She'd been avoiding her phone as much as possible.

Janelle gently guided Roberta to the bed when the news segment finished. Once she was sitting on the side, Janelle removed the moon boot and placed it on the spare chair ready for the next day. "I'll see you tomorrow, Roberta. Well done, today."

Janelle gave a cheery wave as she left the room with Daniel hot on her tail. Which only left Bob in the room. Father and daughter. Neither had anything to say. Bob darted furtive glances her way while his fingers tapped against his thigh in time like a metronome.

"What?" Roberta blustered, trying to cover her nerves.

Bob stood a little straighter. "Roberta, this entire situation is weird. I know, I get it, but I'm your biological dad, and I care about you. It's no secret you and Nate had a thing going on, and—"

"Mind your own business." She cut him off. How could they have a thing going when he hadn't bothered to visit or ring her once? She stared out the only window in the room, watching parrots land on the branches of the tree outside. Despite being fully air conditioned, she wanted to slide the window across and let in the gusty breeze as the dark, menacing clouds intensified.

Rain was only minutes away, and she wanted to be out in it, not watching it through the glass. Everything about the coming storm matched what was happening inside her. Yes, she sent Nate packing. She deserved his silence.

"I'm sorry." Roberta swung her attention back to Bob. The same gentle, hulking man she'd been warming to until she learnt he was her biological father. Before something snapped.

Bob walked around her bed and stood beside the window. "I know I've come late onto the scene and that Sam was the perfect dad. I'm not trying to take his place, I promise, but I'm willing to start from scratch. I'm new at this too, but I'll always have your back, Roberta, even if you never accept me."

Roberta pulled her eyes from the brooding sky and met Bob's. "Is something happening between you and mum?" There was still anger residing, and she didn't know how to shift or deal with it. How could her mother move on from Sam so fast?

Bob ploughed a hand roughly through his hair as he walked back to the other side of the bed, shifting the chair closer. He placed the moon boot carefully on the floor but didn't sit down. With his work-roughened hands, he gripped the back of the chair, the whites of his knuckles showing.

There was the same sadness in his eyes that she was feeling. Seeing their similarities and recognising them at last overwhelmed her. She blinked away the sudden moisture threatening, trying to regain her composure.

"Roberta, life has dealt me the shittiest of hands. People have blamed me for things I never did and I've paid a hefty price. Then, one day when life couldn't possibly get any worse, I'm reunited with a woman I once had feelings for—I'm not going to lie, but that's the truth—and given a daughter I never thought I'd get the chance to have. If you really detest the sight of me, I'll back off. I really will. I don't want to hurt you or Lily, but I care about you both."

Something unfolded inside Roberta. A loosening of sorts. Faced with Bob's reality, her selfish anger dissipated, forcing her to see things from another point of view. A thin trickle of moisture dribbled down her cheeks. For once, she couldn't find her words, and her chin dropped to her chest. Heck, Daniel accepted the situation with Bob and their mother, and he wasn't even related. Why couldn't she do the same?

"Can I give you a hug?" Bob asked, stepping around the chair.

She looked up as he stood over her. Looked at him properly. His arms were outstretched, a vulnerability on his face like he was preparing for rejection. Was this how Nate felt when she'd told him to go live his life free of her?

The thin stream of tears intensified, and she attempted to rise from the side of the bed. Bob was there in an instant, holding her steady when she lifted herself, wrapping his arms around her waist. She did likewise, tightening her hold around his middle, racking sobs spilling onto his chest.

This journey to the north was proving to be a real awakening. Nothing was going to plan. Finding herself crying her heart out to her newly found father had her mentally shaking her head. What a road trip! Had she taken the wrong fork in the road at some point? How did she get here?

She was Roberta Mintello. Confident in herself, her life and, *most* times, the direction it was going. She wasn't perfect nor clueless, but more importantly, she was a realist. These past weeks turned her self-confidence on its head, making her question many things.

She'd lost one dad, only to be reunited with another. Her core family and its values were changing faster than the weather turned in Melbourne.

Bob continued to pat her back gently like a newborn baby. The old Roberta rarely cried, but this new version of her had exposed a vulnerability that was coming out of hiding. This thought resonated nicely with the state she was in. She might just cry again tomorrow if she wanted to. Nothing like her stubbornness to shine through when she needed it most.

When she broke out of Bob's embrace with a muffled chuckle, he stepped back, a worried frown digging into his brow.

"Yeah, don't worry. I've got this. I really have. It's just been a little crazy lately, that's all, and sometimes you have to laugh about it."

Bob's smile lit up his face. A smile she recognised as her own. Another similarity. She wrapped her arms around his back again, nestling her face against his chest. She was down to sniffles now. As Bob gently patted her hair, an overwhelming sense of release washed over her. She could do this.

*My father.*

She was determined to work hard and fully embrace this gift. Treat it like a second chance. Liking the sound of that, she took a moment to breathe in the all-male scent of Bob. Of earth and dirt. Potatoes, as she already knew. Of hard toil and pain. He'd suffered so much for someone not guilty of his crimes. She hoped with time he might forgive her for not accepting him immediately and causing him more heartache. For now, she continued to smile as Bob held her, not wanting to move yet. She enjoyed being surrounded by his strength and security.

Every girl needed their dad.

# Chapter 36

"Are you coming to claim the tractor again today?"

"Sure am. Did you see how good I was on it yesterday? I can almost do it with my eyes shut."

Bob laughed, the lines around his eyes crinkling. "Must get the skill from your old man."

Roberta laughed too as they finished their breakfast. With her ankle still in a moon boot for another week—her fracture was only a low-to-medium ligament injury—it wouldn't be long before she could finally ditch it. The pain was lessening, and her ankle was gaining strength. Didn't stop her from driving the massive air-conditioned tractors Bob's family used on their property. For two weeks now, she'd insisted on working on the farm every day. Up and down the lines she went. Brain-numbing work as long as the stereo was blaring and she could sing to her heart's content, all in the privacy of the enclosed cab.

Lily had returned to Melbourne to sort out her life and make some decisions. There was no doubt in Roberta's mind Lily would return to live with Bob. Weird coming to terms with it, but she was.

For now, she'd put her own life on hold, glad she had the excuse of her ankle. She was embracing the farm life, her newly found grandparents—her real ones this time—who couldn't do enough for her, and her huge extended family. They'd dropped by daily since news of her paternity came out. From aunties and uncles to cousins and babies. So many of them. No one seemed surprised or concerned by the new addition to the family. So engulfed with their love, every single one of them sang the praises of the good fortune that had finally come Bob's way.

Only on the rare occasion since accepting the change in her life had she allowed thoughts of Nate to slip past her defences. She heard nothing more about his environmental warrior activities and never sought any news.

"There's a car coming up the drive. Expecting anyone?" Bob rose from the table, bringing his plate to the sink to rinse.

"No one I know." Roberta stood too and carried her plate to the sink with a slight limp.

Glancing out the kitchen window, she saw a white car approaching. Bob took her plate from her and rinsed it.

"Do you recognise the car?"

"Nope." It wasn't Sally's. They were catching up on the weekend again. Didn't look like a hire car either, and Connor and Liz had already returned to Canada after they enjoyed a farewell dinner only days after Roberta's release from hospital. It wasn't Nate's ute, not that she was expecting him any time soon. If ever. Wait, was it—?

Natasha stepped out of the car just as Roberta recognised it as the white family car always parked in the same spot at the lake.

"Isn't that Nate's sister?" Bob asked.

"Yes, it is."

"I guess she's chasing you. How about I leave now? You can phone me when you're ready. I'll come and pick you up." Bob squeezed her shoulder before collecting his trusty bucket hat off the hook near the front door and walking outside.

What did Natasha want? Boulders tumbled inside her stomach. Any reminders of Nate did this. Seeing Natasha brought an avalanche of emotions and regrets to the surface.

"Hi Bob," Natasha said outside the front door.

"Hello again, Roberta's inside. We've just finished breakfast," Bob replied. "I'm off now. I'll see you around."

With the front door open, Natasha spotted her and wandered in. "Hello, gorgeous. Still sporting the moon boot?" Natasha didn't hesitate to give her a big hug before she stood back and looked down at her ankle. "How's the walking going?"

Roberta smiled, already relaxing in Natasha's company. "I should be able to hand the boot back in a week. I've only got a slight limp now which should completely heal with time. So, all good, I'd say."

As long as Natasha didn't know the full extent of her stupidity that day, she could live with herself.

"Sounds good to me. Can't wait to have you back."

Roberta gulped. Like everything going on around her, she let everyone believe what they wanted to. She had a job to return to, after all. In Melbourne. Far, far away from Lake Barrine and Bob's potato farm.

"Cup of tea?" Roberta asked, trying to distract herself from all the unfinished business mounting up for her in the north.

"Absolutely. It's my only day off, so I can afford a little downtime. I just dropped off the kids at school. Grocery shopping is next, then the day is mine until school pick-up time. Here, let me." Natasha sidled past her to the kitchen, filling the kettle some more.

"Top left-hand cupboard for cups. Top drawer for spoons."

"What sort of coffee do you want?" Natasha asked.

Roberta joined her in the kitchen and made for the coffee machine. "I'll make it. What are you having? Earl Grey or herbal?"

"Earl Grey thanks"

Roberta grabbed the tea bag canister and put it on the sink, then set about making her second cup of coffee that morning. Bob had the full gambit when it came to coffee machines. No surprise their uncanny love of the beverage was another similarity between them. They often joked about their coffee snobbery.

With drinks made and more idle chatter concerning the weather, they sat at the kitchen table. Roberta had a gut instinct that this wasn't a social call to check up on her progress. "So, what's up?"

Natasha took a sip of her hot drink first, then put it down with a sigh. "Look, I know things happened between you and Nate, but he's not saying much. Well, anything at all. Just walking around like a grumpy old bear ready to attack anyone in his way."

Roberta couldn't help the snort that escaped. "Sorry," she uttered, sipping her coffee to avoid eye contact.

"You may well laugh, but I've been handed the biggest dilemma ever, and Nate doesn't want a bar of it."

Roberta was intrigued. "If it has something to do with me, I can understand Nate's reluctance. I'm sorry, but we didn't part ways on the best terms."

"Another stubborn person. I want to crack both your heads together."

Roberta grimaced. "I'm really sorry. I'm not sure what I've done to cause you this distress."

"I'm sure you haven't forgotten the man's life you saved."

"A bit hard to do."

"Yes, well, he's returning from the States and wants to thank everyone involved."

"Surely Sophie and Nate can handle it?" Roberta argued.

"Well, firstly, he specifically asked for you to be there. Secondly, Nate says he won't turn up unless you're there, and lastly, he's some American royalty with more money than you can poke a stick at."

"What do you mean? Is he royalty or just rich?"

"Rich and he's taken an interest in everything we do at Lake Barrine, the measures we have in place to protect our forests, animals and the environmental causes Nate works with. He wants to donate two million dollars to the north's environmental causes, and he wants Nate in charge of spending it. He also wants to donate half a million to you so you can donate it to a charity of your choice."

"What the?"

"Exactly! In his own words, he said he doesn't want to leave all his money to his only son. They already have more than enough."

"Isn't two million enough? Do you really need me there since I could be giving my share of the money to an entirely different charity?"

"Because Nate was very firm. He won't accept the money unless you're there. He wants your help. In *his* words, you got him into this mess, and you can help him clean it up."

Roberta stumbled to her feet, leaning heavily on her chair. "Oh my God, is he serious? I save a man's life and it's my fault?"

"This is why it's become my dilemma. Why I'm here today to beg you, Roberta. I know it will kill Nate to miss this opportunity. There is so much Nate wants to do, but he relies on private donations. To have two million land on his lap and not be taken will give him nightmares forever. Roberta, I know Nate won't waste a single cent of it. Whether he uses it to build road overpasses to allow native life to move or erect signage and fencing to keep sensitive areas safe from too much human traffic or rally and fight the explosion of windfarms, there's so much good he could achieve. He already does so much but always on a limited budget."

"Then why is he being such a pain in the arse?"

"I don't know. Nate's never been like this before, not even when things with Crystal ended. He's different this time, and that's why I need you there. Please."

Roberta sat back down and attacked her coffee again. "When's this man coming?"

"Friday. He wants to finish the boat cruise this time, enjoy a Devonshire tea and make the presentations."

"Oh, fuck."

"One hour of your time, Roberta. That's all."

"What about the helping out bullshit?"

Natasha shrugged, her shoulders dropping like she had no answer.

Roberta tapped her index finger on the tabletop, her mind brewing with suppressed frustration. "We'll kill each other, Tash."

A hopeful smile spread across her face. "After you've killed him, you'll make up with the best sex ever and live happily ever after."

Roberta shot back up again. "Are you serious?" She wobbled on her moon boot before slumping back down on the chair.

"Totally, Roberta. Come on! Where's your spunk? I've loved you from the first day. I'm not surprised Nate fell for you, too."

"Who said anything about love? We fight all the time."

"I've never seen him happier than when you were there, and I need something to happen to get him out of that bloody boatshed where he spends every minute he's not skippering the boat or sleeping. Actually, I don't think he's sleeping."

"Wasn't he down south recently?"

"Yeah, well, apart from that short stint. According to Brent, his heart isn't in the cause anymore. Just so you know, Brent is pointing the finger at you."

"Oh, fuck again."

"My thoughts exactly."

Uncertainty twisted her insides. Even if she never spoke another word to Nate again, she understood the magnitude of this enormous pledge of money. "Okay, I'll be there, but I make no promises. I'll ask Bob if he can drive me over as my replacement car hasn't arrived yet. And ... and Tash, you may as well know if Nate hasn't already told you, I was only ever at Lake Barrine to uncover the box my mother buried. It wasn't meant to end like this, and for that, I'm truly sorry. I like you a lot, and I've had a ball working with you, but I was always leaving. I still am."

Natasha smiled brilliantly this time as though her words meant nothing. "I knew I could count on you. There's no rush to leave, is there? What if your mum and brother decide to move up here? Huh? Have you thought of that?"

Roberta frowned. "Who have you been talking to?"

With one quick final slug of the remains in her cup, she got up and gave Roberta a hug and a kiss. "Everyone, girlfriend. Especially one particular physio who I know very well. She has a thing for your brother."

"Bloody hell! Does everybody know everyone's business up here?" Roberta blurted. Yet another reminder Lake Barrine was smack-bang beside a small rural town.

Natasha waggled her fingers in a casual goodbye as she made for the front door. "Yep, and the American tourist will be there for the morning cruise. See you Friday."

Roberta watched Natasha drive away before limping into Bob's small lounge. She collapsed into the comfortable seater, not sure how she was going to get up again. Not sure how long it would take her to phone Bob to come and collect her. She did her best to tamper down the flutter that insisted on spiking her pulse at the thought of seeing Nate again. Which was ridiculous. They were so not suited. They argued about everything. They ... her muddled mind could only remember how they fit so well all those nights they spent together.

Making up with sex every single night had a weird appeal until common sense prevailed. She groaned loudly, the sound echoing as she leant back against the headrest.

Madness. That's what she was calling her condition.

# Chapter 37

N ate did his usual prelaunch check on the outside of the boat, the early morning sun beating down on his back. Summer was making a show as the date clicked another day closer to the school holidays and the Christmas break when all hell broke loose at the lake. The place filled with the daily bedlam of families, holidaying visitors and tourists from the south flocking to the lake's shore and their majestic boat cruise.

Nothing to complain about if the anticipation of busy days and sun-soaked afternoons were what he was after. He wasn't so sure anymore.

This morning, everyone was in high spirits, and the air was buzzing as the crowds arrived. Included in the growing horde were the local mayor, television news crews, local newspaper reporters and the general hubbub of locals interested in listening to the man who came back to thank them for saving his life. Rumours had spread like out-of-control fires about the gift he would bestow on the local area as a thank you.

One woman had been instrumental in saving this man's life. Nate would never forget her quick actions and her medical skills as she took control of the emergency and brought the man back to life. Her daringness, her confidence, her everything. In all the years of skippering the boat, he'd never experienced an incident like it. He was a fraud accepting anything on her behalf, yet Tash never mentioned reaching out to Roberta, and there was no way he would ever do so after she'd pushed him away. The fact she was still recovering from her accident played on his mind, but Bob assured him, with the one phone call he'd made asking about her condition, that she was fine and doing well. Was she still planning to leave the north? Bob couldn't answer him.

Today, their usual visitor numbers would easily be surpassed after social media spread the word about their special guest and what he was doing for the local environment. Two million dollars was a lot in anyone's books.

Added to this was Nate's reputation. Many people had speculated about how both would perfectly go hand in hand. This only forced his wayward mind to remember how it felt to hold Roberta's hand. To smooth his over her supple skin. Explore intimate places.

He shook off the memories and berated his stupid self. *Move on, dude. She told you to do so and has made no effort to seek you out.* Nothing had changed. If only he could force his mind to change direction, too. To sometime in the future where he was happy.

Usually, something like this huge donation would light a fire beneath him. But of late, he'd been flat, uninspired and lacking energy. Hadn't fully agreed to accept the money, even though Tash was doing a fine job of accepting it on his behalf. Wasn't sure if he should pass the responsibility on to someone who could reignite the same level of passion he once had.

That time barely six weeks ago.

When he was a different man.

He hated being in this slump. Although he'd been there before, somehow, this was different. He avoided the cottage as much as possible. Spent way too long couped up in the boatshed, robotically sanding and sanding. The rowboat was coming along fine. He could begin the exterior epoxy coating soon.

He looked up when his name was called. Sophie, who was tasked with greeting the passengers this morning, waved him over. Every invited guest was now on board, and it wouldn't be long until their special American guest arrived, and Nate promised Tash he would welcome him personally.

He straightened, pulled his shoulders back and found that little store of energy he sometimes called on lately to find a smile. *Come on, man, make an effort. Two million is a shitload of money.* Deep down, he knew he could do so much good with it. *Find it fast! Find the old Nate, for God's sake, and forget about her. She was always leaving; you knew that from the start.*

The small cluster of special guests hovered near the moored boat, along with the television crew interviewing them. Nate moved to where Sophie was standing, welcoming them all aboard while the camera captured every moment. The American tourist—Brian—was there with his wife, their son, and the son's family. It was a long way for them to travel, and it suddenly struck Nate that here was one man who was grateful to be alive. He could take away some valuable lessons from this.

Nate was young and fit, which he'd always prided himself on. Never smoked or drank excessively. Ate sensibly and healthily and would continue to do so. He should be grateful if only there wasn't a sense of 'why bother'. Something was missing. That spark, that purpose, that one person. Twice he'd fallen down the rabbit warren. He wasn't sure if he could climb back up yet.

With their special guests on board, he relaxed his jaw which hurt from the strain of smiling and turned away, allowing his standard frown of late to take over.

Just as he was about to unwind the rope holding the boat moored, something caught his eye. A latecomer was limping down the steps.

He stiffened. He knew that shape. Recognised those curves. Had seen her in that yellow dress before. His mouth suddenly dried as he remained frozen. What was she doing here?

She wore a ridiculously wide-brimmed hat, probably the reason her olive skin always looked so good and well cared for. When she reached the gangplank, she came to an abrupt halt, her eyes cautiously taking in the surroundings.

"Hello, Nate."

"What are you doing here?" It came out sounding harsh, and he instantly regretted it. But he wouldn't be blamed for his rudeness. It was probably all the pent-up frustration from the past weeks of waiting for any outlet. Like right now. He wouldn't take it back. Why *was* she here?

"What do you mean? Tash told me to get my butt here today or else?"

"Huh? You're calling bullshit. She hasn't said anything to me."

"She obviously didn't tell you she came to visit me earlier this week."

Bloody Tash! Sticking her nose in his business, all over two million dollars. "So, you don't really want to be here today?"

"Nate." They both spun around when Sophie approached them from the boat. "Hey, Roberta!" she shouted and galloped over to hug her hard. "Great to see you again. Boy, am I glad to have you back. You look fabulous, by the way." She looked down at the moon boot covering her ankle and then giggled. "Except for that thing on your foot."

Roberta laughing along with Sophie had the same effect as a knife piercing deep inside his heart. He and Roberta had spent all of thirty seconds together and were already at each other's throats. Sophie turns up and it's a lifetime reunion of besties.

Sophie stepped away from Roberta and turned his way. "Uh ... Nate, I've got everyone ready to go, including our special guests. Don't be too long. I'll go and set up the Devonshire tea stuff."

"Are you coming on board?" Sophie asked Roberta.

"I sure am."

"Yay! I better get back." Sophie waved goodbye and spun around, dashing back on board.

For three agonising seconds, Nate stared at Roberta, wishing for many things. But more importantly, he didn't want her here if it was the last place she wanted to be. "Don't come on board if you don't want to be here, Roberta."

"Um ... I'm more scared of Tash, thank you very much. I'm getting on this boat whether you want me there or not."

"And then what?"

"I'll smile prettily. Take my money, and yours, if you don't want it. Administer it if you're too lousy to do so yourself. Organise Brent, Nadia and all the other motley crew." She squared her shoulders and took a step onto the gangplank. "Look, let's just say I'm going to have a wow of a time, with or without you."

Nate's chest expanded with outrage. "You're the one who told me to go live another life," he hissed.

"And I gave you six weeks to do so. Happy?" She tilted her head to the side, a smile threatening to expose itself.

"You've got to be joking?"

"Nope, not at all. Now get this damn show on the road and hurry up." She reached up and brushed his cheek with a kiss before sauntering off with a sway of the hips. He didn't doubt it was more pronounced for his benefit and had nothing to do with her limp.

He swore, and Roberta spun back tutting, her finger tapping her mouth at the same time. "Hurry up, Nate, we have a cruise happening here."

Her laughter rang out over the calm waters of Lake Barrine and carried back to him on the wisp of the breeze brushing his cheeks. The exact spot her mouth touched only seconds earlier.

He unravelled the rope holding the boat moored and jumped aboard. Was this his life if he ventured down this path? What stupid motive could she possibly have to come back and haunt him every day? Surely it wasn't the money? What had she and Tash discussed? When he was finished today, he was going to corner Tash and make her come clean. Then, he was going to drag Roberta over to the cottage and demand answers. Nothing more! God help him, he needed to keep his mind off those gorgeous curves and one incredible mouth that could turn him on in an instant—whether she was kissing him, talking nonstop, or using it to unleash a voice that created magic.

Already his skin was tingling, his mind going to places he hadn't dared to for weeks. How the heck was he going to get through the next hour? Keep a smile on his face the whole time? Accept two million dollars and look grateful for it? All without killing Roberta first for twisting his insides when he most needed to be of sound mind.

The day was doomed.

# Chapter 38

"**R**oberta! Over here!"

As Roberta glanced around, her eyes landed on Nadia, who was waving her over. She almost let out a groan. She didn't dislike the motley crew who campaigned with Nate, but she would never completely fit in with them. Today, though, she sucked it up and walked towards the small group hogging the back of the boat.

The cruise looked to be at full capacity, yet apart from Sophie and Nate, she hadn't expected to recognise anyone else. Now she spotted Brent and a few of the others whose faces she recognised. Brent's frown wasn't unexpected, so in true Roberta style, she upped her smile wattage as she made her way towards the group.

"Excuse me, are you the young lady who saved our special guest?" a man holding a clipboard asked as she walked past.

Roberta halted for a moment and nodded but was saved from replying when Nate's voice vibrated through the PA system. "Ladies and gentlemen, please find a seat so we can get started."

She hadn't considered all that. Heck, did this mean she'd be in the newspapers again? Locals might start to recognise her if she kept this up. She secretly smiled, liking the idea locals might call her a media tart. An apt term she'd heard once for something similar.

"Sorry about your accident." Nadia squashed herself closer to Brent, giving Roberta a small space to sit and remove her hat. "We're so glad you're back on your feet again."

With seating at a premium, it was a tight fit, but it afforded her a seat as Nate started up the boat and let it idle. Just what she needed to get her racing heart to settle down. Had she really been the sassy bitch? No wonder Nate sounded pissed off and confused. What made her kiss him? Her lips still tingled.

To be so close to him again, to be reminded of what they'd shared on those magical nights, had done something to the wires in her brain. Twisted them, tangled them, which resulted in a loose tongue taking over. She inwardly groaned, not sure what message eventually came out and what Nate had ended up thinking.

She twisted her hands together under her hat. A gentle elbow jabbed on her side reminded her she hadn't answered. "Thanks, Nadia. It's great to see you again." Weirdly, she meant it. Being close to Nadia meant Nate was nearby.

Nadia gave her a quick hug in the confined space while Brent grunted. Roberta couldn't help the short gurgle of laughter that escaped. A little bit of the old Roberta was back, and she mentally fist-pumped the air. Riling up Brent was going to be so much fun. She hadn't forgotten Tash's words about Brent pointing the finger at her, and she was going to make it worth her while. If not today, in the future.

"I can't wait to work together and make a difference. This donation is a game changer." Nadia flashed her a smile, her excitement caught up with her words.

Roberta flinched but kept a reply in check. Did they all assume she was staying? Had she pushed herself into a corner where there was no getting out?

She slumped back. *Frick!* Her head and hormones were all over the place. Of one thing she was certain: she missed Nate. There! She finally admitted it to herself after weeks of denial. All it took was five minutes in Nate's presence for the truth to smack her in the face. She loved everything about them being together. Their banter, conversation, craziness, and especially the sex. They were so darn good together. Day and night.

She studied Nate while he was busy talking to reporters. He was a natural and so passionate. It was enough for a light-headedness to settle all over her nicely. Add in some heat, and already she needed to tamper down a build-up of desire. Would Nate have her back?

She pushed that niggling worry aside. For now, she wanted to enjoy the cruise and not misbehave. She had free rein to ogle Nate from where she sat and soak in his words.

Apart from the first cruise where she saved the man's life, she'd only ever been on board one other time to serve Devonshire tea. Forgetting how relaxing it was, she took a moment to enjoy the beautiful, cloudless day.

If she wasn't sporting the moon boot, she'd want to fling her clothes off and dive overboard. It was a thing—that refreshing feel as cool water rippled over your skin—and her skin continued to tingle as the urge to do so with Nate burnt furiously inside her.

She clamped down on those thoughts, looking instead out over the shimmering water. A cool breeze lazily drifted in from the open windows, cooling her suddenly warm cheeks.

Had she really threatened to manage the donation with or without Nate's help? Was this her way of saying she was here to stay? Longer than intended? *Dammit!* She was so confused about what to do. For now, she could only concentrate on what it felt like to be near Nate again. He looked smoking hot with a recent hair trim, all dressed to kill in his neatly ironed khaki skipper outfit. It hadn't gone unnoticed that he'd made a special effort to look good with the television crew and reporters around today.

She scanned the crowd, hoping to identify the American tourist, and spotted him up the front surrounded by the television crew filming and interviewing him. She suspected Nate was waiting a few more minutes, allowing them time to record a short segment before the cruise started.

"We were so worried about you, Roberta. I think Nate was worried the most."

*Huh?* Roberta twisted in the limited space to face Nadia. She didn't mind Nadia, and she smiled warmly in her direction. "Thanks for thinking of me. It wasn't too bad, and I'm coming along just fine." *Nate worried the most?*

There was another grunt from Brent, but she ignored him as the cruise began and she lost herself in Nate's spiel about why the cruise that day was a special one.

*※*

"And lastly, I want to thank this special young lady for saving my life," Brian announced to the crowd as Roberta walked forward to the front of the boat, smiling shyly at the guests as the applause rang out.

"My beautiful wife told me it was Roberta who didn't hesitate to dive overboard and take my life into her hands. Her quick actions saved me, and I'll be forever grateful."

Roberta took Brian's outstretched hand, hers shaking with all the accolades. This was a first for her. She'd saved many lives over the years, but none as dramatic and life-changing as this one. Cameras clicked nearby, but she discarded the handshake and gave Brian a big hug instead before giving his wife one too.

Facing forward to pose for more photos was a weird thing; it took her mind back to the wild brumby night. If her friend hadn't died tragically that night, she might not have taken up nursing as a career. Might not have been at this very spot, this moment in time. A shudder rippled over her skin at the memory. The old saying 'there's a reason why things happen' surfaced to remind her you never could tell which road your life took you on.

On that thought, she turned to Nate who stood behind her. The boat remained idle in the middle of the lake. The cruise was nearly finished, and Nate would only be waiting for the formalities to be over before bringing it back to shore.

During the cruise, he always seemed to have her in his sights, but always with a frown or a look of concern. Now, she sent him a genuine smile, thankful for the chance to make amends. It took Nate a few heart-thumping moments to interpret her smile, but when he did, he transformed like a work of art. One she wanted to ooh and aah over. Run her hands over, feel its stubbled edges, touch his lips with her fingers. Let him nibble her tips.

"Roberta will receive this final donation. I'd like to give her the chance to pay it forward to whichever charity she deems deserving of it. I trust she'll do the right thing because I'd trust her with my life."

Roberta disengaged from Nate, snapping back to attention. The crowd laughed at Brian's unintended pun, and Roberta accepted the gift, still a little awkward with all the attention but burning with a heat that had nothing to do with receiving the sizeable sum of money. A sense of relief washed over her, not concerned at all now about the burden of delivering half a million dollars to the right organisation. She had a feeling she could call on Nate to help counsel her on this decision.

With one of those oversized cheques clasped in her fingers, she now deemed herself all in. Nate held the two-million-dollar donation handed over earlier. *No nerves here*, she joked to herself as she smiled for the photos with Brian and his wife, with the full knowledge they would be splashed all over the news and social media in the coming days.

This was a great day for Far North Queensland and its natural tropical beauty. As much as Roberta was doing everything to deny its magnetic attraction, the special appeal of the north was wrapping its tentacles around her and drawing her closer to its heart.

Melbourne was a different planet.

# Chapter 39

The docking of the boat didn't signal the end of the celebration for the visitors and special guests. There was an all-inclusive lunch after the cruise, and it seemed no one wanted to leave. Tash and the team had set up the teahouse with grazing tables and were kept busy continuously topping up the platters throughout the afternoon.

For the first time in many weeks, Nate desperately wanted to escape to his little cottage and close off the rest of the world. But he was determined not to go alone. He tried not to lose sight of Roberta, but the media was continuously cornering him for questions and interviews in between grabbing a few bites to eat. Two million dollars was a big deal in a small community. He hoped that his show of confidence in spending the two million dollars wisely got through to all concerned. After not wanting a bar of it, he could admit he'd always planned on taking on this task. This type of challenge made up the very fibres of his being.

The only thing holding him back was the unfinished business with Roberta. Even if it ended badly, he needed closure, or he'd never move on. So why did she kiss him before boarding the boat? Hours later, he could still feel the spot where her lips touched. Occasionally, his hand would reach up and touch it. As for that smile while they were on board? His heart had whooshed. Now it tremored with the memory.

Close to three pm, when the crowds were finally abating, Nate made a move and cornered Roberta who was helping Sophie and Hannah clear the tables. Totally not her job while wearing a moon boot and dressed the way she was. It wasn't his place to complain, though. Clearly, Tash and her team were run off their feet. Today was one of those days when anything was allowed. Besides, it gave him the opportunity when he wasn't being interviewed to take his fill of the soft yellow dress accentuating her curves and her dark curls hanging halfway down her back.

He swallowed, remembering how she'd looked with her hair splayed over his pillow. "Roberta, ah—" He coughed to clear his throat.

Roberta was wiping clean a table and looked up in surprise.

"Don't you think you should rest your foot?"

She straightened and winced. "It is a bit sore."

Nate swore. "What are you doing working in your condition? You're wearing a moon boot, or hadn't you noticed?"

"They needed a hand," she protested.

"Come and rest it in the cottage. Can you make it that far?"

She halted for a moment before placing the cleaning cloth down. "I should be able to."

"Bloody hell!" He swept her up in his arms and stormed out of the teahouse, oblivious to the stares.

"Nate, put me down," Roberta hissed. "It'll be this picture that makes it to the papers."

"Well, smile so it doesn't look like I'm abducting you," Nate uttered so only she heard.

Roberta snorted with laughter. "But that's exactly what you're doing. This is against my will, just so you know."

"Don't care. You and I are going to have a friendly chat. Then you can do what you want. Call it what you like."

Within seconds, they were at the cottage door. Nate gently put her down, making sure she was steady on her moon boot, before unzipping a small pocket on his khaki shorts and removing the cottage keys.

"I still have my keys," she offered softly. She was close enough for her warm breath to feather his face and that wildflower scent to fill his senses. There were too many memories attached to it; he wanted to nuzzle his face in the crook of her neck and get high on it.

His chest hurt, like carrying Roberta had tested all his strength. He took a gulping breath, not game enough to look directly at her. He fumbled with the key in the lock. "Were you going to use it today?" His voice sounded unintentionally gruff. "You left some things behind."

He finally got the key in and opened the door, terrified he'd started this conversation badly. He didn't want to upset her before they had a chance to clear the air. God help him, he needed to sort through this shit between them. It was eating at him.

She limped inside, making directly for the small couch. Lying back, she propped her foot on a couple of stacked cushions. "I'm not sure."

Nate remained awkwardly rooted to the spot inside the front door. "Coffee?" he finally spluttered, at a loss for how to start this important conversation.

"Thank you, yes."

She rested with her eyes never leaving his face. It was hard to fathom what was going through her thoughts, but her intense gaze had him burning up. Sweat built under his khaki shirt, causing it to stick to his back. His heart rate picked up, too, his hand shaking a little. He clamped down on his jaw, hoping to steady his reaction to having Roberta in the room with him. He'd been through this sort of confusion before with Crystal until sudden clarity one day made everything apparent.

Well, he needed clarity now! He might come across as confident and assured, but this woman rocked everything, usually keeping him stabilised. Heaven forbid, the word love never entered his thoughts before when it involved Roberta. Crystal had damaged him in many ways, but what if this was the real deal?

When the coffee was made, he brought it over, set it down on the small coffee table beside the couch, and then helped her sit up.

She took the mug in both hands, taking an appreciative sip. "Thanks. It's been a long day. I'll have to phone Bob to come and pick me up."

"Don't!"

Her brows shot up.

He shrugged. "Not yet."

"Well, sit down, you're making me nervous."

She pointed to the other end of the small couch, but he couldn't move to sit that close to her. Not before they talked some of this out of their systems.

As she took another sip of her coffee, her trembling hand caused it to spill on her dress.

"Are you okay?" Nate asked, shocked by her shaking. Did the accident hurt more than her ankle?

"No, I'm not okay," she burst out. "Look at me! Cool, calm Roberta can't even hold a coffee mug to save her life. What have you done to me, Nate?"

"What have *I* done to you?" *Really?* "You're blaming me?" Nate paced in front of the couch, his hands fisted by his sides. "You tell me to leave you alone, go live my life. That I'd be better off without you. How dare you tell me what's better for me?"

"And I meant it—"

Nate stopped, bracing himself to look at her.

"—at the time."

He growled, but the old Roberta looked right back, daring him to hold her steely gaze. "And how is it my fault?"

"Because you didn't stop me from driving away? Didn't snatch the keys from me. You knew I was going through so much crap. My head wasn't working how it should."

"You shut the door in my face. Drove off. Would you have listened to me?"

"Probably not, but that's not the point."

"Well, there you go. Stubborn Roberta would've driven off anyway, ending everything we'd started. Why didn't you phone me when you realised you were wrong?"

"Who said I was wrong? And why didn't you phone me? Come visit me in hospital or at Bob's? Everyone else did, except you." Roberta rose like she wanted to leave.

His heart rate peaked like a panic attack was setting in. "Sit!" He was terrified she'd walk out the door and he'd never see her again.

She dropped back onto the couch. "Well, stop yelling at me."

"I'm not yelling," he retaliated when he knew his voice was raised more than normal. "But I'm a fucking mess, okay? I thought I could erase you from my every day. Get on with my life. Switch off from those amazing nights we shared. Forget a person called Roberta ever existed. I happily wanted to see the back of your car as you drove back to Melbourne." His chest heaved as he gulped for air. He was spent after off-loading, and his shoulders sagged, losing all their tension. "But I couldn't do any of that."

Tears filled her eyes, and he let out a low growl. He dropped to his knees on the floor in front of her, taking her in his arms.

She didn't sob, but her tears gently wet his neck as she nestled against him. Amidst all this sadness, mixed messages and missed opportunity, a light flickered inside his chest. "You are the biggest pain in the arse." He spoke into her hair with a smile on his face. "You're irritating, loud mouthed, sassy as all heck when you know it'll annoy me, and I'm tired of the crazy crap between us, but I ... I ..."

Roberta pulled back, hiccupping once. "Can ... can I please lie down and rest my foot? It's hurting like hell."

"Oh, shit. Sorry." Without hesitating, he picked her up and cradled her against his chest, taking her directly to his bedroom. Placing her on his bed, he asked, "Should I remove the boot?"

"Yes, please."

It didn't go unnoticed how she took one of his pillows and wrapped her arms around it, snuggling up to it with her eyes closed and a smile on her face. Once the boot was off, her moan of comfortable satisfaction broke him. He laid beside her, taking her in his arms. Careful not to hurt her ankle, he hugged her, held her tight and filled his senses with that familiar wildflower scent.

She did likewise. Snuggled up closer. Held him just as tight. They didn't speak a word. None were needed. Making up for lost time. Needing this. Needing her.

Nate lost track of time but didn't care. He was where he needed to be. When Roberta pulled back, he reluctantly loosened his hold.

"Crazy crap, huh?" she asked.

Uncertainty hovered over her face. He loved that hint of vulnerability, even though he rarely saw it. He didn't doubt her actions leading to her accident were tearing bits out of her constantly.

With his finger, he traced a line down her face until it rested on her mouth. "I should've snatched your car keys off you. Yes, I blame myself for your accident. You were so emotional and I should've done things differently, held you back, forced you to stay. That sort of crazy crap."

"I don't understand this. We're so different, yet in other ways, we're so in sync. How do we know if we're a good fit? You know, the couple that makes it until the end?"

"We don't know, but I'm going to work hard at it every day because, without you and your crazy ways, I'm off balance, hurting. I want every bit of crazy around me. Always."

A tiny tear dribbled past her eyelashes, and she blinked to free a couple more. "It's been hurting so much here, Nate"—she placed her hand against her chest with an anguished face—"the entire time we've been separated."

"I'm not going anywhere. I'm here for the long haul."

"You mean that?"

He didn't reply with words; instead, he cradled her face in his palm and leant closer until his mouth found hers. A shock of arousal jolted him, but he directed his energy solely towards kissing. With an unsteady breath, his heart thundered in his ears. He craved so much more but restrained himself with only this, allowing his tongue to dart inside to touch hers. Enjoying her gasps of pleasure. Feasting. Holding back the intensity. Tongues duelling and luring. A kiss to steal his soul. Just how he wanted it. Craved it. Every muscle tightened as he let out a growl of frustration, determined his raw need could wait until later. Not sure how long he could hold out, though.

It might've been minutes, hours or days, but who cared? They were on lake time, and he sensed the sun moving towards the horizon. Roberta dozed a little while his gaze took his fill of her. Unable to let go.

When Roberta stirred an hour or so later, the shadows had begun to creep in.

"Nate"—she rubbed her nose as she slowly woke—"what did the premier promise you?"

"Huh, what are you talking about?" Was she sleep talking?

"After your meeting. Did she make any promises?"

He chuckled, shaking his head at the same time. "You really are crazy." Propped up on one elbow, he leant closer, leaving feather-light kisses along her brow. "How can that be at the forefront of your mind when all I can think about is this?" He pulled back, tracing a line with his finger down her face towards her breast. Her dress was messily rucked up near her waist, and he trailed further down, softly kneading her thighs, itching to move to that magical place between her legs.

His gaze never left her face. Her eyes opened wider, drawing him into their softness the more she awakened.

She reached out and touched his stubbled cheeks, igniting a rush of hormones to emerge and stagger about.

"Tash told me we'd have the best make-up sex ever."

Nate's hand froze. "You discussed *us* with Tash?"

Roberta grunted. "No, it was more like 'he's walking around like a grumpy old bear ready to attack anyone in his way'. She also said you were blaming me for this mess of saving a man's life. It was only after I told her we'd more likely kill each other that she added in that savoury line like this was our life."

Nate moaned, relaxing beside her, nuzzling his face against her neck. He took little bites of her soft skin before letting go and running his tongue over it.

Roberta giggled, and the already enlarged body part in his khaki shorts got bigger and harder.

"So, do I have anything to report back to Tash?" she asked.

Nate smiled as he pulled away. Taking her hand in his, he directed it further down. "You tell me."

"God, I've missed this." Roberta writhed against him with a delicious whimper.

"Me too," he croaked, swallowing back the bulk of relief blocking his airways. Turbulent heat rippled through him as Roberta fumbled with the buttons of his shirt. Her dress was easy to tug over her head. The bra was not too hard to remove, but her underwear required concentration to avoid hurting her ankle.

He dispensed with his clothes quickly, and finally, it was skin on skin, and he could breathe again. He wrapped his arms around her waist and held her tight, relishing the feel of her vibrant body.

"We've got all night, haven't we?" she whispered, rubbing her cheek against his stubble, igniting every damn cell in his body.

"Good luck with that." His body was already on the road of no return as he cupped her backside, drawing her closer. "Can't guarantee it on the first run."

Laugher erupted from her throat, and for an instant, he was prepared to give up the sex to hear her voice in song. Anything.

He stilled, watching the play of emotions on her face as the shadows of dusk deepened. His chest tightened with longing. The need to hold her forever and never let her out of his sight physically hurt all over. But to hold her back would be wrong. She was a strong, independent, funny and caring woman. What he loved most about her.

What you saw is what you got. No filters. Ever.

As the late afternoon breeze lazily floated in from the open window, it tingled along his skin, raising goose bumps, helping to cool his heated body. When she caught his gaze, her smile slipped as they took their fill of each other.

"I've been so miserable, Nate. Sad, downhearted, out of sorts."

Their hands met, fingers entwining. Bracing himself, Nate prepared to ask the one question that had been weighing heavily on his mind. He took a moment to formulate his thoughts and words, watching as confusion clouded her features. "Are ... are you still leaving?"

He witnessed the moment her body shuddered with relief, her confusion fully disappearing. She took his face in both her hands and smiled. Beatific. Blinding.

"I love you, Nate. I have no idea where this will lead to or how it'll end, but I want the chance to work hard at this too, because I ... I was never leaving."

"Good." It came out sounding gruff, but that was how he intended it to. "It hurts so damn much when you do."

He lost himself in her dark pools.

"I'm so sorry, Nate. I know I sometimes get it wrong."

"I'll get it wrong too. I'm not perfect."

"But to me, you are. You're more than perfect." She gently tapped his chest with her fingers, like she was tapping out a tune. "There's a song about being perfect. Would you like me to sing it?"

A burst of joy did a wild dance inside his ribcage. He'd dreamt plenty of hearing her voice again. "Yes, please," he begged on a whisper.

He remained in a trance for the entire time Ed Sheeran's lyrics filtered around the small room, all while the world outside was only minutes away from total darkness. She sang of dancing in the dark with him between her arms. Words of being barefoot on the grass while listening to their favourite songs. That she saw her future in his eyes, and always the repeated line that he was perfect and could he hold her hand.

It made him want to rise from the bed and waltz with her in his arms. But he was spellbound by her words, unable to move. When she sang the last verse and the words drifted off into the ether, he pulled her in firmer along his body. "I love you, Roberta. Your voice is magic, and I'll never tire of hearing it."

He drew her in for a kiss. One that had him bursting with love for this woman. By the time he reluctantly drew back, a thin stream of moonlight washed over them, and he fell into her soft gaze. "Should we get a move on if you want something to report back to Tash?"

Roberta giggled, wrapping her arms around his neck, writhing against him again. This was enough to ease away the last of the tension, dissipate the doubts and bring back the playfulness.

"Yes, please."

# EPILOGUE

*S*ix Months Later

"We are so naughty." Roberta giggled, locking the cottage door behind them and making for Nate's bedroom which they now shared.

"Nah," Nate declared, stripping off his work clothes and leaving a trail from the front door to his room. He toed off his work boots at the bedroom door and bent down to roll his socks off. "But we better make this quick. Dad is coming over this afternoon to give me a hand."

"Well, hurry up!"

Nate snorted as he went to draw the curtains closed.

Roberta loved it when they snuck back to the cottage at odd hours of the day, stripped naked and had fast, hot, furious sex. Her shift at the teahouse finished only minutes ago. Nate would usually still be working until later, but three pm signalled an afternoon break. They could do this!

Her skin tingled once she was fully naked. She pulled back the doona and fell onto her back, enjoying the feel of cool sheets on her skin. She wriggled her shoulders, getting comfortable on the pillow, breathing in moist air drifting past the slowly billowing curtains.

It'd rained for most of the morning, but the sun finally came out by the time she finished her shift, casting its wintry rays over the shimmering waters. Lake Barrine was a long way from the Melbourne winters she left behind with no regrets.

When Nate toppled onto the bed beside her, already sheathed, all other thoughts vanished. This was one time she couldn't multitask. Nate's hands were everywhere, and Roberta moaned in tune with the guttural groan Nate released when he rubbed his hands up and down her back, then to her buttocks, pressing her as close as possible to his throbbing hardness.

Nate rolled over so she was on top, and she deliciously slid onto him. "I've been thinking of nothing else for the past hour. It's been torture waiting."

Nate chuckled. "Yep, you are the naughty one."

"And you haven't?" she asked, knowing it wouldn't take long to reach her climax once his rhythmic thrusting began.

"I never stop thinking of doing this. You are one dangerous addiction."

Roberta couldn't help but laugh even more as Nate playfully nibbled her lower lip, giving it a gentle bite, causing her body to come to life with a vicious roar.

Their mouths joined in hot unison, burning as desire spread through her, heating her blood, urging, pleading for Nate to speed it up a notch. With the rasp of his teeth, light exploded behind her eyes, and she sank into his kiss like a drowning woman.

When he moved to her bare throat, a pulse fluttered wildly, and she inhaled, filling lungs starved of air, readying herself.

She clenched him tighter in her hold and held on to it for one more blissful moment before releasing him, opening her eyes long enough to see the raw need as Nate slammed into her. With her head down, she let go. Enjoying the spasms which set Nate off too.

Flopping down, chests joined, she took a moment to enjoy that sated feeling. Nate's chest heaved in time with hers, his hand resting on her backside providing her with his never-ending reassurance.

"I love you, Nate Surrey."

He smiled back. "I love you, Roberta Mintello."

She enjoyed this quiet time for another minute, knowing she had to duck out and do grocery shopping before the shops shut.

"I have a surprise for you."

Roberta raised her face, eyeing Nate. "What sort of surprise?"

He lowered his head for a hot, searing kiss. When he broke it off, he beamed with his all-consuming smile. "It wouldn't be a surprise if I told you."

Roberta groaned, knowing she'd never get it out of him, but would try her hardest to prise it anyway. "Did TREAT get the landowner to agree?"

"Huh? Why would that be a surprise? We all know he'll eventually cave in and allow us access."

"Well, what then?"

Nate gave her another searing kiss. "Get dressed quickly. I'll show you."

Roberta rolled onto her side, allowing Nate to shuffle out from underneath her and go to the bathroom. Roberta loved surprises, and agreeing to coordinate her half a million dollars with TREAT had been the biggest surprise of her life. She'd never heard of the organisation, but they were a dedicated bunch of volunteers who spent years replanting native trees on the Atherton Tablelands. Coordinating with local landowners and Queensland National Parks, many volunteers over the years had assisted with restoring and joining areas of rainforest by planting native trees in areas cleared by early settlers. This sort of restorative work made her heart sing.

Her contribution felt so right. She only recently learnt that TREAT stood for Trees for the Evelyn and Atherton Tablelands. Their motto of 'the right tree, in the right place for the right reason' resonated with her when Nate suggested them as a possible recipient of her donation. Now she was one of their hardest working volunteers when she wasn't nursing part-time or helping Tash on the weekends, and she couldn't imagine not being actively involved with them.

"Ready yet?"

Still languishing in bed, she immediately rose. Nate was dressed in the board shorts he normally wore swimming, and a small pack was slung over his shoulder.

"Are we going swimming? Because I'm not going anywhere near that chilly water." It *was* winter in the tropics.

"You shouldn't get wet unless you do something impulsive and silly."

"Huh? What's that supposed to mean? What do I wear?" she asked, about to walk out of their bedroom.

"Shorts and tee will be perfect." Nate swooped in for another heated kiss before she walked out. "But hurry up."

Roberta grumbled in response as she walked towards the other bedroom where she kept most of her belongings, even though his kiss was leaving her with a desire to climb right back into their bed. "Do I need a hat?" she called out.

"Yep, won't hurt."

"Shoes?" she checked, fishing out a T-shirt and denim shorts from a pile of freshly laundered clothes.

"Nope."

"Nate," she dragged out his name as she stretched her unironed shirt down over her stomach, "where are you taking me?"

Back in the living room, Nate took her hand and led her to the door. "Just to the edge of the lake."

With the cottage door closed behind them, it took only seconds to reach the water's edge. Roberta baulked when she saw it. The old rowing boat was moored to a stake driven in the ground. It swayed with the gentle swell while a couple of well-intended visitors were also taking a closer look at it.

"When did you get time to finish the epoxy coating?" Roberta knew they'd more than done enough sanding on the old rowboat months ago but had largely forgotten about it when the need to concentrate on the funds took over their lives.

"Dad helped a bit."

How did she not know this? Dealing with her half a million consumed many hours, as had her desire to help Nate with his responsibilities of spending two million dollars. Time was moving at a stupid, warped speed, and the old rowboat had been relegated to the back of her mind.

"Come on, we're going for a row."

"I've never been in a rowboat before."

"Well, allow me to welcome you aboard."

Ooh, she loved this thoughtful man. She wrapped her arms around his neck, squeezing with all her might. The groceries could wait. "This is so exciting. Have you got your phone for a selfie?"

"Nah, we'll take one later." Nate disentangled her arms and helped her step over the high-sided old timber rowboat.

Roberta sat on one end facing Nate. He would do the rowing. A touch of nostalgia from the bygone days. She tilted her head back while Nate untied the mooring ropes. For the middle of winter, the sun still had a touch of warmth as it broke past the cloud cover, allowing its rays to shine directly on them for this momentous occasion. Nate pushed the boat into deeper water and climbed over the side, settling on his seat and grabbing the oars.

"I should post a photo of this old beauty on our social media page," Roberta said.

Nate grinned, the muscles of his arms flexing in time with the oars as he began the rhythm of rowing. "Anything to get your face on social media."

She smiled as memories resurfaced. The odd term 'media tart' popped up again. She'd featured so many times in the local papers over the past six months. The most memorable being *that* photo. She still cringed over it. When Nate carried her out of the teahouse that day, moon boot and all, a reporter had snapped it. It shared the front page with another snap of Roberta shaking hands with Brian and the write-up of that momentous day.

So much had happened since. The promises by the premier led to drastic changes to the controversial wind farm Nate and his supporters had rallied against for months. The number of turbines was reduced, and a new design was to include a minimum buffer to neighbouring World Heritage listed rainforest. The project would completely avoid wet sclerophyll forests adjoining World Heritage areas as well as all known brood frog habitats.

The changes also had to include a First-Nations-led fire management plan, including the control of widespread feral pests. According to Nate, it was a balancing act. Providing more clean energy while significantly improving the habitat for protected species.

For Nate and his team, this was a huge win. One they were still celebrating.

For now, though, Roberta savoured the sight of Nate as he continued to row towards the centre of the lake. "How's the old girl feel to row?"

Nate smiled. "She's rowing like a dream. I've wanted to do this for years."

The strong, steady beat of her heart beat in time with the pull of the oars through the calm waters. This man did this to her, and the intense gaze he gave her as he rowed left her stomach tumbling.

When he stopped, he lifted the oars above water level, allowing the boat to glide.

"This is perfect, Nate. Thank you."

He lifted the bag strung over his shoulder and unzipped it, pulling out a small box. A familiar box. "What the heck? When did that turn up again?"

Nate opened it. She gasped and scrambled for a closer look, dangerously rocking the rowboat.

"You better sit back down."

"But, but—"

The white sapphire, now set in a gold ring, glinted back at her. The sun's rays rained down on its star shape, glittering in the late afternoon. "How, what? Tell me, Nate. What are you doing with it?"

Once she was seated in her proper spot again, Nate left his seat and got down on one knee. Holding the box out, he asked, "Roberta Mintello, will you marry me?"

"Oh, Nate." Dizziness clouded her mind momentarily. "Oh, Nate, yes, of course." She blinked furiously, not believing her life could be so good and she so lucky. "But tell me please before I burst. Oh, my God, I haven't thought of this rock for ages. Oh, Nate, I want to fling myself at you and hug you."

"Don't please," he begged. "We'll tip this thing over and lose this beauty forever."

"Did Billy steal it?"

"He must've because it matched the detailed records of the original rock found."

"Oh, bugger."

"Yeah, a bit rough for his family. I hope they eventually accept the news. But when the station owner heard your mother's story and the turmoil surrounding it, he offered it back to her as a gift. Your mother couldn't believe it and had no idea what to do with it. When I asked her permission to marry you, this was her suggestion."

Roberta sniffed as a tiny trail of tears trickled down her cheeks. Silly Roberta never cried. Or did she? She was now. "Can you please put it safely back in your pack? I can't be trusted at this very moment. If I happen to throw myself at you, I don't want to be responsible for its loss."

Nate did just that. "I'll put it on your finger later. I promise. How about we row back now?"

Roberta nodded, her heart expanding as Nate turned the boat around so she was facing the bank.

As they approached the shoreline, there was a sizeable group of people hovering near the edge. Visitors must've witnessed their launch and were eager to get some snaps now they were only about twenty metres away from the shore. They'd post it to social media way before she got a chance.

She looked up at the teahouse balcony facing the water and spotted Tash, Hannah and Sophie waving to them. Was that Nate's grandfather, Jim, seated at one of the tables? She waved back. Did Nate know his grandparents were visiting today? Why so late in the day? And what were the girls still doing at the teahouse? Their shift ended when hers had.

Waving arms distracted her from the teahouse balcony. She turned to the crowd at the shore.

What the? Why was Sally waving at her?

She squinted, scanning the crowd further and spotted Bob and her mum.

And Daniel and Janelle.

And Nate's mum and dad.

And her grandparents, surrounded by a horde of her cousins.

And Brian and his wife. From the States? *Really?*

And Zia Fiorina. *From Falerna?* What the heck? Fuzziness invaded her head. Was she dreaming?

And … wait … was that Connor and Liz? Holding their newborn baby girl?

She rose from her seat, unable to control herself. "Oh, my God, what is everyone doing here?"

"Sit, Roberta, or this thing is going to—"

The rowboat tilted dangerously with her sudden movement.

"Sit! Don't—"

Roberta lost her balance, her arms waving as she tried to stop her uneven steps inside the rowboat. Too late. She lost her balance, falling over the side with a chilly splash. A collective shout from the shore was the last thing she heard before she disappeared below water level.

Rising to the surface, Roberta quickly freestyled back to shore. The water was freezing, and a chill was taking over her body.

"Bloody hell, Roberta. Only you could make such a drama out of something as simple as a marriage proposal."

Roberta burst out laughing as Connor dragged her the last metre until she got her footing. Standing up, shivering, she flung herself at Connor and squeezed him in a tight hug. "What are you doing here?"

Not impressed, Connor scowled as he disentangled her from around his neck, holding her at arm's length. "Jeez, not all of us want to be sopping wet."

"Are you okay, Roberta?"

Within seconds, Nate's arms were around her. Not even his warmth could hold back her violent shivering. "I'm freezing, that … that's all." A quick glance behind her and Nate's dad was mooring the old rowboat and showing it off.

"Everyone!" Nate shouted to the gathered family as they came closer. "She said yes!"

A collective cheer rose from the group as Nate picked her up and held her shivering body against his chest. "Engagement party starts in half an hour. We'll go get changed first."

As Nate walked off, there were wolf whistles, more cheers and, for once, Roberta was left speechless. Surrounded by so much family and love, she furiously blinked, wrapping her arms around Nate's neck. "Thank you, my love," she whispered for his ears only.

Nate looked at her, shaking his head. He tried to keep his smile in check until it was impossible to do so, and it blossomed across his face. "You've turned my life upside down, woman. How could I want anything else?"

Roberta tightened her hold, drawn to Nate's warmth. "Half an hour, did you say?" Roberta's teeth chattered as she tried to whisper.

Nate's eyebrows rose as he put her down in front of the cottage door. "We could probably stretch it a few minutes. Up for it again?"

"You bet," came her immediate reply. "It'll be the most sensible way to warm me up, don't you think?"

"Can't argue with that," were Nate's last words on the matter as he closed the door behind them, found her mouth, and began warming her up fast.

# AUTHOR NOTE

Lake Barrine is one of three amazing lakes on the beautiful Atherton Tablelands in Far North Queensland. There is one family that's owned and operated a teahouse on its shores for close to one hundred years. Kudos to them, through all the generations, for this wonderful business that continues to thrive today. A visit to the Lake Barrine Teahouse to enjoy tea and scones and the opportunity to experience their boat cruises is a must-do item on every visitor's itinerary to our area.

While my characters are all fictional, a tragic waterskiing accident did happen years ago on Lake Barrine which might have triggered the closure of waterskiing on both Lake Barrine and its sister lake, Lake Eacham. I can't confirm with certainty that this was the catalyst.

The old ramps are still there below water level, and old pictures show a story of congested mayhem on the weekends as the popularity of waterskiing grew in the area.

I can't say I'm too saddened by the closure of the lakes to waterskiing, being a water skier myself (albeit very amateurish). These days, the lakes are beautiful and tranquil, ideal for swimming, paddling and family time. Lake Barrine has the added attraction of 1000-year-old trees and, of course, the iconic teahouse.

By this stage, Tinaroo Dam had progressed as the place for waterskiing, so the outcome was not too detrimental for the diehard water skiers of the area. Whether it was a result of the accident, the option of skiing on the newly constructed dam or just a good idea to move skiing on from such precious natural wonders, it eventually happened.

Waterskiing is still a drawcard to our beautiful area, which I can personally attest to. There were many Sunday mornings when our small family of five rose early, sleepy children included, for a waterski on the idyllic waters of the dam.

The Atherton Tablelands is also renowned for its potato farmers. One family has for many years grown a special variety of potato used by leading Australian potato crisp manufacturers. Australians enjoy potato crisps in many varieties and flavours, and a vast majority of those crisps are made from potatoes grown in our local area.

Wind farms are popping up everywhere in our beautiful north. As my story suggests, it's a delicate balance that we have to get right. Providing clean energy while protecting our beautiful rainforest and animals takes careful consideration by all. Let's hope they get it right.

Lastly, the volunteer organisation TREAT really does exist. They do an amazing job of planting thousands of native trees and joining tracts of rainforest cleared earlier this century, thus giving animals the freedom to move easily from one patch of rainforest to another. Their work is valuable and needs all the encouragement they can get. I hope they remain strong for many years to come.

## ALSO BY FRANCES DALL'ALBA

The **Australian at Heart Series** tells the stories of four interconnected siblings.

### <u>Little Blue Box – Book 1</u>

Regrets, lies, and earth-shattering secrets. When Ella learns the identity of her biological father, nothing will stand in her way. Not even his power. When things don't go to plan, can one little blue box put Ella and Zane back on the same path?  This second chance contemporary romance is filled with suspense, emotion and a life-changing sizzling romance.

### <u>The Stone In The Road – Book 2</u>

Emotional, passionate and heart-wrenching. This suspense-filled captivating romance will have you dancing in the rain and smiling through your tears. Set in tropical northern Australia, we don't always get to choose our path.

## The Silk Scarf – Book 3

An unravelling silken scarf ... mysterious gold ... a breathtaking romance.
An emotional and unforgettable contemporary romance set in Australia.

## Rustic Denim Love – Book 4

Forgotten secrets ... blazing fires ... burning love.
She's busy and diligent, doing the best she can to save her crumbling family.
He's funny and witty, with a solution for every problem.
This one may just beat him.


Link to read more and BUY.

**https://francesdallalba.wixsite.com/francesdallalba/australianathe artseries**

**Sway of The Stars Series** will share the stories of a group of friends.

### The Shooting Star – Book 1

Hidden treasures ... broken spirits ... tangled love. A modern-day treasure hunt where hidden treasures will tangle their love and break their spirits. Duty or love, or can they have both?

### The Glittering Star –Book 2

Shimmering waters ... towering giants ... buried mysteries. She's the no filters chick. Funny, full of life and always ready for a good laugh. Until her mother drops a bombshell. He's the environmental warrior. Passionate, driven and determined to save the world. Burnt once before, he's moving on and doing things his way. So how did they end up hand cuffed together on day one?

### The Giving Star – Book 3

Endless roads ... timeless discoveries ... unbreakable love. She's packed up her life ready for change, with one regret still hanging over her head. He's working his way back from hell, adamant he's never going there again. But one stumble, one discovery, and one hotbed of attraction ... and the entire game plan changes.

### The Priceless Star – Book 4

Forgotten treasures ... a perilous ransom ... shattered hopes

She's chasing answers long buried since the war.

He's content with a steady working life. Until he's not...

Sent to Far North Queensland to research a wartime mystery, Lucia Levorico escapes her privileged life and finds unexpected passion with reserved local, Theo Mather, under an outback sky – until a sudden goodbye and a devastating worksite tragedy tear them apart. When a ruthless ransom plot targets Lucia's wealth, their only reprieve will come from sharing the unravelling of a wartime mystery and its priceless treasure. Unless they're willing to fight for what they have.


Link to read more and BUY.
**https://francesdallalba.wixsite.com/francesdallalba/swayof the stars**

**Eight Seconds**, is a standalone story inspired by Australia's first female open bullrider. She pushed past the barriers and succeeded in a male dominated sport, creating a new legend showcased in two Australian halls of fame.

**Triumph, hardship, true grit ... and one crazy dream.**
**An inspirational story about one woman, with one dream, and one almighty driving passion.**

Link to read more and BUY.
**https://francesdallalba.wixsite.com/francesdalla lba/eightseconds**

**Jack& Eva,** is a standalone contemporary romance set in tropical North Queensland. It showcases our unique and adorable Lumholtz tree kangaroo and the valuable work done by Dr Karen Coombes in her care and continued research of them.

**Broody meets bubbly ... and a bunch of cuddly tree kangaroos.**
When the tempest blows over, will Jack and Eva be able to find a way forward, or are they destined for a train wreck with a bunch of furry animals caught up in the middle?
Fall in love with our adorable tree kangaroo while reading an emotional and passionate contemporary romance set in Australia.

Link to read more and BUY.
**https://francesdallalba.wixsite.com/francesdallalba/jackandeva**

# ABOUT THE AUTHOR

As a contemporary romance author, Frances loves nothing more than losing herself in a good romance. She's all about helping you forget the housework, or the bus to work you're going to miss, if you don't put the book down now!

She's devoted to giving her readers an emotional, passionate, possibly some ugly-cry, fairly steamy love story, that'll melt your heart and have you fighting for the happy ending right until the end.

Frances sets her books in North Queensland. She makes no excuses if some of her settings include amazing lakes and waterfalls, stunning views from tops of mountains, spectacular outback scenes, or crystal-clear creeks shadowed by tropical rainforest.

When she isn't writing, Frances is climbing mountains, searching for waterfalls and swimming across lakes. She loves to exercise, would prefer it if someone else cooked dinner every night, and never notices dust on the furniture.

She lives with her husband in tropical Far North Queensland, Australia, and uses her great baking skills to tempt her family to visit home often.

### Say hello to Frances

Visit her website: https://francesdallalba.wixsite.com/francesdallalba and subscribe to her newsletter. It will keep you up-to-date with everything happening in her author world.

Follow Frances on Facebook, Instagram, Bookbub, TikTok, and Goodreads. To do so, click on this link: https://linktr.ee/francesdallalba

### Still have a question?

Ask her at: https://francesdallalba.wixsite.com/francesdallalba/contact

## Leave a Review

Did you enjoy this book? The best favour you can do for an author is to leave a **review**. If you'd like to leave a review, go to your place of on-line purchase of the book, or search for the book on **Goodreads** and leave a review. Thank you.